I0678298

The Floodwaters in Prittuni

Pur Durance

Aurichalcum Publishing

Copyright © 2025 by Pur Durance

All rights reserved.

No portion of this book may be reproduced in any form without written permission from the publisher or author, except as permitted by Australian copyright law.

Contents

Chapter One
The bare bones of home

Yahvanna glanced around the cottage once more, straining her eyes to see anything that might have been missed in the lengthy packing. The cottage looked veritably bare, aside from the numerous lightweight metal crates stacked about the place; most of them now closed, locked and tagged, their lining sealed against the risk of waterlogging.

There was nothing left on the shelves. Even the lectern and the desks had been packed away. Anything removable, had been. The cottage was a bare rig of what it had been, wind whistling through the grated floor and the eaves; a skeleton, a corpse of a home, smelling of naught but perennially wet metal and the hint of rust.

It had taken considerable effort to gain the sponsorship for its construction, and now it was unlikely to be used again. Few were willing to live out here in the wilds. Few were willing to dedicate years of their lives to the patient, steady accumulation of data whose worth would not be known until she had returned and could properly aggregate it.

Very often scholars who worked in the field like this had teams or colleagues who received the data back in whatever arm of Academe was appropriate; but Yahvanna worked in water. Few people were interested in what detritus turned up in the bogs these days. Much research had been done in the past – frantic, terrified research seeking a stop to the floods – but that had been centuries ago.

Just because there did not appear to be much changing in the recognised patterns of precipitation and similar systems did not mean there would never be. One must accord time and resources for *maintenance*. Knowledge left untested atrophied.

There came a faint creak of the grating where screws had loosened over time, the only evidence of a footfall, and Gus asked: "Is there anything else?"

His words were careful in the manner of a man still relatively new to the language, his accent nebulous to the casual ear. It was not as pronounced as it had been; Vespasien had taken great pains to teach him several sounds not native to his tongue, trying to soften the evidence of his origins. It was a shame, felt akin to an active scouring of history; but Gus was quite possibly in danger, and his safety took precedence.

Even his name had been given by them; Yahvanna did not know his true. But then, he did not know theirs, either.

"I don't believe so," said Yahvanna, and turned to face him with a smile. "You've been very thorough."

Extraordinarily so, in fact. He'd thought of things Yahvanna might have forgotten until she was long home, looking in nooks and crannies Yahvanna had never considered. It was the action of a man well accustomed to seeking that which had been if not lost then misplaced. Perhaps a man with children –

A thought that only made the heartache worse.

He smiled back, though it seemed at least partly reflexive. There had been something drawn in his face ever since they met, though this was not surprising. Never mind the difficulty in communication. In the year since he arrived he had been understandably closed, shielded almost; preferring to watch and listen, and keep his own counsel. And no wonder; if he did have family, children, then they might be lost to him as surely as if someone had died.

As a result Yahvanna rarely knew what he was thinking, though very often knew what he *did* with his time. At first, learning: when Vespasien was not present, there had been no way to communicate beyond pointing emphatically and suchlike. Then there were the waters, the currents, the seasons; the written language; the entire foundation of culture such as Yahvanna and Vespasien had at their disposal.

Listening first was a wise choice, for a man in his position: fallen quite literally from the sky into lands he did not know, an environment wholly alien to him. There were servicemen from the neighbouring states too impatient to learn the best means of living in such a place, who learned only to resent it rather than mitigate their impatience. Gus had not been one such man.

At this point he likely knew more about living in a bog than most. Certainly he was a quick hand with repairs. Forged metal was rare to non-existent above the firmament, Gus said once, and he had already exhibited a keen interest in its manufacture. Since there were no written materials here by which he could study it, he'd studied the cottage itself. Many rattling pins and loose struts, alloys going to rust – things about which Yahvanna knew very little – had been carefully and prudently assuaged under Gus's hands.

Yes, a year on, he knew about the bog, the way Yahvanna had known about it after her first. The floods had been particularly teaching, for everyone.

But he also knew nothing outside it. What he did know came from above the firmament, where skydwellers lived, not here on the waterlogged land.

And that was why the threat to his safety. Skydwellers were, to most, naught but myth.

To most.

The fact that the prospectors who came to see what landed after the startrail seemed to expect a *man* –

Someone knew something. But who, and how, and what? Tyrian had not thus far managed to determine much, and now Yahvanna's permit was due to expire, as was Vespasien's; they were leaving, after five long years of study, and soon there would be no one here.

No one had even suggested that Gus might take over the cottage. He could, of course; it was unlikely Academe would need it or want it in future. As a bolthole it would suffice. But it was hardly a *home*.

And it was hardly *his* home, about which he had said very little on a personal level, and had only recently had the words to speak with at all. The most he'd ever said at once was the first time Vespasien asked him about the stars once he had the words to properly communicate.

For the first time since his arrival Yahvanna felt as though she'd seen Gus truly: unfolding from his reserve and his uncertainty into someone with a focussed kind of passion and a clear love for the subject such that he seemed alight even without the benefit of lamps.

And then he realised he had, and he'd looked stricken, and closed up as easily as he'd unfolded.

Yahvanna could not imagine his position. Regardless of how or why he'd fallen, he was here, far from home, in essential exile among peoples who didn't even believe he existed.

"What are you thinking?" Gus asked, vaguely indulgent instead of vaguely bemused, as he had in the beginning any time he caught one of them watching him. 'What' might have been one of the first words he learned. Particularly when he learned exactly what lived in the water.

His first experience with a leech had been, for a mercy, not as poorly as it could have been; for he, unlike some, had the wisdom to listen to guidance.

"Musing, rather," said Yahvanna, "on how far you've come, if you'll forgive me for saying so." His mouth constricted, a little wry, a little sad; not unexpected in either amount. "I mean it only in the sense that many in your position would have curled up and refused to move for a year."

"Wind alone can take a person only so far," he said softly, in the cadence of a phrase translated. Many of the sayings in his native tongue had much to do with light and air and gravity, and a hundred different words for various cloud and, unexpectedly, stone formations.

Vespasien had whole journals filled with notes he may never be able to show anyone save Tyrian and Yahvanna, and a handful of their closest comrades. Gus had been astoundingly patient, though always held himself back from lapsing into that open exuberance again.

The door snicked, and Tyrian's tread came heavier on the grated floor than Gus's had. Gus stepped away from the door so as not to block it, and Yahvanna joined them at its threshold as Tyrian approached. His expert eye scanned the empty shelves and the blackened furnace, unlit and cleaned best as Yahvanna could manage.

The men weren't quite the same height, Tyrian a couple of inches taller; Tyrian with sandy hair bordering on brown, and Gus's a brunette so deep it might be mistaken for black were it not for the red highlights. When he first fell, under lamp, it glowed like –

Well, Gus said once his hair was likened to a sunset, but Yahvanna, none of them, had ever seen one of those. No one had seen one of those for centuries.

Whatever light he'd harboured upon landing had dulled, so that his hair barely lit at all unless the lamp were turned up as brightly as possible. The only radiance that remained in him was that brief, impassioned love, so swiftly concealed.

It was likely for the best, given how obviously alien his eyes, that he did not himself so easily glow anymore – but nevertheless, it felt like a loss to know the change. If nothing else it did indicate a harbouring of some fashion, that light was if not critical to a skydweller's health then aided it in some fashion.

In any case Gus's hair dulled lacking the brightest of lights, passable. His eyes were more obvious: heterochromatic, one molten gold and the other a shade of indigo Gus said the sky turned at dusk, above the clouds. Both of them were too vivid to be natural here on land.

If they were not careful, he was far too obviously alien. Standing alone he was merely exceptionally handsome; standing beside Tyrian, he was so obviously not nearly as pale or dull in colour. Standing beside *anyone*, he was not nearly as dull. Residing directly under the sun, it proved, furnished the skydwellers with a kind of burnish unseen under the firmament, even excluding the potential luminescence.

Even the scruff Gus bore, in fear of the fact the prospectors might have his description prior to his fall, did not adequately render him *nondescript*.

Then again, Tyrian plied his trade in being fairly forgettable. Handsome yes, in his own way, but in the fashion of a dozen other men: equally handsome, equally forgettable.

If nothing else, standing beside Gus would ensure it.

"The skyride will be here in a few hours," said Tyrian, and glanced toward Gus. "Are you ready?"

"I think so." Gus nodded toward the bag on the crates nearest the door, his mouth twisting wryly. "I know what I'd bring were I sailing on the clouds, but on the water?"

Skydwellers needed water to live, just as anyone else did; but according to Gus they gained it in ways which precluded both rain and the notion of a vast body of water in which one could *swim*. Tyrian had taught him, down by the water's edge; made a week of it, the both of them heading down the escarpment specifically so Gus could learn what it was like before they left. Skydwellers did not swim; no one beneath the firmament neglected the skill.

Tyrian made a quick sweep through Gus's bag, which frankly was not much. Most of the clothes Gus wore were Tyrian's spares, left behind for emergencies or quietly bestowed so nothing untoward was flagged on Tyrian's travel expenses. It had been a hard flood; the cloudwatchers had forecast a low tide which had not eventuated. Although the floods themselves had not broken any records, they can come late, unexpected, and with a cost of human lives.

It was a side-effect, living in the bog and visiting it regularly, that they were those to whom Prittuni turned when travellers went missing.

Yahvanna remembered the hauntedness in Gus's eyes when he and Tyrian came back from finding and excavating the bodies. He'd stayed hidden within the bunker when the skyrides came to collect the remains; barely speaking, not that he'd had much language at the time. Yahvanna's impression was that corpses were not commonly seen above the firmament.

Here, in some places, they were a near-casual occurrence.

"It looks about right," said Tyrian, buckling the bag and pulling the waterproof layer over it. "You're missing a few things I'd recommend, but it isn't as though you had them here to begin with. You've got the compass and the maps?"

Gus patted his belt and the compass-case clunked, the scroll-case thudding faintly against his thigh. His mouth was that wry twist just short of something either aching or bitter. The first time Tyrian showed him a compass, it had been but one more rendition of that question: 'What is *that*?'

Skydwellers, it seemed, did not use or need compasses. The way Gus spoke, the stars themselves were their map. And the way Gus handled the compass sometimes, as though it were something liable to bite – Yahvanna did have to wonder if it was but a reminder of what he did not have.

He was dressed much like Tyrian typically did when out in the bog: linen tunic and leather breeches, the latter with a high belted waist; a leather vest with a high collar capable of being secured; rubber thighboots buckled to the top and rubber armguards similarly secured over sleeves and leather gloves.

His coat was one of Tyrian's old ones with numerous pockets, a hood and a scarf suitable to pull over his face; but it was the goggles that were the most important. They would not help Gus see at all; though his vision had acclimatised some to the relative dimness beneath the firmament he still had a tendency to need brighter lights than the rest of them. But they would hide the colours of his eyes.

Most of these items had not been fitted when Tyrian bestowed them. They were now. Yahvanna suspected Gus of having a hand for thread. Or perhaps simply too much time.

"And your ready food," Tyrian added, and Gus picked up the other bag sitting on one of the crates, slinging it across his chest where it wouldn't be in the way, along with the case that contained the small burner stove. Lighting a fire by hand was not easy, in this kind of terrain, but Yahvanna would not need levinbricks any longer; and those she did have were too old for Academe to care about as assets. Gus had them now, to charge his stove and several small levin-powered lanterns. He had an oil-burner, and associated oil, as backup; but with fortune he would not need it.

Not that his food was of particular quality to begin with. Much of what they ate here was shelf-stable, long-lasting; most of what Gus had packed consisted of jerky and seaweed strips, and the thinly-pressed algae wafers frequently consumed within Prittuni. Fish were, at least, abundant in the mangroves, and there were some few plants on which he could subsist.

Hopefully Tyrian had taught him well enough to survive.

"Alright," said Tyrian, satisfied, and glanced toward Yahvanna. "I'll be back before you head to Passion's place, if not before the skyride shows up. I dare say it might take a bit for them to load your equipment, in any case."

"But not nearly so long as it will to load Passion's," answered Yahvanna with warm asperity. Vespasien was many things, but concise was not among them. Tyrian's grin was quick and flashing and resigned; Gus covered his mouth with the side of his fist, though Yahvanna caught the quirk of his lips. She raised her hand. "Go, then. Be careful, be safe."

And with all luck they would see Gus in a few days, once he'd made his way from the mangroves and into the port city of Lammandan from the coastline, where the state would not be looking.

CHAPTER TWO

SODDEN

"There it is."

Ryan nodded toward the slip of dark-grey that was the canoe tethered to the tangled shadows of a mangrove's roots. The pond in this area was still, out of the current; the roots of the trees were so thick they curtailed any flow, and made it a convenient place to store a vessel. Like dead air, except ... less obviously dangerous.

(Less obviously dangerous, save that Ryan had told Erasmus to never drink from such still water; or boil it thoroughly first, if he must. The best way to tell, he said, was whether the edges of the water was at all luminescent. Which this pond was.)

Ryan crossed his arms, a movement of shadow. His hair wasn't all that bright, but at least it was brighter than the stone behind him. The long narrow stairway leading nadir from the escarpment emerged from behind one of the waterfalls, and they were both damp; but the canoe could only be stored a distance away, so the tide didn't tear it off its line.

Water currents weren't that much different from air currents, in that respect. For a mercy; even the vernacular was often similar.

"I *should* be going with you," Ryan muttered, his head turned toward the canoe rather than toward Erasmus.

"You can't," Erasmus pointed out softly. They had not *discussed* this in so many words; or at least, Erasmus hadn't. He suspected the scholars had, more often when he didn't have a grasp on the language, and a bit later on when he had more of one than they thought. "The city officials are expecting you."

They hadn't explained the logistics, per se, but it wasn't difficult to observe. Ryan was the go-between who brought supplies and took back reports, who kept an eye on the scholars working in the – the bog. He liaised with the people who granted Passion and Yoch the right to work there.

The same people who had come looking for Erasmus, the day he fell.

"I know," said Ryan, sounding grim but unhappy, "but this still isn't a trip anyone should have to make alone. By rights, I *should* be going with you."

A trip out of the mangrove swamp and along the coast to the port, where Erasmus might be able to slip into the city undetected and find his new … companions … at the arm of their school, or whatever it was. Not a highly dangerous journey, Ryan told him, but not something for a novice, let alone someone who'd never been on the open water. Or seen the sea.

Or sometimes could barely see at all.

Erasmus had a sneaking suspicion if he told them *that* part, Ryan would hop in the canoe with him, prudence be damned. He didn't need *coddling*. The world was what it was, and this part of the world gloomy with never-ending cloud-cover. He couldn't *rely* on them. He barely knew them.

They knew about his sight, they knew that the place he'd lived was bright and full of sunlight, that the gloom here on the fundament was dark to his eyes. They were too sharp *not* to know. Yoch had realised it almost at once, before Erasmus really understood what was going on. And his eyes had adjusted to some degree, become more willing to see shapes and colours. Even if only the drab colours that existed down here.

Some mornings he wished they hadn't adjusted at all. Some mornings he woke up and ground the sleep out of his eyes until they were bloodshot, before remembering that ever-present film of darkness wasn't something he could force away.

It almost would have been easier if he *could* barely see at all, rather than this sense of merely having something over his eyes; a veil that refused to lift and show the colours and shapes that were surely, *surely*, underneath.

Maybe the cities would be better. Maybe they'd have more light there, and he wouldn't feel most of the time as though he were walking in a fog that existed only around him, hoping desperately the terrain was as flat as the schematic of shapes suggested; *hoping* that if there was something dangerous nearby, it would move enough for him to catch.

(But they'd given him goggles to wear, apologetically but firmly, in full awareness they would obscure his meagre vision further while telling him his eyes were too noticeable and if he valued his life –

(If he valued his life that much he wouldn't have launched himself off solid isle without so much as a raft to catch him, heart and will warring between the shock of surrender and the certainty that he could survive this, too.

(*What have you done?!*

(*I didn't. I didn't do this. I don't know how this happened.*

(But then, if he disvalued his life so much, he wouldn't have kept walking away from the precipice of the escarpment and the awful thundering force of the water below.)

"I'll be alright," said Erasmus, not quite so firmly as he might have once, before his fall. These people had helped him, without hesitation. They'd hid him from the searchers who came looking, spoke of that fact as if it was *simply a matter of course*: as if naturally they would conceal the presence of a man who was myth to the people who lived here on the fundament, without even asking why he'd fallen to begin with.

They hadn't even asked him if he wanted to go back.

(He did, so desperately it woke him up at night as sharp ache in his chest; struggling to weep only softly so Passion or Yoch, whosever cottage he was sleeping in at the time, wouldn't wake and wonder. Or worse, ask.

(He had to wonder, sometimes, if this was what it felt like for his cousin when he was stabbed; other times, so maudlin that Erasmus could only think that at least Caelestis had died from it, and therefore no longer suffered.)

The long moment in which Ryan looked at him felt rather more sceptical than Erasmus could wish, or perhaps more considering; but in the end Ryan shrugged, a little wryly. "Well, you *did* manage to fall out of the sky and land safely, after all."

Using magic. Presumably, since Erasmus didn't strictly remember the fall. Magic was not well-regarded here on the fundament; aside from the necessity of hiding his eyes, the scholars had been *excruciatingly* insistent on that point. Magic was illegal, here.

(But then, so had murder been, up there –

(But he hadn't. He *wouldn't*. Why would he? Caelestis was his cousin. If only that night weren't just an ice-blighted blank –)

"I'm sure I'll manage," said Erasmus wryly, as humoured as he could abide, had been able to abide for the last year.

And then of course he had to take the bag Ryan carried for him through the narrow stairs, being as there was even less light than usual; and he had to go to the steep bank, gripping the roots tightly and stepping into the canoe.

(It was worse that someone was *watching*. He never used to care about being watched, but now he was clumsy, fumbling; careful and slow about feeling out the roots and the side of the canoe, the water a flat black surface almost wholly opaque to him.

(He used to be able to see islets on the grey horizon and the bright-gleaming blue sky, the shine off the Ascended Westerlies glinting in the sunlight so far distant Christopher insisted he couldn't possibly; and now –)

He did manage to get himself and the bag into the canoe without tipping or dropping anything into the water, so there was that. The canoe rocked slightly as he got himself and his luggage sorted, a kind of slopping up-and-down bob that made him feel queasy the first few times Ryan made him sit in it. It still wasn't his favourite, but at least it was predictable: it was all about weight, and surface tension.

The cross-currents warring around the edges of Bowtip's Declined Arbours were worse. And the dead zone directly beneath Houndspaw? Forget it. The maintenance on the island's lodes was the most dangerous in the Empire; only veteran lodeshapers could expect to jump into that and go anywhere.

Fortunately for Erasmus's life, he was one of them. Unfortunately it wasn't much use this close to the fundament. His sense of the lode felt like something screaming in his nerves, like he was caught in a jumble of winds and he couldn't tell which led.

The lodestone he could feel – the compass, Ryan called it. Like the tiniest ray of sunlight sharpened shadow and heat, holding it made the jangle more acute while failing to pierce it; and then stabbed again, for the echo of the long-ago shame of needing one at all. His sense of the primary lodes had always been – warped. Sometimes he'd still needed a lodestone to guide him even as old as ten.

To need it again *now*, after all the effort he put into not, felt like a bitter salting from ground he thought long ago cleansed. All the more because it reminded him of Christopher, the only other person he'd met who had the same problem, fought to surmount it.

Erasmus couldn't help but reach out, hoping –

(He couldn't stop *stabbing* himself like this.)

– but there was no bracing net arced elegant and intangible and unbreakable from horizon to horizon, only a jangling of tangled cords.

Either way. Erasmus was learning that water was more supple than air, or even clouds; he could expect it to hold him where air wouldn't, even if it complained about it. And so it did now, settling when he leaned slightly into its inverts, until it was quiescent under him. Erasmus accepted the long dual-ended paddle Ryan held out for him, setting it across his lap and pulling up his mask as Ryan tugged loose the rope-line.

"Good luck," Ryan said, and toed the canoe away from the bank, toward the open end of the pool.

Erasmus had practiced this. He pulled away with a quiet sloop of water as he dipped the paddle, almost lost beneath the ever-present thud of the waterfalls striking the earth; dipped the other end to straighten the canoe's slant. It was an odd kind of balance, this, and yet –

Not all that difficult, really. Birds used two wings to fly.

But he didn't dare to crane his head, look around; didn't dare to try and see when or whether Ryan returned to the stairs. He had to focus. On the water. On the narrow but deep stream whose current took hold of the canoe's bottom, and carried him out of the still water into that which flowed. The air became a little heavier with mulch and rotting plants, relieved by the sharp freshness of the water and the soft glow around the edges of the water's dead zones.

Birds called overhead; insects chirped; the canopy rustled. Erasmus paid mind to keeping the canoe upright and not colliding with logs, roots or the luminescent edges of the banks, nadward-reaching mangrove leaves brushing his hair. The banks were high and loose, not exactly easy to climb – especially when the details in any purchase was lost to him – but the mangrove roots were thick and tangled, a better stepping stone. Almost every tree he passed had limbs arched across earth and water. He could see the miniature caves underneath, thick with cirrus roots and cobwebs and the shimmer of what he knew to be beetles and spiders, if he dared to look any closer.

There was so much down here.

That wasn't one of the first things that had struck him after his fall, or even the second. It had come much, much later, struggling through thigh-high water, swiping insects away from his face; putting his hand on reeds to haul himself out of it, and finding among the bristles from far too close a view –

Bugs. Spiders. Lizards, Ryan called them, scattering.

And when he'd stepped out of the water there had been an alarming number of things which dropped off his rubber boots.

His skin crawled for days.

It still did, when he thought about it too hard, all the – *things* – packed into all the little crevices that existed down here, but between gloves and boots and buckles he was well protected against having to *feel* them. Some little creatures existed at altitude, of course, congregating around inhabited islands, but here?

He couldn't step on a piece of earth without stepping *on* something.

There had never been so much life, just casually *living*, in the Empire.

At least here in the mangroves the insects didn't swarm quite so thickly. There were minutes which passed where Erasmus barely even had more than a few flies colliding with his head.

Erasmus ate in several of those extended moments, when the stream was wide enough that he could rest his paddle across the boat and trust that the current would carry him. It really wasn't so different from air; just more viscous. And, in an odd way, more predictable.

"What happens if I meet a cross-current," he'd asked Ryan back when Ryan first showed him the map, vying not to show his panic. *What if I go off-course?* was what he meant; what if the current took him far away from his location, and there were no stars to mark his place, as if he could even risk boating in the night; how could he get back to where he should be, if he was torn off his path?

"You won't," Ryan assured him. "Water flows downhill. All streams wind up in the sea. Keep following the current and you'll get to the shoreline. Then you just want to head south and you'll get to the city eventually."

Downhill took a bit for Erasmus to get his head around. *Down* was a matter of perspective, but Ryan used it like it was absolute. People on the fundament only thought in two dimensions, four directions, despite that they *floated* in *water*.

(Swimming was – strange. Surrounded on all sides by *something* instead of *nothing*; pressure increasing instead of slackening; it seemed like an inversion of float in almost every single way.

(Almost. The thud of heartbeat, the capture of air in his body – that was all the same. He hadn't realised until Ryan pulled him out the first time, neither of them had realised, that when Ryan said 'stay under for as long as you can to get a feel for it', he'd expected Erasmus to come up vastly sooner. He'd been sick for weeks when he first came to fundament, for several reasons including that Yoch said he was oxygen-saturated; but even with that they hadn't put it together, that his capacity for breath was greater, that he stored air more efficiently. The atmosphere was thin above the firmament, and was so very *thick* upon the fundament.

(Some days Erasmus felt like he was breathing something solid, the air was so thick down here.

(At least it meant if he fell in the water and forgot how to swim, he wasn't likely to drown so quickly.)

The tenor of the water slapping against the banks changed, and Erasmus squinted ahead of him, shifting his weight in the canoe. The tug of the current went southward, but the movement of waves against the mangrove roots suggested there was a pool or some other little bay southeast, divided around a tall tree more in the water than over it.

It had been hours, and Erasmus's muscles ached from the seat. Still water would at least be a good place to moor the canoe so he could walk around a bit ...

But the current was good, and it was tempting to carry on, reach the edge of the mangroves as fast as possible.

He almost hesitated too long. The split in the stream came fast toward him, and with a long hiss Erasmus plunged his paddle into the water to turn the canoe out of the current. Its bow scraped mangrove roots as it went, and the length of the canoe thudded broad against them where it turned too sharply; but he was out of the current.

The air hung heavier where the trees grew more thickly now there wasn't escarpment and waterfalls to break them up. Even the leaves seemed heavier. The water was so still the lack of a current felt like dead air, save for the vital fact that it wasn't, that all he needed was the right turn of the paddle to glide toward the bank.

Landing was a little harder, and wholly lacked finesse. He aimed for the roots of the deepest-sitting mangrove, avoiding the glow along the edges. The canoe's other edge scraped along it until it bumped to a stop. It was just as well this was a vessel Ryan laid in for Yoch for emergencies, and which neither expected to use nor would want back, because these weren't the only scrapes it was liable to take until Erasmus got somewhere safe.

At least he wouldn't need a rope to tether the canoe ... presumably. He was surrounded by trees and banks; the only exit was the way he'd come in.

Getting out was as difficult as he remembered. The soil here felt different from the spray-slick banks closer to the escarpment: thicker and more likely to give way as goo instead of mud, more akin to the unpleasant textures of the bog. His boot slipped and he caught himself half in the water, one hand gripping the mangrove roots and the other coming down on something that cracked under his weight, poking fragile-sharp against his glove and armguard.

His heart struck his throat. That hadn't *felt* like a stick. Or a bundle of sticks. And there was a sharp scent that cut through the general wet-earth smell once he'd disturbed it.

He got his foot wedged against a rock about calf-deep in the water, leaning against the mangrove to feel around. Between the clouds and the tree's shade and the – the gloopy movement of the water – the *goop* that was the bank-side –

His eyes refused to actually untangle the mess of – roots? Twigs? – and underbrush and water. At least not until his fingers found the long white root to which they were affixed – that was *not* a root, was it – and lifting it drew the mostly-bared skull briefly out of the water with a thick sucking noise.

Erasmus lowered the bones carefully but the water still slapped more loudly than he could wish. He drew in a deep breath through his mouth; let it out slow. His heart beat fast, his body flushed overwarm; but his stomach, though rolling, stayed where it was. This – this corpse had been here for too long to have that much of a smell beyond what was around it, and that tangy sharpness when he'd disturbed it.

Though judging by the movement a little further under his fingers, there was *something* left for the bugs to feed on.

Water flows downhill, Ryan said.

Water, and everything in it.

Such as the bodies of the lost Erasmus and Ryan had looked for after the floods. There'd been five the prospectors told Ryan and Yoch about. They'd only found four.

Could Erasmus say he hated this place, when it was the only place he *had*, when the thing he actually hated was to be – *confronted*, at every single turn, of the mortality of life and how utterly *grisly it was* when the land was filled to the brim with it?

(There were times he wondered if the prison was better. He hadn't been free, but at least –

(At least *what*? He hadn't had to *think*? To *try*? Just to sit in his confusion and his grief and his guilt and the never-ending hum of wards and never *know*?)

He *could* just leave the body to its decay. Ryan reported to the prospectors months ago. There was no one waiting on news of this person, and they would have to find a way to explain how the body had been found, a way that didn't include Erasmus or implicate Ryan in some kind of collusion. But ...

I'm sorry, Erasmus. There was simply nothing left.

But how much would he have liked just *one* more thing of his mother's, any confirmation of what they'd all known to be true, when there was nothing.

The prospectors had given Ryan a description of the missing people. The only one they hadn't found supposedly carried a mechanical watch, the sort that wasn't quite an heirloom but could be. Ryan had described them to him; they were usually made of metal, which meant they were heavy, but they were also usually secured by a chain or similar.

He'd found the – spine, so he could work down the body from there.

Or.

Erasmus hesitated. He *could* find the watch by hand, but – there was no one around. No one but him. He hadn't dared to lodeshape in the bog; hadn't dared display a sign of magic, even to those who'd warned him about it. They would have questions he couldn't, initially, answer, and without knowing exactly *what* kinds of magic might be most terrifying –

(And because it had ached, the thought of it, of lodeshaping only small and not grandly the way he once *could*.)

It had been easier not to. Almost novel, in a way, to do things without it. And better as a habit, for as long as he was here.

But there was no one to witness.

And it wouldn't take long. He could spend an hour fumbling about trying and failing to find an object he couldn't rightly see.

It barely even took a *minute*. The jangle of lodes was grating, but focused here and now, on such a small scale, all the ferrum in his immediate vicinity practically leapt out. The nails and fittings in the canoe. The small round of metal buried in silt and mud, hidden somewhere under the water. Erasmus dipped his hand beneath the surface so he didn't have to account for the difference between fluid and air, and inside of a heartbeat the watch dragged itself zenith to meet the lode in his palm, fast enough for a satisfying thump against his palm.

And that was that. He had to grope his way down the watch's chain to unclip it from the corpse's water-swollen belt, briefly felt *things* wriggling against his glove, but it was vastly swifter and not nearly so skin-crawling as having to handle the body to find it.

Maybe Erasmus would even try to clean the watch up a little when he made camp, wherever that was going to be.

Pity he never had been good with fire, and there wasn't any sunlight to spark one with. He wasn't all too convinced of his ability to do so with the flint and steel Ryan taught him to use, but what else did he have? The burners gave off more heat than illumination.

But that was a thought for later, and he did not particularly want to linger in this place.

Grimacing Erasmus straightened, stretching all his limbs one by one so he didn't topple over in the water, and awkwardly got himself back into the canoe. The vessel splashed, the water sloshing. He'd wait until he was further along before trying a walk again. Light forbid there might be *other corpses* waiting him at every reservoir.

He was half soaked, half-nauseous, and his skin itched in places he didn't particularly want to think about. How much worse would it have been, if he'd actually tried to do something by *hand*? How did anyone bear to live their entire lives doing things by *hand*?

(How did anyone manage to *live* down here?

(How did he have any choice *but* to?)

If there was Light here to hope with, Erasmus might have done so. All he had was to push himself off the bank with the paddle and find his way out of the damned bay in the hope the edge of the mangroves weren't too far off, and that the sea, whatever fashion of water it was, was kinder.

Chapter Three

A confusion of motivations

The annex in Lammandan was shaped as the city in which it was built, while evocative of Schecheyan architecture. It was made of metal, unusual against the backdrop of Lammandan's tendency toward mortar and stone, and yet: the clean lines echoed the manner in which Lammandan had in many fashions been hewn from the side of a cliff.

Still visible from a distance, bright-gleaming such as anything could under perennial cloud; standing out like a piece of statue polished by the touch of many hands, while the rest tarnished.

Lammandan was not a water city in the same fashion as the Thalassocracy's, but its homesteads had grown downward, rather than up and over the cliff, and the water had in the past risen high enough that any rocks which had been at the cliff's base were no longer shallow enough to be of danger.

Some of them remained – but they were also the ones on which dwellings were built, boardwalks strung between them and kept in line with anchors on steel cables dropped deep into the water. For a mercy, Yahvanna and her companions did not have to suffer them. They weren't onerous to any degree, but it was nice not to have to forebear the presence of water after so long living in it.

The skyride's launch was at the height of the cliff, and so instead of winding their way up they had to walk down and across steel-cabled bridges.

The annex was among the cluster of wealthier buildings on the sturdier parts of the cliffs, which had the mien of stone that had at some point in the distant past been struck with a hammer so half of it had fallen and lodged, craggy and upthrust, from the sea. The main fort, where the viceroy ruled on behalf of the baroness, was constructed atop and whittled through the thickest part of the cliffs, and it was within one of its highest courtyards that the launch was built. Anyone using the launch must therefore parade through the fort itself, passing through checkpoints and either out of the city or deeper within it.

There lay the danger for Gus. If the prospectors suspected something, anything, about the startrail, it had to have come from the civil guard; and if the civil guard knew anything, it was given to them as a suspicion by –

Well, it could have been any number of people, actually. The baroness herself could have suspicions; someone else could have been the one to tell her so; it could be any number of her officers or courtiers. Lammandan was the second-largest city in the state, and its being a port meant a great deal of political business was conducted here.

More so in recent years.

The capital was drowning. The plateau on which Aulerin was built had not once been considered lowland; but that was many, many years ago. Even the baroness lived here in Lammandan in some seasons.

They'd sent ahead for some of the porters from the annex to meet them as the skyride came down, to transport their equipment and what remained of their research while Yahvanna and Vespasien dealt with paperwork and permits. Vespasien, as expected, had a significant number of books.

... A *significant* number of books.

"You really don't have to bring him everything he asks for," Yahvanna had said to Tyrian as Vespasien's crates were being packed, and Tyrian only shrugged ruefully. As pragmatic a man as Tyrian could be, occasionally he was ... not. Very often pertaining to specific personages. Such Vespasien.

"Who am I to deny a scholar his reference?" Tyrian had asked blithely.

"The man who must justify each of them as a transportation expense," Yahvanna had answered with asperity, but the point was moot. They must needs wait for Vespasien's things to be loaded, but for a mercy did not need to wait for them to be un.

Or so Yahvanna assumed. She had not returned to the port before, not in such a way. Nor had Vespasien. Tyrian, of course, had liaised with numerous scholars over the years, and nothing he said indicated anything that might be construed as unusual.

"Sign here, Scholar," said the customs agent with a brusque sort of efficiency, setting a thick parchment scroll on the counter by Yahvanna's elbow, along with a cartridge pen.

"I believe I have signed half the paperwork in the building by now," said Yahvanna dryly, vying not to frown. She had signed and countersigned both her permit and the office's copy to confirm her return; her claims to resources brought from the bog; her luggage; outstanding expenses still sitting with the state, including transportation. "What is this?"

"Consent to open the crates and your understanding as to forfeitures," said the customs agent, and Yahvanna's eyebrows rose.

"Prithee," said Vespasien softly, "for what reason must the state unpack our luggage?"

"New regulations," said the customs agent stoically, his square face barely changing in its expression. "Stops people from slipping in and out over the border using crates."

For a mercy they had not seriously considered *hiding* Gus inside their luggage. The crates were sealed against water; they were not conducive to *breathing*. Even for a man who could hold his breath an alarming length of time.

"*Who* would risk that?" Yahvanna asked irritably. "They would only suffocate."

And why did he specify that consideration, when he had also stipulated *forfeitures*?

The customs agent shrugged without unfolding his arms. "Be that as it may, it's the rules now. We can't release your luggage until it's been checked, permit or no permit."

What an awful nuisance.

"My possessions may suffer such an intrusion well enough," Vespasien murmured, but his brow was crinkled and his mouth crimped.

"Mine would not," said Yahvanna irritably. "I have far too many delicate objects for others to go rooting about in them unattended." She held up her hand. "I would go to Academe and arrange for some oversight, if it please you. I shall not have my samples broken by mishandling after all the years I've spent accumulating them."

"I too shall return forthwith," Vespasian agreed, his voice steady enough but with a trifling edge.

The customs agent shrugged again. "That's your right, Scholars."

He let them leave the room, at least, square stony thing that it was. The launch itself was a broad cobblestone courtyard on the fort's upper terrace, the ride's span marked by flags. There were doors off the fort's wall where cargo was stored prior to being shipped elsewhere either in the city or the state.

Their things were, currently, a broad low stack in the yard beneath the ride's stern, unloaded but also – unmoving. There were porters loitering, but none of them belonged to Academe; and they hung back from the several civil guards currently standing by the crates.

"What's going on?" Yahvanna asked as she and Vespasien crossed the yard to meet Tyrian, standing feet planted and arms crossed, watching the crates and the guards on them. "I thought the permits granted us rights through customs."

"They have every other time," said Tyrian tersely. "They know where you've been the last five years. I freighted some crates through after the floods, and no one demanded to look in them."

"Perhaps the size of the crates is at fault?" Vespasien offered delicately. "The gentleman within the building suggested someone might be hiding in them."

"They'd be dead by now," said Tyrian grimly, and that was precisely why none of them had seriously considered the option. He jerked his head toward the guards. "And they'd be significantly more eager to open them. Contraband seems more likely."

"Such as *what*?" Yahvanna demanded, and all Tyrian did was shrug. "Is there nothing to be done without causing a scene or allowing them to paw through my equipment?"

The larger hardware, she did not much care about – but the vials and other samples were very often delicate.

"Not right now," said Tyrian. "I want more information before I start throwing weight around. We'll have to leave your crates here."

"Bother," Yahvanna muttered, but Vespasien looked – strained. And if she called attention to it here, it was only likely to cause trouble. "Let us go, then, and see where Academe's porters got to."

If the annex knew this was a consideration and had failed to tell them – or *Tyrian* – no. Even if this was a recent change, Tyrian ought to have known about it from when he was last in the city. Something *odd* was going on.

Yahvanna did not like leaving their crates here with no one to guard them; but they were locked, not rented but owned by Academe, and therefore the state should not have access unless they broke the locks. *That* would be a presumption liable to cause trouble with Schecheya, particularly as there was significant risk of breaking the contents thereby.

If the agent had meant to slide the paper in with the rest of those they had to sign, he had done a poor job of it.

The walk to the annex was ordinarily a pleasant one, as the fort's walls and city's breaks reduced the prevailing wind to something more comfortable while providing a sufficient viewpoint to watch the bunting and the flags snapping, the ships far below and the gliders soaring from gust to gust, cliff to cliff.

In this instance the walk was merely an opportunity to stew and therefore source of irritation, as they only had what they'd been allowed to keep on their person. Tyrian had his binoculars, but none of them used them to watch the gliders, or indeed paid much attention to the view. No guards stopped or hailed them, and there were not so many people as to clutter the path this high in the city. There were others with a better vantage lower in the city, and most people with intent to watch went there so as to avoid the walk.

And yet Vespasien looked veritably anxious the further they walked.

"Alright," said Tyrian as they came to the first of the heavy steel bridges, cables groaning in the wind, punctured by the distant boom of surf below. "What did you put in your crates? No Prittune will be able to tell your notebooks about Gus from your notebooks about stars, as long as they're mixed in."

For a long moment Vespasien was silent, his chin held if not high then steady, his gaze ahead and pace – a little rigid. Then, quietly, he said: "Do you recall our mutual friend's attire when he arrived?"

... Ah.

"I do," said Yahvanna grimly. "I forgot about it."

The fabric had been so clearly nothing similar to what was available in the states surrounding, and equally clearly unsuitable for the environs. Given all the mysteries Gus presented, this – artefact – had slipped Yahvanna's mind, but of course Vespasien would think to keep such items.

"So did I," admitted Tyrian, knuckling his brow with a sigh as they stepped from the bridge onto the first outcrop serving as a crossroad, making way for several other commuters. Several benches had been drilled into stone; there was a rigid canopy to cut off the wind; beneath it were several boards on which to leave messages, tourist information, and other community posters.

Tyrian drew them closer to the cover, so as not to get in the way of anyone accessing the three bridges, and turned toward them, frowning. "Not *exactly* what you'd call contraband, and if they're already suspicious I can't imagine they'd overlook alien fabric during a search, but I don't see why they'd be searching luggage for something like that alone. Something else is going on."

"Perhaps Prittuni is still looking for remnants of the last startrail," said Vespasien quietly.

"A year on?" Yahvanna asked, and silently Vespasien pointed toward the board past Tyrian's shoulder. Yahvanna sidled sideways to see past him; Tyrian turned.

There, black ink running at the edges where water had seeped beneath the transparent protective sheet, was a poster bearing Gus's clean-shaven face.

"Well," said Tyrian finally, "I think we know they're looking for him."

"How could you have missed this?" Yahvanna demanded, marching over to the poster. She did not snatch – it was nailed down – but the water damage indicated it was very recent. Had they simply replaced it recently, or –? "Was this *not* here before?"

"No," said Tyrian. "I've come this way since. This is new."

"Someone else knows our friend walks upon the fundament," said Vespasien quietly.

Yahvanna whirled, folding her arms across her chest. "But why *now*?"

The poster had a few details; a reward for information, a claim about murder Yahvanna was not going to read too much into. There were a great many reasons for a man to have to flee, and accusation of murder was such a useful tool to condemn a stranger in the eyes of strangers.

Gus had not been lying to them. To fall from the sky, the grief in his tone and bearing and the absolute confusion of his state – it was impossible to imagine him a murderer, let alone subterfuge.

And he had been here for a year. The prospectors had already searched for him. The timing made little sense.

There was another group of commuters coming up one of the bridges, not even bothering to glance their way as they stepped onto stone. Labourers, most likely heading up to the fort or one of the steads outside the walls to be of aid to those outside the city. It was late in the day for it.

Tyrian held up a finger and went to the lead, a wiry woman with broad shoulders and grizzled hair. "Excuse me, madam. We've just recently arrived in port, and wondered." He pointed toward the poster. "What's the story behind *that*? I didn't see that last time I was here. Should we be worried?"

He *sounded* convincingly concerned, and the woman glanced toward the poster.

"Oh, aye," she agreed, her words rendered nebulously audible by the wind. "They've been looking for him for months now – some killer from another state. Subtle, like, until late this morning. My cousin in the guard told me he was sighted somewhere up the coast." She grinned. "That's north and on the shore, so as long as you're up on the cliffs you don't have to worry your pretty head about it, lad."

Tyrian bowed. "Thank you and your cousin, madam. Maybe I should learn to fly."

She laughed and he backed away to let her crew over the bridge, and they waited until the labourers were well away before Yahvanna demanded low: "*How?*"

"I don't know," said Tyrian grimly. "There wasn't anyone close enough to see, I'd swear to that, and Prittuni isn't so advanced as to have drones capable of observing someone without being in view itself."

"Magic, I deem possible," Vespasien offered softly. "There are forms of magic capable of scrying a person from a far greater distance, though *who* would take such a risk, I cannot currently imagine."

"And if so, why wasn't he observed before this?" Yahvanna demanded, and Vespasien's shoulders rose in a helpless shrug, his long arms dangling.

"Perhaps there is something about the bog which prohibits magical observation."

And the implications of *that* veritably made Yahvanna's heard beat faster. What could possibly cause magical interference? It had not occurred to her as a possibility, and she had not read anything unduly magical about the bog. Aside from that, Vespasien's point was true: who would dare? Few were the people who still dared, lest it taint their relationships with others, but there were some. None of them made sense as pursuers ...

... Save, perhaps, one. Academe did not, officially, condone magic: but it was not above the study of it, either.

"We'd need to speak to someone familiar with such forms of magic," Yahvanna observed. She had heard of them offhand, coupled often with magical properties relating to water, but had not examined them in great detail. Not enough to know much of value, at least.

"Maybe Gus himself," said Tyrian, "assuming we can *get* him here."

And a great assumption was that, if the guard was already searching for Gus along the coast. He was not familiar with the terrain; it was difficult for Tyrian to describe boltholes and safe places when land itself was so very alien.

"We may need to request assistance," Vespasien murmured.

"From who?" Tyrian asked. "Schecheya won't interfere even if they can be trusted with the information, and someone in Academe is just as likely to be guiding the search as anyone from a state; and the Owls are too far away."

If they were even contactable without tipping their hands. *Especially* if Academe was behind the search.

"We'll do what we can," said Yahvanna grimly.

"This also doesn't explain the new customs regs," Tyrian added grimly, crossing his arms. "Conveniently timed, don't you think? Just for *us*."

They all fell silent, and it felt as though the wind vied to steal Yahvanna's breath from her lungs. They were tucked into a cliffside lee, where wind was lessened to breeze, but the howl from among the cliffs, the rattle of the bridge, gave the impression of their being in the eyes of the storm. Or, perhaps, about to be swallowed by it.

"They let us go from the fort," said Yahvanna finally.

"That makes me wonder what's awaiting us at the annex," said Tyrian.

"How far along before we can see it?" She couldn't remember. It had been five years. She knew the route, of course, could walk it with some thought; but she also couldn't remember ever seeing the annex from afar, save from aboard a skyride.

"You don't, on approach," said Tyrian, and grinned. "But I happen to know a place on a different road."

"If we elect another path, our decision may be construed as an admission," Vespasien pointed out.

"If we're already under suspicion, then tiderise I'll walk blindly into it," said Yahvanna. "If we aren't, then we can merely say we went for a stroll to stretch our legs and see the city first, and it should hardly be an issue."

For if they were under suspicion, it would be foolish to the extreme to go directly to the annex.

Vespasien inclined his head wordlessly and Tyrian beckoned them along the third bridge, the one which led not faintly curving up but down. "This way."

***

The path Tyrian chose led down into the port's bowels, to the harbour and the ships and the vastly less wealthy residents of the city. Well before they struck sea-level he turned them off the landing, behind one of the watchtowers and onto a path carved into the cliffside itself. It was a dark, damp little thing, narrow enough that Vespasien edged along it nervously; overshadowed by the loom of the city above and wet with spray from below. Those houses built in front of it turned it into a corridor stable primarily owing to the buttress of eaves and roofs, on which Yahvanna glimpsed the silhouettes of people, stowed out of sight save their eyes.

And the path inclined slightly upward. By the time they emerged they were higher than when they'd got on it, and on the far side of the city – the annex's side.

"I don't see how we'll get any visibility like this," Yahvanna noted, but Tyrian's smile didn't falter. It was the sly half-a-one he wore, faintly mischievous, when he was doing something most likely illegal and most certainly exhilarating.

"We're not there yet," said Tyrian, and took them to the long pillar piercing nearly half the cliff, unheeded and unstopped by the grubby and salt-encrusted residents of the lower city.

The pillar looked very nearly like a spear, if one gargantuan in size; a natural shaft which had begun to fall away from the cliff sometime in the long distant past and then was somehow jolted up so it towered above the cliff's edge. It was too far for the fort to make use of it, and yet as Yahvanna recalled there were rumours one could climb it, and that there was someone who lived at the top.

As it transpired, there were stairs. Narrow stairs, curling around the outside, with barely a guardrail to keep them safe from the wind, of such dull metal it was invisible from a distance. Even partway up it took Yahvanna's breath away, until she dared not look down the long chute toward the white-frothed waves hungry against the base of the cliff.

Vespasien gripped the rail with white knuckles, his breathing laboured and eyes wide; but he did not turn back and he did not look down.

"This is high enough," said Tyrian, for a mercy with a good third of the spear still above them, and paused at a concrete outcrop which allowed them to step off the stairs onto a viewing platform mostly hidden by the spear's width. Vespasien edged onto it carefully, with a two-handed grip on the rail.

"There it is." Tyrian nodded toward the annex.

Like many wealthier buildings it was perched on a narrow cliff with its rear hard against the cliffside, a broad wall preserving the grounds from the threat of its inhabitants tumbling over. The view was had from the building's upper levels and balconies, inset and tall. The annex itself did not have towers, though they were common among many of the wealthier buildings, but since it was made of metal it stood out among its grimier neighbours.

From this angle they could see the gate, and part of the garden leading up to the building entrance.

"Those are state guards," Yahvanna noted clinically, for they were: not guarding the gate but standing with the Schecheyan guards *at* the gate, and with another pair by the annex doors. "Someone important is inside."

"I'm starting to get the feeling this was a conspiracy of some kind," said Tyrian grimly. "Prittuni can't do much to us without Academe's blessing, but if they have it –"

"I do have to wonder exactly how Academe knew."

Among other things. Magic was taboo, but that didn't mean there weren't those in Academe who studied it; and if there was plausible deniability enough, nothing need be said of its study or potential use. Only a reporting of sighting a murderer. With experimental technology, perhaps; Schecheya's was more advanced as a rule.

Possibly technological oversight was how they'd even managed it, but if so, it was using devices Yahvanna didn't know.

In the meantime Yahvanna's research, *Vespasien's* research, was stuck in the fort awaiting to be opened. If Academe was working with the state, the crates may not stay shut for long.

They could not presume to trust anyone currently in the annex. Though they also needed to know what Academe was doing within it.

"We need more information," said Yahvanna to Tyrian, "and then we need to get out of here."

"Agreed," said Tyrian, "in spades, and especially to the first part. I need to get into the annex, for one thing."

Yahvanna frowned. "What for?"

Tyrian's gaze slanted sideways in Vespasien's general, but inexact, direction. "Remember when we were wondering whether our mutual friend's propensity for light might reveal him on footage?" She did, in fact. "I left the camera and the photographs in storage."

Ah. Because he hadn't dared bring the pictures with, owing to the need to declare them first; and if they were in the annex then they were subject to the annex's rules.

"If the photographs are seized it would prove beyond a shadow of a doubt that we met with a skydweller," said Vespasien faintly. Not necessarily that skydwellers existed, because either Gus appeared as an ordinary man or he'd ruined the photographs, and lens flare was not precisely evidence on its own; but anyone who already knew would know, and that was vastly more dangerous.

"If we can arrange for a ship," said Yahvanna eventually, "we can secure an escape route and search for Gus up the coast after we've retrieved what we can here. Perhaps to Schecheya."

Academe might be working with Prittuni, but the Schecheyan Ministry and Academe no longer agreed on a great many things. The former would not extend their hand to aid them; but they also would not extend a hand to aid Prittuni, provided the three of them reached Schecheya first and unmolested. And presuming they could get through customs without Academe's observation.

"A ship might be difficult, unless it belongs to the Thalassocracy," said Tyrian slowly, scanning the harbour below. "And I don't see their flags in berth. They might be at odds again."

"Perhaps we ought to find what information we can and then make our way north before discussing the subject," said Vespasien with that faint note in his voice.

"Good idea," said Tyrian, "if by north you mean 'higher up the tower'. I have some gliders stowed up there and they'll get us into the annex more easily than anything else." Vespasien's eyes closed, and Tyrian patted his arm sympathetically. "You can go down the way we came. See what ships you can find; Yoch and I can manage breaking into the annex."

"Ominous," Yahvanna muttered, but Tyrian was already making his way further up the stairs, and she had no choice but to follow.

Chapter Four

Unexpected everyday choices

There were an awful lot of Prittune in the annex, currently. This, Britt didn't necessarily mind, depending on what sort. The schoolchildren were *meant* to be here. They were being taught. Likewise the youths and young adults, and assorted other students of various ages who were enrolled.

Prittuni's guards, though?

It was *passing strange*.

"Birdie?"

"Coming," Britt called through the door from the kitchenette to reception, and gathered up the tea-tray. Paused to take a few extra deep breaths and survey its contents. The pot was steaming (not quite the best they had at their disposal, but it was porcelain instead of clay), the cups were neatly upturned (matching, of course, not a single chip), and the plate was loaded with huffkins (they called them something different hereabouts, but to Britt a huffkin was a huffkin was a huffkin).

It was a little awkward, what with Britt being so short, but she was sturdy. She had to be. Prittune tended to look down on someone with hands like hers, evidence of a childhood scraping clay and silt out of the riverbanks, but Schecheya was a *little* more open-minded than that.

A little.

If nothing else, they'd respected her gumption.

The headmaster of the annex, known primarily as Master Cheya (Britt knew no other name), was in Britt's experience a little bit fussy, a little bit pointed, fairly jovial. Amazingly organised, especially with Britt as his right-hand, though sometimes – a little dismissive. He had so much to do (his own research, making the ambassadorial-type decisions, that sort of thing) that the act of running the school at the annex very often slipped by the wayside. Or off his list entirely.

Britt didn't mind. It meant *she* very often helped run the school. The senior professors often had locally-hired assistants to help them, and the teachers were evenly split between Schecheyan and Prittune, but someone had to organise all of *them*, didn't they?

It was what she'd been hired for. Hadn't quite been specified in that way, or detailed how much work it would be, but it was what she'd been hired for.

Master Cheya's office was on the ground floor on a corner of the building onlooking the gardens, but had a stairwell leading up to the next, so he and any guests could overlook the cliffside. He hadn't taken *this* one up there, though. Upstairs was where he kept his special items.

'This one' may have been, if Britt wasn't mistaken, very possibly General Ell Burnstone, whom Britt recognised firstly due to the stylised L embedded in her House's coat of arms and secondarily, with an uncomfortable jolt of pounding heart, as having been there the day the county fell into the sea.

Britt didn't remember much. Didn't try to, all that much. But she remembered hearing a commanding voice, remembered looking up frozen and shivering to the searchlights, and seeing the silhouette of the tall woman with greying red hair, almost emblazoned in the light.

Search the east! There may be more survivors.

Pity there wasn't much the guard could do to *stop* the waters, before they swallowed the land.

That was why Britt's hands shook as she set the tray down. The *only* reason why, honest.

Porcelain rattled and she winced.

"Are you quite alright, my dear?" asked Master Cheya, stopping himself mid-sentence – whatever the sentence had been – to ask.

"Quite alright, sir," Britt answered quickly, and eased the tray down the rest of the way. There. Not a single spill. It was fine. She was *fine*.

(Never mind that all she could smell was salt, and her skin goosebumped with phantom chill, the cold of a day's worth of waterlogging.)

Britt straightened and found the general's eyes on her – more specifically her hands, before they dragged upward to her face. For a brief moment their gazes met, and the general's were grey and clear-eyed and sharp. "Cantlondish, are you?"

Britt curtseyed and it felt like a turn on her axis deep inside, her heart beating quick and hard against her ribs. "As a matter of fact, I am, General."

The general's mouth thinned. It didn't seem to be hiding a smile. It probably wasn't hiding anger, either. "Dismiss your secretary, sir," she said directly to Master Cheya. "I seem to bring up bad memories."

But that meant Britt wouldn't get to find out what the general was *here for* –

We can't find anyone else, General.

Then look harder, tiderise take you! There has to be more than this!

Her nose smelled *gossip*.

"I am *fine*," said Britt firmly, and set out teacups for them both, and poured them tea without a single clink of porcelain. For a mercy there wasn't anything else on the table at which they were seated, or her hands might have betrayed her again.

"Please do take your leave if you must, my dear," Master Cheya said with gentle admonishment. "This is not the sort of meeting in which I need notes taken." He sat up, resting his elbows on the table and his hands clasped. They were by the window, but he did not look out, despite that the wall allowed the garden to if not thrive then condescend to cultivation. The neat row of bushes flanked both the building and the wall itself, lit faintly orange by the discreetly-placed sunlamps over them. "You say they've arrived?"

"Yes," said General Burnstone, her gaze on Master Cheya rather than Britt buttering their huffkins for them, "and they left their luggage with customs without much of a fight, so they didn't seem to suspect much."

"I see." Master Cheya frowned, heavy fingers tapping the table beside his teacup. "I suppose now you want the passkey."

"If you want us to look inside the crates," said the general with asperity, "it would be useful."

Master Cheya's frowned deepened, and he picked up his cup of tea. "I'm not fond of the thought, I confess."

"You were the one who told us to hold them," the general answered, and did not remotely sound sympathetic. If anything, there was a derisive curl to her lip. "How easily you turn over your own people to a foreign nation."

"If they've got themselves unknowingly embroiled with some kind of killer, it's for the best," Master Cheya shot back. Britt's heart skipped, but her hands remained steady as she set out the huffkins before them. "They may not even *know*, in which case, being taken into custody is the best thing for them." He spread his hands. "Scholars, you know. Very rarely do they have their eyes on the real world, and Passion in particular has never quite had his feet on the ground, if you take my meaning."

This time, the thud of Britt's heart was not for the clawing of memory, but a jolt of real concern. She had never met Passion in person, but he sent such lovely flowery letters back to the annex, describing the world around him in a way only he saw it.

Never addressed to *her*, specifically. Always to the staff of the annex, thanking them for their time and their efforts and whatever new items they'd sent along with Ryan. It was ... nice. Endearing. Endearing enough that Britt, and she was not the only, made efforts to put some small special things in the next supply run, even something so simple as a shelf-stable fruitcake.

She had spent a long time not being seen. Few people remembered the staff. That Passion made the effort –

It was meaningful. Even though he didn't, couldn't, know them. Unless Ryan mentioned the rest of them, and perhaps he did; for Ryan was a talkative fellow himself. Always brought back flowers from the depths of the bog

Britt hadn't realised *could* have flowers. Always returned with a smile and Passion's letter and gratitude on his behalf.

Carefully Britt set out the huffkins, her head whirling too quickly to have heard the conversation which came next, and only coming back on Master Cheya saying: "*Do* be gentle with them, won't you? I truly don't believe they mean any harm."

"What *will* you do if it turns out that man is a genuine killer," said the general, her mouth still with that bitter curl. Britt wasn't sure which part of the situation, or the conversation, was doing it.

"*What* man?" she asked without thinking, and withdrew the tray unthinkingly to her chest. It wasn't as though she was unaccustomed to bandits or murderers – she was Cantlond-born, after all! On the far edges of the state. It seemed as though there were more and more people turning to violence just to survive. The state couldn't keep up with them all. And of course when Cantlond fell –

It wasn't as though Britt had never seen a dead body before.

This sounded ... different. Different to bandits who killed for coin or to live, different to an accident on the street caused by a row over food or lodging.

Master Cheya patted her arm with his much larger one. "Don't you worry about it, my dear," he said firmly. "He hasn't been sighted in the city. Now, you keep the personal possessions of scholars out in the field, don't you?"

"Yes," said Britt, which Master Cheya *should* know but possibly didn't, owing to that being one of those small logistical details he didn't particularly concern himself over. He knew it needed to be *done*; he just didn't pay attention to the details. That was what staff were *for*.

"Would you be so kind as to fetch for us those belonging to Scholars Passion and Yoch, and Mister Ryan?"

... Oh. Britt's mouth thinned before she could stop it.

"With all due respect, Headmaster," said Britt with the grim determination of knowing this was going to be A Fight, "it's against policy to release personal items to anyone other than those who put them in there, or someone who's been authorised to sign on their behalf."

Master Cheya patted her arm again. "The annex is under my authority, my dear," he said gently. "That includes all items within it, in an emergency. The general may need them for her investigation. The scholars' lives may depend on it."

Britt blinked huge and slow, more at Master Cheya than the general. "How?" she asked with as much obtuseness as she could muster. "If they truly have been – suborned by someone with ill intent – it would have been after they left their possessions in my care, in which case, there's hardly a need to look at them, being as the scholars haven't returned in the interim."

There was a loud pause. Master Cheya sat back in his chair and folded his hands over his lap, and regarded her silently. The slant of General Brimstone's mouth, if Britt wasn't *immensely* mistaken, had the tenor of a savage grin more than disdain; but it was a little hard to tell, since she hid it behind a cup.

"And Mister Ryan?" Master Cheya asked eventually. "Has he added to his box since?"

"Yes," Britt admitted, "though I couldn't tell you what. I bring the box to them and don't pay much attention what they do with it, though I do stay in the room."

She was most concerned about someone getting into a box that wasn't theirs, though there had to be some measure of trust involved. As well as privacy. The scholars who went into the field had a right to know their items were left untouched in their absence, however long the absence.

"Then perhaps you might bring us Mister Ryan's belongings?" Master Cheya suggested delicately.

Britt tried very hard not to frown, or otherwise purse her lips. "Master Cheya," she said, "if you don't think that the three of them are knowingly involved, then I don't see why we have to go rifling through their things, or have them arrested. Why can't we welcome them home the way we would anyone else, and ask them to stay in the annex? Why are we treating them as conspirators, instead of witnesses?"

"Mistress Birdie."

Oh, now that wasn't a tone Britt heard very often. It made her raise her chin and straighten her back, for all the good it did, with how short she was. She looked Master Cheya directly in the eye. He looked distinctly unamused, and yet: said nothing more right away, regarding her again silently.

"Mistress Birdie," he said, gentle for all the use of the title, "you're quite correct. What I fear is that they may be doing something they view as a tad outside the law for the sake of their science, when in reality their actions are contributing to something *vastly* outside the law, and which puts them, and anyone nearby them, in danger. Were they to remain here at the annex, we would have to evacuate the school entire. The man with whom we suspect them associating is a cold-blooded killer." Britt's gut plunged. "As distasteful as it is, they and everyone around them would be safer were they in the custody of trained guards."

"Even so –"

Even to herself, her voice sounded uncertain. It was true they may not be wholly unaware; just unaware enough not to realise. Mister Ryan especially was not *particularly* attentive about rules, and how many times had Britt herself been obliged to task a scholar for ignoring managerial procedure? And yet –

General. We've been ordered to withdraw before the floodwaters rise again.

And how long will that be?

Almost certainly not before dawn, General, but –

Then don't you dare move those ships a sodden inch before then, is that clear?!

Unaware, unsought-after, Britt's eyes met those of General Ell Burnstone, grey as the firmament overhead; steady as stone underfoot. When the floodwaters were rising, despite being ordered to evacuate herself, the general had remained until the very last moment. Seeking survivors. *Searching* for those who yet *lived*.

"I just don't like it," said Britt finally, to Master Cheya but without shifting her gaze. "When we keep possessions for people, sir, it's with the understanding they'll be left undisturbed. We don't have exemptions for that."

It wasn't right to bend the law in a way that would make someone *suffer*, instead of alleviate their suffering. She wasn't sure who was right, but – well, *surely* they could evacuate the school if they must, and make arrangements for those who had nowhere else to go. Certainly it would be more disruptive, but surely the scholars' rights mattered too. Especially if they were being somehow tricked.

"We don't expect our scholars to be charmed by a charismatic murderer, either," said Master Cheya, kindly but with an edge; and then, pained: "Please don't oblige me to *order* you, Mistress Birdie. I have long thought of us as partners more than employer and employee."

That hit, digging in like a barb. It was true that in many things, related to the school in particular, people came to Britt before they went to Master Cheya, and accepted her response even without his authority. It was *true*. Britt had felt it too, on many occasions, and he had not minded; indeed, declared his satisfaction for not having to deal with such matters.

And yet –

Britt dragged her gaze from the general's to meet Master Cheya's squarely. "If that's so, sir," she said quietly, "then why wasn't I consulted before you decided that it was too difficult to manage the school with the relevant scholars here?"

He had never said such a thing to her until this moment, until he needed, *wanted*, her to comply with a request she did not agree with.

It might be foolish, digging in her heels like this. But it mattered, to not treat people like criminals until they were. It *mattered*. She thought Schecheya was *better* than this. She'd certainly thought *Academe* was better than this.

Master Cheya sighed and covered his eyes, and for a moment – oh, he seemed tired. "Please fetch Ryan's belongings, Birdie, as an order with which I expect you to comply. I realise this is a sordid, unpleasant affair, and your concerns have been noted. Would that I could grant them more weight than that."

... It occurred, very suddenly, that Master Cheya himself may not be the one making the decisions here, only the conduit through which they were passed.

Britt's lips compressed, but this time it was with a sudden burn of tears, a lump in her throat. She had to comply – for one thing, she didn't know what would happen if she didn't. Probably he would ask for her key and get them himself, or ask someone else to, and if they didn't know how storage was sorted they might breach someone else's privacy in pursuit of Mister Ryan's –

And likely they would take Passion and Yoch's thereby, instead of just the one.

None of it seemed very *fair*, but if Britt was to be complicit against her wishes, she could at least try to mitigate the damage.

"Very well, Master Cheya."

Her voice was soft and still didn't erase the hoarseness, and without another word Britt turned on her heel to exit the room and cross the entry. The storage room was behind reception's expansive polished desk, *her* desk, made of broken timber the floods smashed to pieces, and still retaining the knots and sanded fittings where it had been put together like a puzzle.

It was a work of art, wholly unpractical, and she'd fallen in love with it from the very first moment she crossed the threshold in search of education to replace that which she'd lost. That someone would put in the effort – that

Schecheya would choose to take the shattered remnants of what had once been whole and make it whole again in another way –

Until that moment Britt had not truly understood what desire was.

It was from behind this desk she, and her junior staff, organised the annex *and* the school. Empty of all but Yas, right now, because most of her people were out on errands so as to get them away from the unnerving presence of the state's guards in the vicinity. Many of Britt's staff were Prittune; but many of them were Schecheyan too, daring to experience the world or the family of senior ambassadorial staff seeking something to do with their time.

Storage was down the hall behind the door, at the far end where there was the most space and it was closest to the stone of the cliff. The annex wasn't built right up against it, but it was a near thing and a narrow area, and a great deal of the building's less flattering infrastructure was built in the space. The boiler, for instance, and the generator, and other such necessary machinery. Storage itself was kept at a constant temperature, in case of delicate items, though it wasn't strictly an archive.

Britt was the only one with the keys, but spares were available from the key-chest in case of an emergency. No doubt Master Cheya would have asked for that, and received it. And been able to remove any of the boxes therein.

It was better this way. This way, it was only Ryan's being removed. Britt had won that fight, probably. Maybe. If it didn't occur to Master Cheya to use the spare keys after the fact.

Even still, Britt's jaw ached with the force of her clench as she fitted keys to locks and turned them both, then the handle, and entered the room at a brisk walk while trying not to think about what she was doing. The long-term storage was at the back and around the corner. The larger metal crates were down the bottom, the smaller up the top; the floor was absolutely clear. Even the ladder she used to reach the higher shelves was tucked away, a clever little thing whose wheels bent down to let feet on floor once weight was plied.

She rounded the corner and there at the far end was Mister Ryan, halfway climbed up the metal shelves for the dim concealment of the uppermost, and paused in the motion of looking utterly guilty.

Britt stared. Ryan winced.

This. This was not even the most egregious thing she'd ever seen him do. The man had a habit of skulking across the rooftop, and twice she'd caught him climbing through windows instead of a door.

"How?!" Britt demanded. "The door was locked!"

He slid back to the floor and sat back on his heels, gazing up at her with not quite enough chagrin and nowhere near the wry smile he should have had. His hair fell across his eyes and there was nothing sheepishly amused or coy about it, only serious and withheld.

Belatedly Britt remembered that Master Cheya wanted to give this man and his friends over to the general, and she blurted: "The state's here to *arrest* you."

"Oh, I know," said Ryan, and craned his head up toward the vent on the uppermost part of the wall, its grate removed. Out from the narrow rectangular hole Yoch extended her arms and rested them crossed against the wall, her head poking out like a – a – perhaps a bird hatchling from its tunnel-bored nest in the cliff.

Her short black hair was windswept, grey with dust and gold skin grimy; but there was never anything except keenness in her dark eyes. As there was now.

Of course. Aside from Britt herself, and the children who could neither dare nor reach, Yoch was perhaps the only person slight enough to fit in the vents. She certainly seemed *comfortable* there. And the door to the storage room was only locked from the inside; anyone within could open it without a key.

"Why are they arresting us?" Yoch asked bluntly. "I'm curious what excuse they've made."

"That you've become accidentally embroiled with a stone-cold killer," said Britt; and added belatedly, more stern than fearful: "You *haven't*, have you?"

"A *stone-cold* killer wouldn't keep his heart on his sleeve the way he did," said Ryan grimly. "I've met enough of those to know the difference."

"You and I have different observations of his stoicism," Yoch observed dryly, and Ryan craned his head up.

"He kept himself to himself," he said, "but it was restraint, not emotionlessness. I won't say any man isn't capable of killing under the right circumstances, but him and *stone-cold*? Not a chance."

Britt sighed something long and unravelling, her hand pressed to her chest. "Then the state's wrong, or misunderstood." Oh, what a relief. It was exactly as she'd thought – some horrible misunderstanding. Even if this man *had* killed someone, surely it was manageable. Desperate circumstances often mitigated sentences. "Then you can explain to Master Cheya and General Burnstone, and we can stop this nonsense here and now."

"Would that we could," said Yoch grimly, and Britt's gut shrivelled sudden enough to make her feel mildly ill.

Even so, her voice was the firm censure she used on students being where they weren't supposed to be. "And why not?"

They exchanged long speaking-without-speaking glances, and Britt crossed her arms. "All I need *do* is shout. *Please.*" Her eyes stang very suddenly. "I don't want anyone to suffer more than they must. Tell me why I should help you. Surely you *aren't* in conspiracy with someone who means us ill?"

"No," said Yoch softly. "Certainly not that."

Ryan sighed and reached around to the pocket flat against his back, beneath his pistol. It was where he always kept important documents, though these were smaller than Britt expected. It wasn't until he'd passed the envelope into her hands that Britt felt the stiff edges and realised what they were.

"Photographs?"

Only a few, but some. She threaded her finger beneath the unpressed flap and let them slide out into her hand. At a glance of the sides, they all looked to be of the same general area – a metal room with a corrugated ceiling, and all taken of the same wall, presumably with the same man as on the topmost.

Britt studied him. It was a dark picture, taken without a flash, which was an odd choice; and it made him look darker and tireder. His face was not precisely sallow – his skin had a healthy kind of brownness to it quite unlike someone with naturally darker skin – but his face was drawn and weary, his hair a little lank, in the way of a person just from some terrible illness or other travail. He looked directly at the camera, or the person behind the camera, and yet his stare was fixed.

His eyes, though. His eyes were *striking*. Even blank and tired, and with pupils entirely too round. Different colours, one a shade of blue just short of purple and the other a kind of gold, neither of which Britt had ever seen in a person before.

He didn't look remotely like a murderer. He looked like someone who'd just lost his entire world. Gods knew Britt knew that feeling well enough; just the sight of him put something taut and sympathetic in her chest.

And yet, that didn't explain his pupils.

"Is he alright?" she asked. "Did you have to give him something? His eyes ..."

"He's not accustomed to our light levels," said Yoch enigmatically, and then: "That's one without flash, isn't it? Find one with."

The first few were all dark; finally there was one with bleached-white shades, where the flash shone off metal and –

Her heart skipped beats, her limbs suddenly buzzing. "What under –"

He *glowed*. It was as though the flash reflected off him as much as metal. He was still human-shaped, but brighter even where clothes dulled the light, until his edges blurred with lens flare and his exact features were obscured. His hair blazed deep red and his eyes –

They could have been deep wells of gold-and-blue light, for all the humanity in them.

Britt's hands shook, and numbly she watched the photographs drift to the floor, her fingers too paralysed to try and stop them. Ryan kneeled by her and scraped them together, tucking them back into the envelope.

"It turns out," he said matter-of-factly without looking up at her, "sometimes a startrail has a skydweller on the other end of it – or at least that was the case here."

"The prospectors knew they ought to be looking for a man," said Yoch, her voice low and throaty, "which begs a number of questions, though currently I'm primarily concerned about one: who told them he was a killer?"

"And why?" Ryan added, and reached behind him to slide the photographs back in his pocket. "I assume at this point it was to add urgency to finding him, but there's no telling. Whatever the case, it's clear someone knows *something*, and expects a skydweller in particular."

Britt swallowed hard, her mouth dry. "Master Cheya said Prittuni could take you into custody ..."

Did he know? Gods below, did he know what the man was that they were looking for? And if he did, then –

The scholars couldn't come in and 'solve this'. It would be their words only, and in the meantime, if this poor man was found –

He looked so very heartsick. The long fragile stare of a man who had, in but a moment, lost *everything*. Britt knew the look. She'd seen it in the mirror often enough. And *someone* was slandering him for no other purpose than to get him in their grasp, for no other reason than – than –

Than fear or hatred or some kind of foolish religious spite, or even worse the clinical academic interest which divorced myth from *personhood* –

It wasn't fair.

Abruptly Britt turned toward the shelves, reaching down for Ryan's on the lowest shelf. There was no way for them to know he had removed anything. After all, Britt herself wouldn't have known what was in here before.

"I have to go. They've asked for your things. They might ask for the scholars', yet." She had already been, perhaps, too long already. Surely it wouldn't take this long for someone to collect a box and come out again. Her heart pounded with ineffectual rage and fear in her chest, and she turned her back on the pair of them. "The door will be locked when I exit."

But they would be able to open it from the inside, and Ryan surely knew of avenues away from the annex no one had even considered. How else could he get *in* so easily?

Britt did not wait for an answer, only marched toward the exit; but behind her came Yoch's voice, soft and full of warmth. "Thank you."

Britt made no answer. Her throat was too tight, and she had to spend her energy on not weeping too tellingly before she went back to Master Cheya's office.

CHAPTER FIVE

DROWNED

From a distance the end of the mangroves had not been visible, at least not from the top of the cliff. Erasmus had never realised just how swiftly grey the horizon became, how easily obscured, with naught but cloud cover. That, and he was much closer to an ... an absolute *ground*.

There wasn't really a word for *ground* in the languages above the clouds; only variations on *grounding*: the opposite of *weightlessness*, the antithesis of *falling*.

In retrospect, the concepts might be related. Passion had oodles of evidence the languages from above and below the cloud cover had the same root. You could fall off a cliff, but you couldn't fall off the *earth*, not here. It was as nadward as a person could get. Even naddier than the most nadward part of the Empire.

So Erasmus didn't know what he was looking for, not exactly, and all Ryan had laughingly said was: "You'll know it when you've reached the other side."

The scent caught his attention first. Everything about the mangrove was pungent and sharp in equal measures, but the sharpness became more and more overt, cutting past everything else. He'd never smelled anything like it; it was so crisp he could almost believe the wind had become a blade, did he not know exactly what that looked like. It seemed familiar, but he couldn't place it.

Somewhere after that the air took on a scent even more overpoweringly pungent than that of the mangroves, or even the bogs. It reminded Erasmus of something rotting, but combined with that sharpness. He was still trying to imagine what kind of flesh or plant-life might be responsible for *that* when the mangroves opened up very suddenly and the vast expanse before him was naught of dingy froth-topped green and cloudy grey.

Even dim and through the goggles, it was so ... *big*. The weight of the waterfalls had been shocking enough, but all this – all this *water* – it couldn't possibly *all* be water –

And his canoe plunged out toward it, gripped by the eastern current with the mangroves fast passing. To one side, cliffs and a hollow boom like that of sails being torn apart as the ... the water collided with its base; to the other, a long grey stretch of something too flat and featureless to be natural rock, the occasional bar extending into the water like fingers.

Go toward the beach, Ryan told him. *South, toward the beach.*

What exactly is *a beach?* Erasmus had demanded, and Ryan paused.

Do you know sand?

No. Erasmus didn't know *sand*, at least not in a way Ryan could describe. In the end all Ryan could say was to turn away from the cliff and go south toward the beach.

The water jostled suddenly, the canoe bobbing in a manner even more unpleasant than on the river. The breeze heightened as Erasmus emerged from the safety of the mangroves. The air here was so – *fierce* – but there were no cross-currents colliding, just the wind savage against the water's surface, pulling it up until it frothed and slammed itself against the earth in a wash of white.

The banks peeled away suddenly and Erasmus's heart pounded high in his throat at the thought of being drawn into that – that monstrous unknown. Without thinking he thrust his paddle into the south-side, bracing against the weight of water. The canoe turned so sharply that everything tilted.

His heart and stomach jumped higher. The wind-ragged water slammed against the bottom, washing over the side; the low edge of the canoe broke surface and water swamped in sudden and heavy, drenching fabric and seeping beneath his rubber linings almost at once.

In a tangle of paddles, luggage and canoe Erasmus went into the water, from blustery wind to a cold obscuring throb in his ears. His shoulder collided with the shoreline, and earth gave under him; he flailed until he got his feet under him in water that was barely a few feet deep.

But with a steep drop. He felt it in the way the earth moved under him, the sudden evaporation of anything under his feet if he drifted just a foot further.

He couldn't hold onto all this. He hadn't got a chance to take a real breath, and the water's pressure tried to squeeze out what scant air was locked inside his diaphragm. Altitude would never have been like *this* –

Erasmus dropped the paddle and lunged for his bags, groping for the earth with one hand and getting only particles that gave under his desperate grasp. Nevertheless, he managed to flounder his way to something solid enough underfoot, dragging the rapidly weighted bag after him, and clawed his way to air.

Breaching the surface left him buffeted by waves, threatening to send him tumbling over. Everything was heavy, unpleasantly wet, scraping against skin. He staggered to his feet and fell over again when he tried to lift his bag and the water sucked at it unexpectedly.

For all the tiny grains, the earth felt as hard as stone when he struck it. The coarse soil felt like a thousand tiny daggers pressed against fabric, nothing like the clean icy winds of altitude; grimy and gritty and *unpleasant*.

Everything on the fundament seemed to be unpleasant.

For a few moments Erasmus lay there, wearily pulling down his wet mask to breathe deep and as slow as he could manage, staring up at the blurry clouds veiled by drops on the goggles. Water washed up against him with a soft hiss, gentle on this shallow edge of it.

Alright, *as a sound* that was pleasant. As a reality, it very much wasn't.

It was so tempting, now he was wet through, laying still, with that soft hiss in his ears – it was so tempting to let himself fall asleep. His limbs ached. His everything ached, his chest maybe most of all. At least in the bog he'd had people to watch for guidance, but here?

He couldn't be more alien to the location if he *tried*.

Eventually he pushed himself upright, as heavy as if he'd been caught in an antipodal lodeshaping. The canoe was a shadow on the water, probably closer than Erasmus could tell, and yet – a thousand miles away as far as his ability to retrieve it was concerned. And swiftly growing harder to see.

... It occurred, belatedly, that this might not be due to distance but the fact the day was dimming, and he was still here on the – the beach – with no idea how he was meant to find the location Ryan tried to describe as a safe place to camp.

With a curse a little too fragile to do anything but catch tears in his throat, Erasmus hauled himself upright on shaky legs, and his bags after. He wasn't sure where he was going except somewhere that wasn't *here*, so close to water. Somewhere he could dry out, if not light a fire.

For a mercy whatever fabric lining Ryan insisted on covering his bag with, which Erasmus painstakingly restored every time he opened it, kept his things from soaking the way Erasmus himself had. Without the suction of the water – well, it was still heavy to pull onto his shoulder, but at least wasn't unbearable.

This damned soil was, though. This – *sand*. Too wet to be anything but hard when he landed on it, but giving under his feet with every step until his pace was more like a lopsided attempt not to fall at every moment. The wind didn't *help* – pushing at him like its only purpose was to send him over.

The longing for the moored stability of the isles was a hard, sharp-edged knot in Erasmus's chest. Without a word, what was there to *say*, he trudged away from the water and followed the slope.

It wasn't yet dark the way the scholars saw it, but it was dark enough to his eyes there didn't seem a point in trying to remove the goggles. Or … looking around in any fashion. At least if he ran into something he'd know he'd found the top of this … beach.

For long inexorable moments he felt as though there was nothing else in the world but the horrible boom of water against stone, the hiss of it over this sharp-edged soil; a ringing in his ears that wasn't just the clawing wind, but fatigue and chill and misery.

"Hoy there!"

Everything here on the fundament seemed cruel and full of jagged edges.

"Stop!"

The shout came at several removes. Erasmus didn't actually realise it was directed at him, only stopped and turned with the kind of dull disinterest exhibited by a passerby looking to see who might need assistance, an act which in itself failed thanks to the darkness. All he saw was shadows; the movement of foliage, the long unyielding wasteland of the beach.

Except –

Those figures weren't just *trees*, were they? Or even illusions. They came at him more swiftly than he thought possible on this kind of horrible yielding terrain, and it wasn't until one of them seized his arm that Erasmus figured out they were *real*.

He flinched and shied away –

He *never* shied away. He wasn't *Christopher*, for Light's sake.

"Is that him?" came from higher on the slope, demanding in the way of someone with authority, feminine-voiced. Roughly his hood was pulled down, and at once the wind yanked his hair.

"Who else would be out by the mangroves at this time of day?" came the answer from another of the shadows, deeper and masculine; and finally, *finally*, it filtered in that Erasmus may be genuinely in trouble.

"People fish near here," someone else offered. "Fish like the mangroves. My uncle's got a boat –"

"Who else would be out by the mangroves at this time of day *half-drowned and with luggage*?" growled the second man, and shook Erasmus. Gently – but something twisted and mewling and surprised still came out of his throat.

He pressed his fist to his mouth and breathed in the abrupt silence.

"I dunno," said the feminine voice dubiously. "He looks too pathetic to be a stone-cold killer."

Erasmus's gut plunged so fast he nearly choked on the bile before he realised there *was* any, his shoulders hunching. The ringing in his ears became more acute, and with an awful chilly horror knitting up from his core he realised – he probably shouldn't have ignored that – or chalked it up to ... to just *misery* –

The sensation gripping him from within wasn't *just* horror.

He wrenched himself away from the man's grasp, stumbling on numbed feet and just barely catching himself on the sand as he fell.

"Hey now," exclaimed the pedant, reaching toward him. Erasmus flinched again, curling in around the horrible yawning knot in him; one arm out and flailing to smack the offered hand away, seeking words that didn't come easily to his mouth. When they came they scraped raw and terrified.

"*Don't touch me*. I don't want to –"

It was an agony that came from somewhere inside him, swamping as much was water. *Worse than*, because this threatened to carry him away until he didn't have a body left to feel, only that awful ringing and the sensation of being *crushed* beneath weights he couldn't see. Voices spun through his ears too quickly to catch the words, if he knew them at all – a long liquid babble of grim fear and desperation, as distant as the sand beneath him.

"– hurt you –"

His words came so very faintly.

Breathe. Just breathe.

He shouldn't have gone in the water. It felt too much alike.

Just breathe.

The first time this had happened, the very first time –

What have you done?!

I didn't ... I didn't. I don't know how this happened.

– he'd come to sitting stunned next to his cousin's still-warm corpse, and Christopher's horrified shout ringing in his ears.

Just breathe.

He didn't *wholly* lose himself this time. Not wholly. Enough to feel the crushing weight; enough that he was dimly aware of himself curled in the sand, clinging to consciousness by his fingertips. When the yawing distance eased it was with a pounding head, rattling breaths, and a huddled, hurried conversation above.

"Called out, maybe? It's been known to happen. They say it's like a man gets possessed, doesn't know what he's at and doesn't remember it after."

"Don't be stupid," said the brusque man, scornful and rattled in even measures. "Everyone knows that kind of power doesn't actually exist. It's just an excuse for criminals to get off."

"Then why's we all got a damned nick, eh?" snapped the feminine-sounding voice. "Face it, it's got to be true in some way or nobody'd bother. And there's no way this bloke's a stone-cold *anything*."

"Not *stone-cold*, maybe," said the brusque man, "but he's wanted for *something*, or someone who looks like him, and if it's not him he's better off in a dry cell than the sodden beach at night."

"You're not wrong there," said the pedant, a little dubious but assenting.

Erasmus drew his breath in slow and deep and shuddering. Let it out slowly. Tried to unclench his stiff aching arms from around himself. Relief wasn't an unravelling thing, didn't ease the tautness in his chest; but the ringing in his ears subsided some.

He hadn't wholly lost control. He hadn't hurt anyone.

Tell me your name.

Christopher. Please.

Whatever was in him hadn't hurt anyone.

Someone crouched by him, and the pedant's voice came if not kind then at least a little sympathetic. "Alright, mate. Think you can get to your feet? We'll be taking you in now. It ain't much, but it's better than out here."

After all the time and care the scholars had taken to try and keep him *out* of the state's hands –

But perhaps it wasn't him they were looking for. Perhaps there genuinely was a killer hiding somewhere nearby, who resembled him at a glance, and he just happened to be noticed. That seemed likely, in fact. The last people looking for him had been a year ago. There was no reason for anyone else to look for him in particular.

And he.

He was afraid to be alone tonight. He hadn't realised the water, the ocean, would do that to him.

Erasmus's breath shuddered in his chest, but he managed to nod, and didn't even fight as the guards hauled him to his feet.

CHAPTER SIX

A gentle capsizing

Tyrian found them rooms for the night in one of the inns lowest in the city, over the water. It was a sailor's inn, so they weren't likely to be looked-for; if nothing else because people forgot that scholars could very often be more accustomed to the rigors of living than most others. Depending on the scholar.

It ought to be logical that those just come from bogs might be willing to dare the crass inhospitability of a sailor's inn, but few people thought in terms of logic.

If nothing else, Tyrian knew people here, so they were unlikely to be in danger, at least from ill temper. The fetid smoke of poor-quality tobacco, on the other hand, was surely an asphyxiation hazard.

Then there was the booming shudder of the tide against the inn's stilts. The sensation of the floor shifting underfoot, the sound, reminded Yahvanna all too well of her first floods in the bog; the complacent daring which ended in her huddled in the loft of the cottage, clinging to the walls and praying to whatever gods who would bother to listen while cursing her own arrogance.

"Sorry," said Tyrian when he saw her flinch at a particularly robust boom of water against the building's foundation. "This is the safest place I could think of."

Yahvanna took a deep breath and let it out slowly. "The foundation is far more robust than the cottage was."

It was a truth, and: still did not quite unknit the tension in her chest. The tidal indicators visible on the beams below the porch as they entered suggested the waters had, over time, risen. The floorboards were damp underfoot, and every so often – as with the wave that made her flinch – spray jetted visibly above the windowsills, and water sluiced beneath the slats in the gutters beneath.

Still not the rampaging, relentless wash of water.

Still a little too evocative of it.

The innkeeper was among Tyrian's acquaintances, so although Vespasien and Yahvanna stood out while awaiting arrangements – Vespasien more than Yahvanna, it had to be said, partially due to his anxious hunch and knitted brow – in short order Tyrian beckoned them toward the stairs. A few people called out Ryan's name, but Tyrian only waved back, and did not allow himself to be deterred.

"He only had one room," Tyrian said as he took them up the narrow stairwell very nearly crushed between the inn's wall and reassuringly solid cliff. (Reassuringly solid, so long as one did not remember what happened to Cantlond.) "Too many sailors in berth."

"I'm *sure* we'll somehow manage," said Yahvanna with great asperity. It wasn't as though she hadn't abided with these two men, both separately and together, during far more inconvenient instances. Having to wash her cycle linens with Tyrian sitting across the way while they were both trapped in the bunker under the cliff sprang to mind.

He'd actually helped, the second time. And he knew more about the herbal qualities of plants than Yahvanna had quite ever bothered, specifically those pain-related. Tyrian was the sort of man one *needed* nearby when survival was in question, and *wanted* nearby when it came to any possible comfort therein.

The room was at the top, very nearly an attic; only avoiding it by dint of the fact that it was not big enough to store much of anything. The bed filled nearly the entire space, barely large enough for all three of them and that mainly due to Yahvanna not being so tall as the others. As it was, Vespasien had to bend his head to get in the door, or stand down that end.

It was so close to the cliff that Yahvanna was certain she could have climbed out the unexpectedly large window and scaled the yard to the roof; and from there been on a narrow walkway with a rusted rail, clearly not in frequent use, not far above.

"You absolutely could," said Tyrian when she mentioned it. "That's the point. This is the room with an escape exit – just in case."

"I pray such an escape will not be necessary," Vespasien murmured, looking a little green as he glanced toward the seething froth of the ocean below them, and clutched his bag closer.

"You're not meant to *look*," said Tyrian with fondly indulgent exasperation, and Yahvanna patted Vespasien's arm.

"I rather doubt you'd fit down such a chute," she pointed out pragmatically. The space was so narrow that although Vespasien was not himself a naturally wide man he had broad enough shoulders Yahvanna rather thought he'd get lodged before he ever hit the water.

For some reason, this only made his face whiten. "I believe I shall sit down."

Which he did, somewhat heavily, on the bed.

There was not much point in staying up. They could not discuss much here, where it was so easy to be overheard; and what light was available through the firmament was swiftly departing. If they'd been in the annex the lights would have stayed on for hours longer, scholars and students bent over their studies, books and research according to preference and stage of education.

"We could," said Tyrian when Yahvanna mentioned it, each of them turned away in the act of pulling off their damp outer layers. "We're low enough on the water that the inn has a sluice pulling from the tide. But it'd cost."

"In bribes to ignore the light, no doubt," said Yahvanna dryly, and stripped off her trousers to pull on some dry woollens.

"In cost to cover the expense of maintenance," corrected Tyrian. "This isn't Yhedilitt. There aren't regulations prohibiting people from building their own hydrolevin systems."

That couldn't be cheap, and did beg the question how an inn on the water could afford to have one built and maintained, particularly given the additional risk of damp wires.

As well as other questions, relating to the undermining of the baroness's power and rule of law. One of the only means by which a sovereign *could* maintain authority was by ensuring the people benefited from governance. Without that, Prittuni was one step closer to either anarchy or a violent military state. If an inn could safely harness its own power, it had no use for infrastructure provided by the barony; and if it could gain wares from the ships at sea rather than inland ...

Perhaps Yahvanna would carefully ignore how near to the proximity of pirates they might, in fact, currently be.

Or perhaps merely the Thalassocracy, which was little different in the eyes of many. If anyone *did* know how to protect levin from the damp, it would be them.

Regardless, the point was an academic one: they could not afford either the additional expense or the attention. So to bed they went, Yahvanna letting the men get comfortable first before finding a place of her own, primarily across and between them rather than on the bed proper.

At rest the occasional shudder was not *so* much like the floods. The cottage had, after all, stood over the waterfalls at all times; this was not too different from this height, where the wind rattling the eaves was far more overt and reduced the water below to a soothing regularity.

It was perhaps the warmest she'd slept in weeks.

***

They were all of them accustomed to rising early, the morning still grey even to their eyes. The innkeeper had food ready as they went downstairs, nodding them toward a spare table away from everyone else. The taproom was not so much empty as listless, a dozen bleary-eyed sailors either up early and unwanted or having just come in from a night of leisure elsewhere in the city.

"You said you were looking for a boat might take you up the coast looking for summat," said the innkeeper to Tyrian as he brought over a loaf of uncut day-old bread, along with salted pork and a pot of pickled seaweed.

"That's right," Tyrian agreed amiably.

"And then a ship out to sea."

"Aye," and this time the word was a little more cautious.

"Well, my gal was on the docks this mornin' prepping for the outgoing tide," said the innkeeper, setting down plates with a clunk, "and sent back with a lad that she saw a guard's barge pulling in from the north."

They all of them sat up. What cobwebs of sleep remained were swiftly chased away by adrenaline as Yahvanna asked: "Has it docked yet?"

"Not when she sent back," said the innkeeper. "You've time for the vittles. Wouldn't loiter on it, though."

There wouldn't be time for tea, more's the pity, not that Yahvanna was sure they served it here. The innkeeper went off, then, leaving them to eat. And to speak in relative privacy.

"How common are barges from the north?" asked Vespasien quietly.

"They aren't," said Tyrian grimly. "It's only the beach and the mangroves. They'd use rides going north, if they weren't certain of finding something on the shoreline or just off it."

Like a man lost for a year somehow, inscrutably, found from a distance only once he left the bog.

They hurried in breaking their fast, such that Tyrian still had a piece of bread in his mouth when they rose and left, pulling bags on shoulders and holding them close against the risk of some unknown patron not realising Tyrian's comrades ought not be touched.

The inn was on the water, but to reach the other side of the harbour they had to wind upward over the cliff, and thereby reached an overlook off one of the bluffs. It was close enough to see details, but not so close as to be noticed unless some enterprising guard was using binoculars on the city's own walkways; and even then, there were handfuls of people watching the view strung all the way along the paths. There always were.

Tyrian cursed just as Yahvanna's gaze found the state's flag snapping over one of the boats, even now with passengers disembarking.

It was a middling-length train of people, clearly an escort, not the sort done with respect. Though they also weren't being cruel, as far as Yahvanna could see. Simply – direct. One of the guards walked alongside Gus, hand firmly around his arm, while Gus himself clutched his bags to his chest and walked with head down.

He had the mien of someone who'd been in some way crushed, if not cowed, relenting wordlessly as his escort tugged him toward one of the mechanical lifts by the cliff. It was a long corded pulley of a thing, dingy-looking by dint of the excrement of seabirds and the constancy of salt air. Gus didn't even look up at it, which was – surely, surely, it was alarming.

But he was still wearing his goggles. Perhaps he was simply reticent to show anything that might be too alien a reaction.

Tyrian's fist struck the rail so hard it vibrated under Yahvanna's hand. "*I should have gone with him.*"

"There was no way of knowing our friend might have been observed by some unknown means," said Vespasien, low-voiced and gentle.

"And blaming yourself for it is hardly going to aid him now," Yahvanna added.

"He doesn't know the land," said Tyrian bitterly. "He's never seen the ocean. How could we have thought it was a good idea to send out an absolute stranger to the world beneath the firmament, *alone*? Just because he could light a fire under supervision doesn't mean he was going to be safe at night. Just because he could swim in the delta doesn't mean he knows what to do in the sea."

He was working himself into a right fury. Tyrian did have a tendency to turn his sword on himself, when it came to circumstances he believed he should magically foresee. Never mind that he'd deliberately and overtly eschewed magic on numerous occasions.

Without a word Yahvanna turned and strode away, and Tyrian said sharply: "And where do you think *you're* going?!"

"That lift goes to the fort," said Yahvanna without turning, "and it shan't ascend at speed. It's unlikely we'll beat it to the top, but we may yet see where they take him, and who meets him." Burnstone was said to be the decent sort, if nothing else; if indeed she was the one in charge of his capture as well as theirs. "It seems a better course of action than standing here shouting into the wind."

For a long few paces there came no response, and Yahvanna had made the walkway nearer the cliff by the time Tyrian's footfalls came abreast of her, with Vespasien's heavier behind them.

"You're right," said Tyrian more calmly, with a quirk on his mouth that was so wry it was hard to tell whether it was amused or grudging.

"I frequently am," said Yahvanna dryly, but turned her head so he could see her smile, and took his hand to squeeze it gently. "Come. Show us the best way."

CHAPTER SEVEN

THOSE SODDEN CROSSROADS

"I'm very sorry, my dear," said Master Cheya at breakfast that morning, seated at the same table beside the windows where Master Cheya had received General Burnstone.

Britt usually served it, which was not strictly among her tasks but one she enjoyed doing; and very frequently Master Cheya invited her to join him. She didn't *ask*, no – but it was one of the subtle delightful overtures in what they'd wrought.

Quite technically he was her employer, on behalf of the annex, and didn't need to extend these endearing little courtesies. And yet it was hard to deny that their foundation, like the beams of a ship, had quivered.

Which was perhaps why he felt compelled to say so. Though Britt had accepted his invitation in this instance, she was – quiet.

After all, whose confidence had been betrayed in this instance? Ryan's, certainly; and Master Cheya, by Britt's withholding of information; and yes, perhaps her own, in the expectations she'd held rudely torn aside.

General Burnstone had at least seen fit to unpack the box within Britt's viewing, though Britt could not be sure if that was because the general agreed with Britt or was simply being courteous in response to Britt's insistence about the scholars' right to privacy.

There had been nothing of suspicion inside.

Nothing that hadn't been *removed* before either of them could witness it. And so the secret beat like scraping wings on the underside of Britt's locked throat. As it did now.

Britt mustered a smile and if anything it made the way Master Cheya patted her hand more anxious than his apology had been. "No, don't force anything you aren't feeling. I just want you to know – I *am* sorry."

"I simply don't understand the need, I suppose," said Britt, trying to be steady and accidentally achieving a state of miserable fatalism. "Surely any of our scholars, and a man of Mister Ryan's worldliness, would know if they were assisting someone so terrible. And if they are, oughtn't we wonder whether the man they might be assisting is perhaps being slandered in some fashion?"

Master Cheya's face pinched, his hand resting on Britt's unmoving, and Britt took a deep breath. "I simply think we should consider their judgement in lieu of any strict facts, is all. After all, if this man has been under suspicion prior to entering the border, then he hasn't committed a crime here in the state. How do we know the accusation from outside the country is real?"

"It's real," said Master Cheya softly, with an aching kind of careworn resignation. "It is quite real, I assure you."

"The fact that you won't tell us how you know makes that assertion more alarming, not less," Britt answered simply.

He had not even when General Burnstone pressed him. Yes, there was some measure of – of security, given that Master Cheya was Schecheyan and not Prittune; some measure of national procedure. It was wholly possible whichever state the supposed murderer was from had a delicate situation of their own, one that prohibited disclosure to other states even as Academe attempted to mediate between them behind closed doors.

The situation may well *be* that delicate. But if so, surely something of such import allowed some *modicum* of explanation beyond 'the man is a killer'. Who, and how, and what weapons, and what *dangers*, at the very least! No private details need be disclosed.

It was the absolute refusal to provide any context at all which was most alarming.

And Master Cheya didn't provide any here, either, only looked more tired still; taking back his hand only to pass it before his eyes.

"I suppose it would be uncharitable of me to wish another Cheya was responsible for this," he said wearily, and his own smile was rather visibly mustered. "One never thinks the most difficult situations will land in one's own lap, or prepares for difficult choices. ... Not that this one was particularly foreseeable, I suppose."

All of which was *extraordinarily enigmatic*, and Britt's heart panged more deeply; this time for the man she knew instead of one she didn't.

"Would that I could help you with it," she said quietly.

If she could, perhaps she could mitigate whatever fear drove him to overlook the rights of those who depended upon the annex. Surely, surely, whatever was happening ought to be done on the foundation of that which had sustained Schecheya for so long, instead of overruling them for the simplicity.

Rumination was interrupted when Yas tapped a little anxiously on the doorjamb, entering before either of them had even called.

"Master Cheya, forgive me –" The way Yas bowed was hurried, uncomfortable, anxiety written large in the nervous flap of hands. "We've just received a message from General Burnstone."

"Ah, that would be the state guard we saw trotting up the walk, no?" said Master Cheya lightly. The same guard which had, indeed, spurred Master Cheya's apology, likely in response to whatever face Britt had made unknown at the sight of the uniform.

"The general begs your presence at the fort," said Yas, brow knitted, still anxious. "*Immediately.*"

Britt's heart thudded uncomfortably hard against the inside of her ribs. Master Cheya looked down at the crust of his scone and the drips of cream and jam.

"Well, I wasn't likely to eat much else, I suppose," he said whimsically, and rose, pulling his napkin from his collar.

Unthinkingly Britt rose with him, folding her own napkin so as to catch the crumbs. Master Cheya paused in the midst of stepping out from behind the table, an act which took rather more care than Britt herself had to worry about.

The way he looked at her –

Tired. Considering. Perhaps even yearning, after a fashion.

"Might you come with me, Birdie?" he asked finally, and the fond warmth that knitted up Britt's throat brought a sting to her eyes even as it collided with the heart-thump of worry.

"Of course," she said quietly, and watched with heart-aching fascination as relief scrolled tellingly across his face.

***

'Immediately' still had enough give for them both to fetch coats and for Britt to wrap some sugar cookies in waxed cloth for them to have later, in case snacks were required before they were able to return.

There were state guards awaiting them outside the gates along with a carriage. It was not the first time Britt had ridden in one, though it was the first with escort and directly up to the fort. There were roads sufficient for carriages, at least from this elevation, but the carriages themselves were different to those which ran overland: being narrower, built of more delicate rods, and with lead-shod chassis so as to keep them on the ground.

Though there were some fairly lovely views on the way up, and a glider who followed the bend around a bluff with a perfect arc sweeping upward, Britt would be lying if she said she wasn't pleased to reach their destination. Something about wheels on a cliff-side path made her nervous, however sturdy and strong the ponies.

Then again, there were many once from Cantlond who scarce understood how she could bear to *live* on the side of a cliff these days.

If nothing else, Britt's clipboard and notebook were a soothing weight in the fold of her arm as she followed where Master Cheya was escorted, overlooked as a part of his equipment more than as his retinue. A secretary was, in many cases, furniture. Sometimes that was a grievance; in this instance, an abject relief.

The fort, like many things in Prittuni, was built of rugged stone, no shape set apart; each cut only as much as they must to fit together. It was as cold and grey as the city must no doubt appear even from a distance, and this not even a rainy day; but it was *sturdy*, and that was reassuring, despite the sameness of the courtyard through which they were hurried.

There were no gardens here, at least not in easy public view. A right pity, that was.

They were led up some stairs and ushered into a hall, and then nearly at once into a room overlooking another just about the same dimensions, except tall in a chute-like way. The balcony had the kind of pillars that ought to hide a person, and in this case did: General Ell Burnstone stood with her arms crossed beside one, in the shadow where no one from below was liable to notice.

She glanced up the moment they entered, her sharp grey eyes drifting consideringly across Britt before arriving on Master Cheya.

"You came with alacrity," the general observed with a clinical kind of edge, and inclined her head toward the balustrade. "Well, have a look. Is that him?"

Britt's heart vaulted into her throat and stayed there, sharp-edged. Her legs felt numb as she followed Master Cheya unthinkingly, sticking close by the pillars to avoid being observed themselves – but in Britt's case it hardly mattered. She wasn't sufficiently tall to see over the rail, and so she looked through it.

Her chest twisted tighter at the sight beneath them. The entry door must be under the balcony, with a table and chairs situated well within view. In one of the latter slumped a man, dark in hair and clothing, his reddish highlights showing in the lamps.

Several times overnight it occurred to Britt to wonder whether the photographs had been doctored, that perhaps someone had manufactured the glow in him, used the pictures without flash to create the illusion of integrity. Then she remembered *who* had given them to her, who had surely taken them; and, most of all, she remembered how tired the man had looked in the photographs.

As tired as he looked now, weary as if only the chair held him, his hair tangled around the rubber of the goggles he wore. He'd have to, with those eyes, but it was a wonder no one found that suspicious.

It did suggest he was thinking more clearly than his overall mien indicated.

As did the fact there was a tray containing a plate half-filled with buttered scones, just plain butter, along with a sugar bowl and a small clay jar of milk. It took a moment for Britt to spot the cup being cradled in his hands, almost wholly obscured in the way he clutched it close.

His bag, it had to be his bag, was on the table, opened; its contents laid carefully about, still in the process of being sorted and carefully tagged by prospectors.

"There's nothing really suspicious in the bag," said General Burnstone very nearly conversationally. "Nothing but the usual things. Food, supplies. Flint and steel, a camper stove, some old levinbricks nearly past use. Everything a man would want in the wild. A knife, but the utility sort, and it hasn't been used – no sign of blood, not even an animal's."

Britt dragged her gaze from the man to look up at Master Cheya, and caught the wrinkle of his brow. It wasn't thought. Britt knew by now what *thoughtfulness* looked like. This, she rather felt, was confusion. As if even to Master Cheya, the man was not as expected.

"Except one thing," General Burnstone added, as if the pause was only to judge their reactions; but the only reaction she *got* was for Master Cheya to turn toward her, his expression one of bemused interest.

The general unfolded her arms to unfold the handkerchief she held in turn, already stained with rust and dirt. Inside was a rusted pocketwatch, the sort that had fallen out of favour just before the Levinstrike and fallen back into it afterward. This one was quite large, and if Britt wasn't mistaken silver instead of brass, though it was difficult to tell given its state. That made it valuable on its own merit, if not for the tarnish and the mildew, and there was certainly the shadow of an emblem or coat of arms there, though Britt couldn't see it properly without cleaning.

"I'm afraid the significance is lost on me," said Master Cheya carefully.

"He said he found it in the mangroves," said General Burnstone. "On a corpse washed up in one of the pools. It seemed like the sort of thing someone would want back, so he took it to try and find the owner when he arrived in the city." She folded the handkerchief carefully back over the watch before Britt could figure out the emblem on it. "Five people were lost in the unexpected floods up north last season. Of them, four were found – by your Mister Ryan, no less. The fifth was a man of the Yew and Pigeon."

Britt held her breath unthinkingly. That particular House was not as wealthy as some – but wealthy *enough*, primarily owing to the fact of having care over the roads and the post. It wasn't 'old money' the way some Houses still put store in it: but the Yew and Pigeon was well-known, and well regarded, all over the state. They were among the Houses who'd risen by dint of the necessity of their trade, and their obstinacy in plying it.

Even when Cantlond was on the brink of fall, the Yew and Pigeon still brought their ponies forth into the rain and the flood to bring messages and mail.

Master Cheya looked surprised, and glanced again down at the man by the table. "That would indicate truthfulness on his part, no?"

"It would," confirmed the general. "The people who found him have expressed their doubts that he is the man you're searching for. Too frightened, they said. Too willing to come along. They got the impression he was just as glad to be out of the rain and the wet."

"Perhaps the report *was* mistaken on some level," said Master Cheya uncertainly. "Though at a glance he does appear to fit the details. Or perhaps –" He fell silent suddenly, his brow furrowed and breath half-caught, his fingers rubbing together as though he had paper between them to fiddle. It was a habit of his. "You're certain he exhibited no violent tendencies?"

"None," said General Burnstone with a curl of her mouth less about mirth and more about sardonic, her gaze steady and almost unblinking on Master Cheya. "If anything, it was the opposite. He seemed terrified of harming them by accident. Almost as if he was afraid of losing control."

... Oh, *no*. Britt's heart plunged, deep and cold and sinking, until she was obliged to swallow down bile. Her eyes dragged back to the man beneath them, who had not seemed to move since they entered.

No wonder no one had tried to take his goggles. It could not be comfortable, being arrested for something he may or may not have done, but it was in everyone's best interests to keep him as comfortable as *possible*, if the side-effect might be – something no one could control.

"Schecheya does not officially endorse the existence and threat of possession," said Master Cheya carefully, so that it felt like a pounce when General Burnstone spoke on his heels.

"But Academe does acknowledge the potential."

"Academe does not rule out anything which lacks evidence as to its existence or nonexistence," said Master Cheya.

"And in the meantime you've got a man who may or may not have killed someone," said General Burnstone, and the sardonic in her tone was even more pronounced. "Or may simply be psychologically unsound and framed for it, and Academe is refusing to provide information as to his alleged crime, his accusers, or indeed even the event itself."

"General Burnstone." Master Cheya's voice was firm. "You would not even know about this man if it were not for Academe's efforts. We are attempting to unravel a mystery, here."

"Are you?" said the general derisively. "It seems to me that you're attempting to maintain one." Her voice came waxing through Britt's ears, as if from a great distance. "First it was 'there's a man who will crash in some kind of experimental aerial technology' but neither man nor the technology could be found. Then it was 'take my people into custody for their safety', in the same conversation you asked to take custody of the man standing accused of *murder*."

"It would have been delicate at best to hold the man in the annex if some of our own scholars might be moved to – impractical actions," said Master Cheya, and now his voice came strained. "General, there is only so much I am permitted to *say*. This man fits the description, and I am obliged to have him held."

Below them, one of the prospectors came around and knocked gently on a corner of the table, far from the man. The man still jumped, a jerk of head that looked as though it might have caught his neck, and a moment of mouth-half-open breathlessness that spoke of someone jarred out of deep thought or worse.

It was probably worse. His entire demeanour – it was just like that night. Of people too shocked and weary and heartsore to respond unless prompted.

The prospector spoke too quietly for Britt to hear, but she held out her hand and the man glanced down at the cup in his grasp as if surprised to find it still there, and then gave it over. Hurriedly, as if to risk touching the prospector for too long might just infect her.

Britt's heart ached with sympathy, and she turned around as General Burnstone said with flat resolve:

"Be that as it may, Master Cheya, at this stage Prittuni has been given no reason to hand him into Schecheyan custody. I am inclined to take him to the capital with me and proceed from there."

"General," said Master Cheya, not wheedling but absolutely humourless, "if he *is* possessed, that means he's been practicing magic. As I recall, it's been some time since Prittuni has had to deal with such a situation. Is Prittuni prepared to contain a magician?"

General Burnstone's smile was not polite, not at *all*. "Is the annex?" she countered. "A *school*? Let's not pretend you're any better equipped to face that risk."

The way Master Cheya drew up his shoulders and drew in a breath – Britt was struck by the abrupt certainty that he was about to invoke the Treaties, which might force the general to relent but would *not* make him *friends*, not at all –

"Excuse me, General," Britt interjected before Master Cheya could ruin the annex's reputation at least in General Burnstone's eyes, if not the state at large. *Possibly* the state at large. Master Cheya startled in her direction; General Burnstone didn't move an inch. "I believe Master Cheya is simply concerned about adequately representing whichever stakeholders reported this man to Schecheya to begin with. If you're amenable, I should like to accompany him with you to the capital, so I might keep a record of events and oversee his care on the annex's behalf."

She turned directly to Master Cheya's white-faced stare, curtseying. "If that suffices for Master Cheya's needs, of course?"

"It might," said Master Cheya, sounding a little faint, and rather strained. His eyes were not precisely popping, but if Britt didn't know better she might almost think him suddenly *terrified* for her. "Yes, Mistress Birdie, it very well might."

Now General Burnstone looked at her, piercingly considering and mercifully without that sneer; and Britt held her gaze without flinching.

Plainly General Burnstone did not think much of Schecheya, or Academe, or both; or perhaps simply the power they wielded in the Treaties and the mechanisms therein. But Britt was not Schecheyan-born, even if she'd worked with them for quite a while now, and perhaps that would be enough.

Finally General Burnstone inclined her head. "That satisfies me. Since it's his care about which you're concerned."

"I intend to report on all matters pertaining to him," said Birdie firmly and with her chin raised.

"I'm sure you will," said General Burnstone, but it did not sound sarcastic, though she didn't smile. "I intend to leave tomorrow morning with the inbound tide." The one that passed upriver, south of the city. It would not take them the whole way to the valley – the current in the river shifted easily – but it would get them going, at least. "Do you wish to see him now, or return after you've packed your things?"

"Now, if you please," said Britt. "Or rather, after you've shown me whatever rooms he might be kept in, so I can see what he might have and what he might need."

If she wasn't mistaken, the general's mouth quirked. "He isn't a student, Mistress Birdie."

Britt firmed her back a little harder, raised her chin a little more – *stared*, with all the boldness in her, daring this general to be obstinate about so petty a detail. "Nevertheless."

The general's mouth quirked more deeply, and the bow she sketched was shallow, but courtier. Relenting. "As you please, Mistress Birdie." And she turned toward one of the guards stationed on the inside of the door. "Fetch me the lieutenant."

Britt exhaled slowly, and Master Cheya gripped her hand unexpectedly tight, leaning down. The lantern-light struck his forehead sheened with sweat, and it struck Britt in turn just how worried, perhaps even *afraid*, he must be.

"Be *careful*, Birdie," he whispered. "Some things are not as they appear at first glance."

"I know," said Birdie quietly, looking him directly in the eyes, and didn't know whether she was reassuring him as to the risk of a man possessed or indicating that she knew the man was a skydweller. Master Cheya blinked, then frowned; then opened his mouth –

Said nothing.

But he didn't quite let go of her hand, either, not until he was absolutely obliged.

CHAPTER EIGHT

BEACHED

The guards' barges had been some way down the beach, well beyond Erasmus's ability to see, and drawn alongside the sand by several ... oxen. A word Erasmus only picked up by listening, while trying not to stare at the massive beasts yoked by long, laughably narrow ropes. So narrow he didn't see the ropes at first, until they flexed with the movement of the oxen themselves.

Such beasts simply did not exist in the Empire, not even on the largest landmasses; not even in the capital. They were too big, too – lumbering. Too heavy. Something about the slow sway of their heads, the dull uncaring gaze, sent chills down Erasmus's spine.

He did not have to try too hard to skirt them, since the guards had taken him directly to the first barge and put in a cell, which while barred was also laughably insecure and, more importantly, dry.

It wouldn't have been hard to get out. Erasmus didn't try. The barge was small, so he had the benefit of their small stove just as much as the guards did, and there was a sheet partway across the bars for him to hide behind while he changed into something dryer. They fed him some of the dried seaweed and jerky the scholars seemed to subsist on – Erasmus made the connection, finally, that when the scholars spoke of *beef* they were referring to the very beasts pulling the barges – and then he fell on the cot and went to sleep.

When he woke he felt the pull of the water against the bottom of the barge before he felt anything else, like the tug of the wind undership but heavier, and for a moment –

For a moment he saw the hazy, black-on-shadow silhouette of the bars and his heart stabbed so cleanly tears came to his eyes, convinced for a moment he was being taken again to the prison; that Christopher was but rooms away, believing Erasmus was a killer, or worse –

Heretic.

And there was nothing Erasmus could say except to plead that he *hadn't*, he *wouldn't*, why would he; none of which mattered, because his every word was suspect.

(But the worst part, the very worst, was that Erasmus could not be certain Christopher was *wrong*. He didn't remember the end of the interrogation. He remembered Light so bright it seared his eyes and made his head throb; he remembered pleading. He didn't remember how it ended.)

But the booming crash of water against docks was nothing like the cutting wind, and Erasmus was at least capable of obeying the guards' commands when they escorted him off the barge. And of making sure he still wore his goggles the whole time. The damned things reduced him to a head-down trudge, squinting at the varying shades of the deck underfoot, but he didn't dare take them off. The scholars had been insistent on it.

As a result he didn't see much of the city. Not that he *would* have seen much, most likely.

He tried to ignore the jangling, like something scraped unpleasantly against or in his ears. The barge alone wasn't a bother, but a city –

It hadn't occurred to him until this moment that a city might be even more cluttered. It was tolerable, but surely – surely they were aware how discordantly their cities were built?

To say the guards were gentle was an overstatement, but – kind. Perhaps. The room they put him in was more of a meeting room than a cell, and they didn't ask before going through his bag, but they gave him something simple to eat and hot to drink, and Erasmus didn't have much in the will to refuse or try to take command of the situation. What did it matter? He had no authority here.

They found the watch. He told them the truth.

He couldn't tell if they believed him or not. They seemed more inclined to accept his word than Christopher had.

(And wasn't that a stab, one of his two best friends hearing him speak and knowing it for something else; while strangers seemed to believe him.)

Any gentleness was clearly a side-effect of trying to keep from making him feel threatened. It was almost funny, that these strangers did what Christopher never had (but the *look* on his face, the taut mouth and the hardness in his eyes poorly concealing anguish and fury).

Finally the prospectors packed the bag, better than Erasmus had ever managed to keep his luggage but not quite as well as Ryan had packed it to begin with. The watch and the knife were the only things they took out of it.

The door under the viewing balcony opened. He'd heard people talking up there, but hadn't tried to listen too closely. Save the obvious, that the conversation pertained to him. Erasmus was the only subject in the room.

Two people entered. This time, the briskness of one of their paces sounded so much like Christopher's impatience to *proceed* that Erasmus looked up in spite of himself, squinting behind the goggles.

It wasn't Christopher, of course. Neither of them were Christopher.

The taller had dull red hair, with enough flashes of lantern-light off buckles that Erasmus suspected a military uniform of some fashion. Many people here seemed to use metal in their clothes as a standard, but those with training, such as the guards and the prospectors, seemed to use more. Most of it had no lodes to speak of, but – could.

The shorter was – short. Even compared to the shortest of the guards Erasmus had seen, this person short, and stocky enough that Erasmus couldn't immediately tell gender by general shape. *Not* wearing a uniform, though. Or at least, flashing less.

It was the short one who came forward, dragging a chair to sit opposite Erasmus, albeit with the table still between them.

"Hello," she said, brisk but kind, and with a round sort of accent unlike the rest of the Prittune, or the scholars themselves. "You can call me Birdie. I'm here representing the Schecheyan annex here in the city, to oversee your care while here in Prittuni. May I have a name for you?"

Christopher. Please.

Tell me your name *and we can* end *this.*

Erasmus bit his tongue on – he didn't know *what* was going to come out – maybe just the knives suddenly in his throat. Took a breath, as discreetly as he could, and knotted his fingers together on the table to conceal the tremble.

"... Gus."

It was what the scholars were calling him. It had a similar sound, at least on the ending.

"It's my pleasure to meet you, Gus," said Birdie in the warm fashion of a person who was saying something rote – but convincingly. "Do you know where you are?" Wordlessly Erasmus shook his head. "You're in Lammandan's fort. Do you understand why?"

Wordlessly Erasmus shook his head again. He knew the people here didn't like magic, and that his eyes would give him away, and that they were – somehow – inconceivably – familiar with the concept of heresy. They called it something else, treated it differently, but that was one of the things that had stuck in his head. They were familiar with the *concept*.

How strange it was that above and below should share that same fear.

"Given his state, the guards didn't attempt to explain," said the taller woman briskly, standing far back. Outside of easy reach. Inside of range to intervene. "He made no resistance. Fresh from falling in the ocean, they said. He seemed to be having trouble swimming."

Something dull panged Erasmus's chest. Was *that* too much of a suspicion? He'd managed it – Ryan taught him – but he wasn't particularly graceful about it. Would someone who'd been born here be more accomplished by default? Maybe.

"And he seemed to be afraid of hurting them," added the taller woman.

Birdie nodded thoughtfully, and she might have smiled, reaching out. It didn't occur to Erasmus until she took his hand that that was her goal.

He flinched and pulled back before he could stop himself, halting just short of putting his hands in his lap. Birdie paused and settled her hands over one another on the table instead.

"The authorities here in Lammandan received a description of a man who resembles you who might have committed a crime," said Birdie matter-of-factly, and at least this time Erasmus managed to keep the flinch internal. "The guards thought you might be him, and since you seemed in need of aid regardless, they brought you here."

"... Alright."

None of that was total surprise, except that they suspected him to begin with. If they knew where he was, why did they wait until he was out of the bog before trying to find him? Was there something about the bog that prevented them from observation? That followed; there were any number of ways a scry might be interrupted one way or another, and they were always hardest around things like fountains. The fundament had considerably more running water.

But that meant someone had used magic to find him, which didn't make sense in as far as the scholars' representation of the fundament. Besides, the mangroves had more running water than the bogs did.

And what had happened to the scholars? The fact they might be in trouble because of Erasmus came as dull thud to his ribs; but he couldn't ask, lest that draw suspicion to them directly.

They all waited a beat, Erasmus staring at Birdie and wondering how much she could, in fact, see through the goggles.

"Would you like to tell me where you're from?" Birdie asked eventually. "If there's someone who might be waiting for you? The Prittune Annex can ask the annexes in other states to make contact if you have friends, or family."

The snort was wholly reflexive, as was the faintly hysterical scatter of laughter. It took effort to rein it in, and even then it sat aching in his chest, contained and salting, *salting*.

What friends or family would be a lie; but at the same time so close to not-a-one that it almost tripped off his tongue anyway, and twisted the metaphorical knife harder.

Erasmus had tried not to think about them in the past year.

(Tried not to wonder about that play Alexander was supposed to lead four months ago, they'd been rehearsing for weeks already, did it still go on? Tried not to wonder about the twins' birthday, how badly they wanted a pet, how poorly Chris had hidden the yearning. Tried not to weep himself to sleep for days after he realised Areth was turning thirteen and he was *missing it*. Tried not to wonder whether Christopher –)

He couldn't help but *stab himself*.

This time the touch of Birdie's hand was so light that Erasmus didn't realise at first it was there, or that a hand was pressed to his chest, or that his mouth was drawn tight in rictus grief.

Deep breath.

Deep breaths and he managed to wind it all down with an exhale, relax his shoulders and his face and return his hand to the table as if they hadn't *both* just seen the scream caught behind his teeth.

This time he had no will to stop Birdie from touching him. He hadn't flinched.

(It'd been worse.)

"Is there anything I can do to help?" asked Birdie quietly.

Erasmus's voice came hoarse with the tears he had not shed, but sat heavy and constricting in his head nonetheless. "I don't think anyone can."

These people didn't even know where he was from. And the scholars had been clear that they weren't convinced anyone from Schecheya might actually *help him*. If there was help to be had. Help the scholars seemed to assume would be – possible – in some way. Somehow.

As if there was something to go back *to*, when at best his family and dearest friends believed he was a murderer; and at worst knew that he was somehow heretical. Even though he didn't ... remember doing that. He didn't remember *asking* for that.

Cease this taunting. We both know this wouldn't happen unless Erasmus asked for the power.

But how could he convince Christopher he *hadn't*, when it seemed so clear that he *had*?

"Well, I don't believe *that*," said Bride firmly, and Erasmus blinked, drawn out of reverie by the firm matter-of-factness of her voice. She smiled and patted his hand. "I won't pretend there are times it certainly *feels* like that, but that doesn't equal truth." She turned in her chair without releasing his hand. "The general here has a room for you. It isn't much, I'm afraid, but you'll have a chance for a proper shower and someone will wash your clothes for you. Then tomorrow we'll all be going to Aulerin."

'Shower' was a word he'd heard before, mainly in terms of either water falling lightly from the sky and the scholars reminiscing wistfully about the comforts of civilisation. He wasn't sure what it referred to but he didn't like the implication in the disparate but seemingly-connected uses.

Rain had been terrifying the first time.

"... What for?" Erasmus asked, not quite faintly; so distant and clinical from his own mind that he was almost surprised by the hoarseness of his voice. He could almost believe there was a different man speaking.

... His ears were ringing as down a long, long tunnel.

Hurriedly Erasmus yanked his hand away and flattened them both against the table, taking a deep breath and letting it out even slower.

"For one thing," said the general grimly, "there's cells there built to contain someone like you."

His heart jolted and it was – grounding. If he could *feel* his body he was probably fine. Probably.

"I don't know what that means."

Was she referring to his being a skydweller? A lodeshaper?

A heretic?

Even the specialised wards of the Heights hadn't been enough. Whatever was here, Erasmus could probably get out of them. Even though the thought of being *in them* made his heart try to ricochet off the underside of his throat.

He'd never thought of himself as being afraid of small spaces before, not the way some people described it, of nightmares trapped in a space that closed and closed and closed. But then, there weren't any spaces small in the Empire the way they were small down here on the fundament, with the entire crushing weight of water or earth threatening to swallow a person whole.

There were places down here where a person couldn't even see the clouds. For *days* on end.

Erasmus still didn't know how he'd fare if he'd been forced to live in that small bunker under the waterfall for months during the flood season. For a mercy, he hadn't had to; he'd been staying with Passion when they began, and stayed there until they were over.

(And to think that until then he'd assumed Passion's house was built above the trees in the hope of seeing the stars.)

"Hm."

The way the general stood, Erasmus could believe her gaze was as piercing as Christopher's was. But although she watched him for a moment, in the end all she said was: "Mistress Birdie is your liaison. If you have any needs left unmet, ask for her. If you feel that you might be – perhaps we'll say, 'having a turn' – she will attend you. Understood?"

What a lyrical turn of phrase that nearly made Erasmus smile. Nearly. They had a similar phrase in the Empire, but – he suspected it meant something different.

Or not. Maybe it was just coming at it from different directions.

"Yes."

The general unfolded her arms and turned, pausing only to nod to the guards beneath the balcony, a motion most exhibited by the movement of her braid down her back. "Show him to his cell. Mistress Birdie will be accompanying."

The rustling motion of salutes was oh so familiar, even if the salutes themselves were alien.

Erasmus swallowed hard. *Cell* was not all that inspiring, but – maybe it would be alright. He'd been alright on the barge. It had only been bars, after all. If it was only bars, he might be alright. They didn't seem likely to be using wards, or magic. It had probably been the wards at the Heights that did him in. He was ... fairly sure.

It was the humming.

And the containment.

But there wouldn't those kinds of wards here. He'd be alright.

He'd be *alright*.

CHAPTER NINE

WHAT CONSTITUTES COMPLACENCY?

The first time Britt saw the man in the photographs, she thought he looked like he'd lost his entire world. Seeing Gus face-to-face only convinced her of that fact.

She couldn't see his eyes, not with the tint on those goggles; but there was a fragility to the way he sat, the way he moved; a terrified flinch just in the act of being reached to. As if he thought he might drag someone into the suffering, if they got too close.

Even when they were going to the cell Britt looked-over prior to speaking to him, he walked in a huddle. His bag clutched to his chest even though there hadn't been anything truly personal in it; head down, following quietly on the heels of the guard sent to show them the way.

It was the exact kind of self-contained suffering Britt had seen in so many after Cantlond fell. Like being wrapped in a veil, and even if someone reached out, it couldn't possibly be enough against the inexorable pull of grief.

I don't think anyone can.

She'd been wrong then. He was wrong now.

She'd *make sure* he was wrong now.

At least Gus was reacting, and able to talk. Not that he said much, unless asked a question. And it was odd, the kinds of things that made him flinch. The shower had. Perhaps it was the cold.

They were keeping him in one of the guard barracks, one without many people in it, where he could use the showers before being escorted to the room. There weren't prisoner cells per se, but the sergeants' rooms weren't all that much bigger. Solitary, though, with a bunk only for one person. It was just about as good for a prisoner as it was going to get.

Britt, obviously, did not remain present for his personal attendances, but she waited in the barracks offices until one of the male guards came to escort her so she could see with her own eyes that Gus was as comfortable as he could be.

"He hesitated," the guard said in undertone as he took her down the aisle between the bunks, "but then he went in willingly enough. My partner's got the key."

"You know when we'll be leaving tomorrow?"

"Yes'm. We'll have him ready."

"I'll be here before then," said Britt firmly, gripping her clipboard to herself so tightly the clip dug into her chest as the guard by the door unlocked and opened it.

The barracks wasn't particularly well wired; that was why it wasn't being used. Something about blowout a few months back, still in repair. The rooms themselves were alright, but it meant there wasn't much light besides a levin lamp on the desk beside the tray of hot just-delivered stew, casting Gus's silhouette against the wall. There was a decent window, but it overlooked only a corner of the courtyard and was currently locked. And the bed was almost certainly better than anything Gus had had recently.

He mostly seemed to be picking at the food, however, swishing the spoon around in it more than eating it. Bent low, most likely to avoid anyone catching his eyes, because he naturally had to take the goggles off for the shower and apparently had not had a chance to put them on again. Maybe they were being cleaned.

"Is the food not to your liking?" Britt asked, and the swishing stopped.

"It's – fine."

Britt had seen young students more convincing than that, but he did raise the spoon. Paused. Tipped it to drop a chunk of meat or offal back into the bowl before putting the spoon in his mouth, all without presenting her with an easy view of his face past his hair.

Mentally Britt calibrated his social status upward. At one point, most likely wealthy enough to have the pick of cuts. Britt had seen the children of wealthy houses come through the annex shocked by the food on the table – not because it was bad, but because it wasn't something they'd had to eat before. Very often, she found such children had difficulty with certain textures less-wealthy people couldn't afford to refuse.

It wasn't their fault, and Schecheyan cuisine was such that the Schecheyan cooks were in fair raptures at finding textures such children found palatable.

Prittuni as a rule couldn't afford to be quite as accommodating. The way Gus squinted down at the stew, picking around it with buttered bread in his off-hand, held exactly the same doubt, with an adult's self-awareness. And he wasn't complaining about it, so he understood there were limitations.

"If you say so," said Britt, "but if there is ever something you cannot eat, please do tell someone. It's no good giving you food if you can't get it in your belly." His nod was short, a split-second belated. "Is there anything else I can help you with until tomorrow?" The shake of his head was just about the same tenor as the nod had been. "Then I shall see you then."

She made to step out of the room –

Stopped, and turned, and went to the desk, reaching into the bag at her belt to withdraw the cookies she'd stowed long ago at breakfast. The guards had fed her well enough, so they hadn't been needed, but perhaps –

"Here." Britt set the bundle on the edge of the desk. "I brought these with me from breakfast, but I can always get more."

For a brief moment Gus raised his head, staring at her or the bundle as arrested as someone who'd taken a fall. For that brief moment his eyes were not at all hidden from her, as vivid in hue as she'd only ever seen in paint, and the breath caught in her chest.

Then his head jerked sideways and down, and he swallowed hard – again and again – and said almost as hoarsely as down in the meeting room: "Thank you."

"You're welcome."

Britt pulled up a slightly crimped smile and stepped out of the room, and the guard pulled the door to. The sound of it locking behind her –

Well, she wasn't the one who was in there. But it made her heart ache nonetheless.

That look on his face, like he'd never expected kindness again.

Britt let herself be escorted from the fort in something of a daze, winding up in a courtyard with a carriage and pony drawn up and the tall driver hunched in the seat. The guard standing by the door saluted, his scarf pulled up and visor low against the gusty afternoon. "I'm to escort Mistress Birdie to the annex."

… The timbre of his voice was oddly familiar. It drew Britt from her thoughts as her escort saluted back. "Over to you, then."

The guard by the carriage bowed and held open the door, the tone of the courtesy and the ironic lilt in his voice *acutely* familiar. "After you, Mistress Birdie."

"Thank you," said Britt, suddenly straining not to unleash the helpless giggles throttling the words, and with as much dignity as she could muster she climbed into the carriage. The guard followed her after, drawing the door closed, and rapped on the wall between himself and the driver.

Inexorably, a little ponderously, the carriage pulled away. Britt held her breath until they were across the courtyard, through the gate, and then could hold neither her breath nor her giggles any longer. She dissolved into rather hysterical laughter, pressing her fist to her sternum. "You're – *terrible*."

"I rather think I'm not, or we wouldn't have got away with that," said Ryan lightly and with a crooked grin, pulling off the guard's helmet.

Something thudded on the underside of Britt's seat and she jumped with a twisted squeak.

"Do you mind moving to the other seat for but a moment?" Yoch demanded, voice muffled.

Britt obliged by just about falling on Ryan's lap, laugh-crying in fits as the seat-cover pushed up and Yoch climbed out, looking flushed and miffed and rumpled. Decorously she put down the seat and used it for its intended purpose, all as if she did not have a dust-bunny in her hair and a smudge of grit on her cheek.

It wasn't helping. Britt gulped down wheezing breaths, hand pressed to her chest, leaning into Ryan's supporting elbow. "Wh- where's – Passion –?"

"In the driver's seat," said Ryan.

That effectively took the wind out of Britt's inappropriate mirth. "I – didn't realise he know how to handle a pony."

Her words were punctuated by the carriage bucking over some rock on the road, sending them all jostling. He had not struck Britt as the sort of person to want to learn, though he most certainly could not have fit under the seat the way Yoch had.

"He didn't used to," said Yoch dryly, pushing herself upright, "but he has a vested interest in keeping wheels on the ground, and is too tall to blend in save where everyone expects a body to be."

Britt spent all of a second debating whether she wanted to know exactly how and why the three of them had come to that conclusion, and the only reason she *didn't* ask was because Ryan asked his question first.

"How's Gus?"

The twinkling amusement was gone from his eyes, his face sombre. Any lingering incredulity wiped away as swiftly as an unhitched cloth under wind.

"I'm not certain how he was before," said Britt honestly, "but I don't think he's well at all. He's talking, but only in as far as someone talks to him. And eating, which is a better sign. Mostly, he seems caved inward. Physically, emotionally – in every way."

"About as he has been, then," Yoch murmured.

"He took off his goggles to shower," Britt added, "and kept them off, but he's really only spoken to me since. It's getting on in the afternoon and he seemed tired, so I expect he'll go right to sleep after this."

She'd slept, after Cantlond went under. Sometimes it felt as if all she did was sleep, and yet somehow never woke feeling rested. Some kinds of weariness couldn't be solved by mere sleep, for all a body pretended as though it could. There was a point one had to grow accustomed to action even when so deeply fatigued that going to sleep forever seemed the easiest course.

"If he's been keeping his eyes covered as a rule then at least he's thinking," said Ryan grimly. "We saw you come up with Master Cheya. Are you willing to tell us what happened?"

Britt sighed long, and it felt like it unwound at least part of the tautness in her chest, even despite the bumpiness of Passion's inexpert driving. So long as he wasn't about to run them over a cliff, she could weather it.

"I really shouldn't," she said, but she shouldn't have let them go the first time, either. "Master Cheya is so *immensely* worried. Perhaps even afraid. He was about to invoke the Treaties, I'm sure."

"I can't imagine that would have gone over well," Yoch observed. "It's one thing for Schecheya to moderate a peace using carrots, but too many of the states are feeling the yoke to safely exert that authority."

So much of Schecheya's good will, through Academe, was founded on agreements made in decades past. The states still adhered to them for now, but the means by which Schecheya's diplomacy had stabilised the states now in turn seemed more of chains than aids. In Cantlond there'd been talk of ignoring the Treaties, going on their own as it were; a sense that the Treaties hadn't really done much good by them, and therefore they weren't obliged to hold them even if Prittuni at large did.

After all, Cantlond was barely even a part of the Prittuni. Prittuni itself was barely part of Prittuni. The remnants of a once much grander nation, lost to flood and ruin, until all that remained was Aulerin's Honour and the family who ruled it in service to a crown that no longer existed. Cantlond, long ago, had grudgingly submitted to the barony's authority for lack of any other and the desperate need for stability at the time – but its people had never *really* considered themselves as belonging to it.

It was one of the reasons why Academe's increasingly urgent warnings and entreaties to evacuate had been ignored.

And then Cantlond had gone under.

For that reason, no one was willing to test the Treaties yet, at least not in Prittuni. But it might not matter, if one of the other states did, and obliged a response. For all the benefits, it did seem sometimes seem as though the states had each traded sovereignty for an increasingly vague promise of security.

And sometimes it seemed as though Schecheya was the only one with any ideas at all. Thus the rest of them abided.

"I wonder how much he knows," Ryan murmured.

"More than he wants, less than everything, I should think," said Britt. "He was *very* worried for me – but I think he was surprised by Gus, too. I don't know what he was expecting, but it wasn't what Gus actually is; he expressed some doubt in whatever report had been initially given. And he told me outright that things aren't what they seem, and that after clearly knowing things he wasn't allowed to tell me at all."

She frowned, wiping hair off her brow. "Although I do wonder if that's because he already knew about the potential of possession."

There was something else other than that, of course, because he'd only said so *after* raising the topic of possession himself, but perhaps it related to something Academe was researching –

"I beg your pardon," said Yoch sharply, "the risk of *what*?"

Britt blinked at her, her fierce-focussed face, the attentiveness with which they *both* plied her.

"Master Cheya seemed to think if Gus had hurt someone, it was because he's possessed," she said blankly. "Gus seemed to believe it as well. The general said when the guards found him he told them not to touch him, because he didn't want to hurt them; and every time I reached out, he flinched or pulled away, or both."

Ryan and Yoch exchanged glances.

"We've both touched him," said Ryan, baffled. "He never reacted like that before."

"A trigger, perhaps," Yoch suggested. "Something in the mangroves. Something that made it feel close."

"He never said anything about it," said Ryan, his voice growing terser by the word. "Not even a suggestion. He didn't act like a man who might be possessed – or was even afraid he might be. Why would he keep that from us?"

Yoch spread her hands with a shrug. "Why else? Fear. If not of us directly, then how we'd react."

With a long hiss Ryan slumped back in his seat, folding his arms across his chest with his fingers tapping his forearm like a man who'd like to be rather more physical than that. "I *should* have gone with him."

"And *shoulds* will help him now, will they?" Yoch countered irritably, and sat back with a sigh. "It's Passion who needs to hear this; he's the one with the adjacent field. His professor is a physician." This last was toward Britt.

"Academe has performed some studies on possession from a medical perspective; Professor Al has worked on most of them. Of the three of us, Passion is the one most likely to know something of value on the subject."

"It's a little telling to stop the carriage partway," said Ryan, glancing out the window, "and I'm not wholly sure Passion knows how on this kind of terrain, to tell you the truth. It'll have to wait until we've delivered Mistress Birdie." He returned his attention to Britt beside him. "What does the general plan to do with Gus now?"

"Take him to Aulerin," said Britt. "I'm going with, on Master Cheya's behalf. After that, I'm not sure. Possibly exams. If he is possessed, that means he's legally a magician by default, but he hasn't shown any actual signals yet."

Just the extreme fear of them, or possibly half a fear with the other half worrying about being discovered as a skydweller. Who only knew what the general would do about *that*? Prittuni had no laws allowing for such a thing. No state *did*.

... Come to think of it, he might simply be written off as a magician, in which case he may be no worse off than he was now. They might be able to work with that.

"Then we'll have to make our own way," said Yoch, and craned her head out the carriage window. "It's getting late. Night will be falling soon. There's a late tide into the river at dusk, is there not?"

"There is," said Ryan, rummaging in his belt until he found an odd-looking coin and flipped it toward Yoch. "And we'd better get on a barge taking advantage." All barges upriver used oxen to lead them from the shoreline, past a certain checkpoint. It was safer to catch a night tide to the stables upriver than it was out into the ocean proper. "When we reach the annex, you go and find us a barge while Passion and I bring the carriage back up to the fort. We'll meet by the river docks."

"Understood," said Yoch, and tucked the – it looked to be more a medallion, rather than a coin – into her own belt. "Is there anything else you're willing to tell us, Mistress Birdie?"

"I don't think General Burnstone knew the prospectors were looking for a skydweller," said Birdie thoughtfully. "She accused Master Cheya of perpetuating a riddle. It sounded as though the Prittuni searching for Gus thought he'd be falling in some kind of experimental craft."

"Which once again begs the question," said Ryan grimly, "who among Academe does know, and how, and how far up does it go?"

"Questions whose answers must remain for later," said Yoch, her eyes nearly black as they passed under a cliff. "Mistress Birdie, thank you. Some might consider aiding us to be treasonous, or adjacent."

"It's not as though you're plotting anything ill toward either Prittuni or Schecheya," Britt pointed out, and mustered a wry smile. "Unless you've been lying to me, but I think you'd have done a better job at it." They hadn't known about the possession. She was certain about that. "Besides, there are no laws about reporting skydwellers that I know of, so it's not as though I'm helping you do anything illegal by keeping that unspoken."

And Master Cheya seemed out of his depth. Even he knew he was out of his depth; otherwise he wouldn't have looked so relieved to be rescued from the act against which he was bracing himself.

Britt didn't quite know what was going on, or why, or how, but these people weren't bad people, and Gus wasn't a bad man. He needed *help*. Help he might not get if he was put in positions where he couldn't speak for himself, and had no one to speak for him. And if in helping him Britt could help the annex, and Master Cheya, well –

It wasn't all that difficult a choice.

For a while they rode in silence, in the descending switchbacks and over the sway of steel-twanging cords. Britt – did not recall being discontented with her lot, not really. She had a place to stay, a job she liked, respect. Friends with whom to share tea and cakes. Contacts, with whom she negotiated arrangements for students and the annex at large.

It was just that now she was thinking on it, perhaps of late it had all become a little … rote. A little too comfortable.

Or maybe that was just the act of being *able* to look back, and not remembering the last person she truly, directly helped. Oh, there were the students and the staff, all of them depended upon her organisation; and yet. Most of the time, she didn't see the results anymore. She didn't have to *stretch*.

She hadn't noticed that perhaps she might be getting a bit restless. Restless enough that she'd trusted Ryan and Yoch with barely a moment's thought, for the sake of a man with vivid-coloured eyes and a thousand-league stare.

"How *did* you come to be accompanying Gus to the capital, anyway?" Ryan asked eventually sometime as they were crossing the final bridge, his expression still sombre but with a note of amusement in his tone. Britt raised her hands with her shrug.

"The general wanted to take him there instead of turning him over to the annex. Volunteering to watch him on behalf of Master Cheya seemed like the best way to stop anyone from doing something stupid. He – he seems to need the help."

This, Britt said rather helplessly. It seemed a vast understatement if one just looked at him.

"On that," said Yoch softly as the carriage pulled up, "I cannot but agree." She laid her hand on the door opposite the annex, nodding toward Ryan. "I shall see you anon."

She slipped out the door, closing it behind with a soft thud, and vanished into the cliff's shadow as easily as if she was Ryan himself.

Chapter Ten

The longest ways

There was no time to speak until they were well on their way. Using Tyrian's medallion at the inn, whose meaning she only barely guessed, Yahvanna secured berth at speed on one of the merchant barges heading upriver toward the Aulerin.

Night had well fallen by the time the barge was due to cast off from the river dock, some ways south of Lammandan's main bulk and around the curve of the cliffs where they descended rapidly into something too rocky to be delta. The barge was still moored, but riding higher every moment; all the crates were loaded, and the passengers had nearly all boarded.

The clouds had thickened in the few hours since, turning darkly grey and heavy, until the night itself was but dim splotches of lamplight against the darkness. The smells of salt and increasingly incipient rain hid everything else.

Yahvanna stood waiting by the gangplank, watching the darkness under the lamps flanking the road from the city.

Not watching the last other passengers as they walked past her, coats buttoned up against the drizzle which promised to turn into a rain and hurrying amidships as fast as they could.

"On you get, miss," said the sailor by the plank, but Yahvanna pointed.

"There they are."

Down from the curved road around the cliff, a pair of shadows running – one visibly taller than the other, and trailing – neither bothering to defend themselves from the drizzle.

Yahvanna turned to the sailor. "Just a moment longer," she said. "Please."

The sailor sighed. "So long as *you* get on board, miss, and they don't mind the plank being taken out from under em."

Vespasien might stumble, but Tyrian never had. Yahvanna hurried up the plank and then turned to wait by the rail, brushing damp hair off her face. Gus would be all but blind in this kind of light and weather – but he would be travelling in the morning. Perhaps the rain will have eased by then.

Perhaps.

Casting her mind back, Yahvanna couldn't help but remember how long he'd taken to stop flinching when anything dripped on him from above. Even drizzle, a common and ordinary misery, made him react as though the droplets were ants. All Yahvanna could think at the time was that they must not get much rain, high above the clouds.

But he'd never complained. He'd never told them of his fears. For all he spent a year with them – they were still strangers yet.

The barge lifted on the tide, moorings groaning. The sailors hurriedly cast off even as Tyrian sprang up the gangplank, barely touching it or so it seemed, and vaulted over the rail. He turned as he landed, and both he and Yahvanna seized Vespasien's arms, hauling him bodily onto the barge as the sailors turned up the gangplank from either end.

"Move!" one of them barked, and the three of them flung themselves against the wall to give the sailors room in the aisle while they hauled the gangplank onto the deck.

"Lucky," said another with a sharp laugh, "and quick on yer feet. Get below, then, get."

They got, just short of scurrying around the cabin and through the door. The stairs beneath them surged as the tide took hold, and both Tyrian and Yahvanna gripped Vespasien tight before he stumbled. If Vespasien went over, they were all going over – there wasn't particularly room on the stairs.

Barges such as this were wide and wallowing, most of the cargo lashed to the deck with any passenger cabin being amidships and a little lower on the draft. There were no separate rooms; cubbies at best, cordoned by curtains on lines, and communal washing-areas beneath the stairs and on the far side of the room.

Their being the last on meant all the cubicles were already taken, and all that remained was to find a seat in the public area and attempt to dry off as much as they could.

"Did aught go amiss?" Yahvanna asked as she hung up her coat on the long seat remaining near to the stairs, wholly un-private and the most likely to become waterlogged.

Just as well they only had what luggage they could carry. Just as well they were all three of them accustomed to keeping a bag for emergencies.

"Nothing dire," said Tyrian, shaking off damp. "Just little nuisances."

Vespasien looked the most miserable as he sat heavily on the seat, wiping hair off his brow and running a hand over his beard, in the early stages of looking unkempt. He may not have been any more miserable than the two of them – it was only that he looked out of place any time he wasn't in a library, and between his hunch and his frame he contained a kind of gauntness which turned all physical travails wretched regardless of his actual resilience.

He was, if nothing else, significantly more out of breath than Tyrian.

"I told Passion what we figured out," Tyrian added, since Vespasien didn't seem about to, "but there wasn't a chance to discuss it."

Vespasien nodded, still drawing in ragged breaths.

It was a social nicety to ignore conversations occurring in one's vicinity on a barge or a ferry; but it was still public, and not particularly secure. They'd have to be circumspect, at the very least.

"How high is the actual risk?" Yahvanna asked, reaching down to unbuckle and scrape off her boots. These were not the equipment she wore actively into the bog – but living in the bog, they were still rather higher than most, well-made, and deserved the night to air, since most of them would be sleeping.

Vespasien held up a finger, and his next breath was deeper. Since she was down there anyway, Yahvanna kneeled proper to unbuckle his boots too.

"My thanks," Vespasien managed. Tyrian sat next to him, already unshod, tucking his boots under the seat with his heels, as Vespasien drew one last deep breath. "I am not particularly concerned."

Yahvanna sat back on her heels with a relieved sigh. Vespasien was not habitually so definitive. "Why so?"

"Such behaviour as our friend exhibits has a multitude of causes," said Vespasien. "Of the numerous studies undertaken on the subject, Professor Alvin's medical conclusion is that the vast majority of such examples are naught more than a range of reactions to identifiable stimuli. Given our friend's recent history, panic attacks are by degrees more likely to explain his responses than any other cause. Perhaps our friend is less accomplished at swimming than he pretended."

Tyrian dropped his head back on the couch with a low grinding sigh. "I should have –"

"Gone with him, we know," Yahvanna interrupted before he could sail down *that* river. "He hadn't sailed on the ocean before. I suppose it's possible capsizing or falling in might have frightened him?"

"Such a hypothesis is extremely plausible," agreed Vespasien.

"And his fear of hurting anyone?" Tyrian asked irritably.

"Such a fear could be caused by any number of possibilities unrelated to the topic," said Vespasien, "though given our friend has been less than forthcoming, we cannot adequately hypothesise without knowing more details about his emotional state. A fear of harming others could, indeed, be unrelated to the cause of our friend's panic attacks."

It hardly seemed likely, but then, he had neither panicked nor feared their touch since he fell. How were they to know? They hadn't witnessed what Birdie described.

... Except, perhaps, that first day, when Gus had laughed despair on the edge of a cliff, and only seemed to keep himself upright by clinging to whatever they put in his hands. Perhaps he was simply good at *hiding things*, a task made simpler by only ever seeing three people at most. A sudden influx of others with whom to contend may well have been too much in his grief, and that not accounting for the fact of life here being so very different.

In retrospect, they had not been very kind; and yet: what else could they have done? Their best knowledge at the time was that Tyrian's absence would draw more attention, and Gus had seemed capable enough to function.

"We'll discuss it more when we reach the city," said Yahvanna finally and reluctantly. Reluctant, because she would like to make plans before then; and because Tyrian seemed more inclined to brood if he weren't being distracted.

"Perhaps we might eat," Vespasien suggested, rumpling in the inside pockets of his cloak, "and perhaps a game?"

Yahvanna forced her shoulders to relax, an easier task than it seemed a few seconds ago. "Only if Ryan does."

"Only if you both don't pretend at being as obtuse as a hardwood log while I'm cheating the pants off you," said Tyrian with fond exasperation, and swiped the deck of cards from Vespasien's hand as soon as he'd withdrawn it from whatever pocket it was currently stowed. "Listen. Palming a card is *not* that difficult to learn."

"But how *ever* will we learn if you don't *teach* us?" said Yahvanna in her most saccharine tone, and it was worth it for the fact that Tyrian threw a button at her head before he shuffled the cards.

***

It rained all night. Yahvanna was unbothered by it, but the other passengers complained about the noise and the dripping, and the leak in one of the corners. Five years in a bog; one grew accustomed to both the perennial damp and the sound of water thundering.

The one interruption was when the barge reached the stables, halting to be hitched to the oxen leading them the rest of the way upriver and then passing step by step through the locks. Yahvanna remembered the faint shudder of the movement as they stopped and started, and then rolling over to go back to sleep against Vespasien's shoulder.

The rain was still falling the next day. The misfortune of it was that most people declined to take the fresh air on the deck, and instead turned the public cabin into one of sulky malaise. The other was that it slowed their pace, owing to the oxen drivers needing to take care on the banks. It would not stop them any – these banks had been built-up and stoned-over for years – but the roads were old and the risk to the animals was worth mitigating.

Late in the afternoon Tyrian came down from a turn upstairs and said in a low voice the sailors were worried about the deck swamping.

"How likely?" Yahvanna asked, curled up in a corner of what was now, temporarily, their couch, with a cup of tea Vespasien had just passed her from their burner.

"More so if the rain keeps up," said Tyrian. "They've got all the sluices open, but the deck's not a particularly safe place right now. The captain asked me to let people know to stay below for the time being."

Not a particularly titillating request, particularly for – or perhaps because of – those who were queasy; but what could they do? The three of them split the room, Vespasien with the pot of hot water in hand for the sake of those who had not been prepared for the lack of ability to boil it.

For a mercy the rain eased overnight. Although it only moved ahead of them onto the plains, promising they wouldn't outrun it in the city, at least it meant better visibility for the oxen and their drivers, and a chance for the deck to dry. The river was so swollen that Yahvanna watched as waves lapped the road-tops, occasionally washing across the oxen's hooves. Much higher than this and the roads might flood entire.

This situation was neither new nor unique, on Prittuni's plains.

Aulerin was not, by strictest terms, beneath sea-level; indeed much of it was on a hill, with fertile soil surrounding. But the valley in which it resided had been created with the judicious use of dams, and in heavy rains, such as these, the lower quarters of the city were prone to flooding.

The city itself was encircled by walls: one higher up, bounding the castle; another lower where it encased the wealthy of the state; and finally the one around the city at large, through whose gates the barge sailed into the moat. Within those walls it was also split into rings, staggered according to elevation and built such to drain each ring into the next and thence into the moat.

Aulerin was not below sea-level. But the plains had ceased being strictly grassland years ago, and the perennial wetness of the lands surrounding was evident in the fact that under these persistent rains the water sodding the grass was higher outside the walls than it was within. On the approach to the docks a recently-fitted lock allowed the barge to descend the yard – *if* that – into the city's moat; and the water-level within was already quite high. There was some minor flooding around the warehouse district, where pathways drained into the river.

If the moat itself became much higher, it would not be the rains flooding the lower city; but that was why the lock. It allowed the city to discharge moat-water into the river.

As well as providing a means for departing barges to do so expediently.

There was yet another wall further off, encircling not only the city but the farmland around it; an incomplete dream intended to serve as a bulwark, the hard labour of recent years. It was not uncommon for the farms to waterlog year to year, or so Yahvanna heard, such that the farmers remaining outside the walls tended toward growing crops which thrived in water. The reason the outer wall was so large, so incomplete, was due to the baroness's firm promise to encase as much of the farmland as she could. And, no doubt, the fact that doing so would make greenhouses easier to maintain outside the city.

It was wise, Yahvanna thought, to consider how she would feed the capital, to ensure there would be land enough for it; even if it meant the security of the wall would take longer. At least it kept the state's armies busy, and not considering whether their neighbours might have better fortunes.

Though if it took so long as to be rendered useless ...

They were building the side facing the dams first. Only the future would tell if they'd built it tall enough quickly enough. The rest, facing the ocean and downrivers to the west, was still an open circle yielding water unto the sea, and the barge had not needed to pass through anything from the stables to the city.

The plains were not yet a bog, owing to the persistent and considered drainage works, but they were not far off one.

They came up slow and sodden, delayed but within expected parameters of the weather, and to a one glad to be docked.

"Where are we going?" Yahvanna asked the moment they were off the barge and away from the risk of being overheard. The street-curb leading off the docks was a long gargle of water draining into the river, which made it annoying to have a conversation and safer to have one here than nearly anywhere else.

"Not too far off the hill," said Tyrian slowly, gazing toward the streets. "If they suspect magic, they'll want to take him to one of the bunkers built for it back in the day."

In the day when many of the states were vastly more violent about excising all traces of magic from their lands, and not always too discerning about how they proved culpability. Nevertheless, there were *enough* mages who exerted enough force to make plain the necessity of robust prisons, in case someone proved to be precisely that powerful.

Yahvanna did not know how powerful skydwellers might be as a rule, but a man who managed to land safely, if unconscious, with naught more than smoke off his clothes, was almost certainly powerful by their definition.

That did not mean he was, by extended definition, *dangerous*. Or that dangerous meant *threatening*.

There were times the nations of the lowlands baffled her with their blind zealotry and insistence on condemning tools as evil.

"Where are they?" Yahvanna asked, and Tyrian swivelled, glancing down the way.

"As I recall, most of them have been commissioned for other uses in the intervening time," he said, "such as food storage. But I believe there's one still here on the outer ring." He paused for a moment, eyes distant, and then finally nodded firmly, striding off down the docks. "This way."

CHAPTER ELEVEN

EXCHANGING OF KNOWLEDGE

For simplicity's sake, and because Britt had promised, she presented herself to the fort guards early in the morning before even the sun had risen. It had begun drizzling overnight, though the rains moved inland, so by the time Britt rose and was on her way the streets were naught more than sheens of grey stone reflecting lantern-light.

The fort courtyard was already a kerfuffle of movement for the general's escort and the vanguard's early departure. Britt was given to understand listening to the shouted orders that there was no barge necessary for General Burnstone's movement; she had come here with her entourage on foot and by pony. But a barge was more secure for holding prisoners. And there was that old tale about magicians and water.

So this time, General Burnstone travelled by barge, which judging by hurried whispers was not particularly welcomed by several people, up to and including the general herself.

None of that was Britt's concern, despite that her mind tried to latch onto the logistics of it all. The only person about whom she must be concerned was Gus.

Unexpectedly, Master Cheya had already been awake and waiting for her when Britt came downstairs to meet the carriage. In his dressing-gown and nightcap, perhaps, and with a drawn anxiousness that suggested he had not slept particularly well; but he'd been there, and worried, fair wringing Britt's hand.

But in the end he said nothing she didn't already know – only exhibited more keenly the trap he felt in. Whatever he was not, could not, say, if nothing else perhaps Britt's actions here might help relieve some of the pressure.

Britt had eaten at the annex, but quickly. When the guard escorted her into the cleared barracks, it proved they had already woken Gus, or perhaps he'd already been awake. He was already sitting on his bed, tray empty save crumbs on the desk and detritus at the bottom of the teacup.

And the folded remains of the paper in which Britt had wrapped her cookies. That it was empty made her chest feel warm. Her kindness, however unexpected, had been received in the spirit intended.

For a mercy, Gus had remembered his goggles. He did look better, washed and beard trimmed and hair combed; but none of that quite lessened the drawn grief on his face or the seemingly permanent crimp in the corner of his mouth.

"I'm sorry," Britt said, "I thought I'd be earlier than this." For all how early it was; but she'd misjudged how swiftly the guards actually made their preparations, and forgotten they must needs move to the docks. "Have the guards told you how you'll be moved?"

Wordlessly Gus nodded.

"There'll be a carriage, mistress," said the guard behind her. "A secured one, a guard with the driver and a guard inside."

"Then I shall be inside as well," said Britt. If there was a guard there, they could hardly claim she'd be in danger, and she was supposed to be looking after Gus.

"Yes, mistress."

She chose to ignore the tone of helpless resignation. As if she'd had to twist their arms at all!

"I brought some books for myself," said Britt. Her luggage was mostly outside, handed over to the hostlers, but she'd kept a knapsack for herself for travelling, and sat it on the bed a fair distance from Gus to open the flap and go through it. "You're welcome to borrow something, if you like. I dare say you haven't much in your bag already."

In fact, she knew for a fact he didn't, thanks to the list provided to General Burnstone about it.

Gus hesitated and then said very, very softly: "I don't know how to read."

"... Ah."

Guiltily Britt looked down at the books. All of them were paperbound, owing to it being easier and Schecheya having some stable way of producing it compared to other states; none of them were teaching books. She should have thought of that.

Gus was speaking Schecheyan, because most people did if they wanted to communicate with someone other than their own. It had become the linguistic benchmark for international education and trade, much the same way the Thalassocracy's coin had for currency. Presuming the skydwellers spoke something else, the scholars would have taught him whatever language was most likely to be useful.

But that didn't include teaching him how to read and write it. Out in the bog, there wouldn't have been much to read, aside from Passion's many books; and those were not conducive to teaching.

Britt looked up. "Have you had any lessons?" she asked. "So I have some idea where to begin."

Another hesitation, and Gus looked at the wall across from her; not toward her, not toward the guards. "... I know some letters."

He might have learned a few basic things as notes from the scholars. Reading and writing were harder than speaking. Left alone with no one who knew his languages, he would have been galvanised to learn, just to be able to communicate; but speaking would have taken up that time.

They could start slow. Britt pried her fingers between the books to hook tips around the slate's edge and pull it out, along with the chalk in her side-pocket. Gus's head jerked around as she climbed onto the cot; a little too high for her feet to touch the floor, but that didn't matter.

She put the slate on his lap and he drew back from it, hands and body alike, as if it might have been infectious – or perhaps as though he was afraid *he* was.

"Alright," said Britt with determined cheer, "let's start small, then. Can you write your name?"

***

Preparations did not take long enough for a full lesson; barely more than to find that Gus had a grasp of the letters of his own name, as well as a smattering of others Britt suspected might spell, variously, 'Passion', 'Ryan' and 'Yoch' if he had not so laboriously put them out of order.

Or perhaps that was simply the act of writing them alone.

He was not unfamiliar with chalk in his hand, at least, that much was obvious; his lines were not the shakiness inherent in a person who had never had to use his fingers in such a fashion. Just unfamiliar with these shapes. But he squinted toward the slate surely more than was warranted even with goggles on, even when Britt brought over the lantern.

That, perhaps more than anything, lengthened the time needed for such a basic task.

Then a third guard came down and they were, if not bundled, then moved with alacrity out of the barracks and into the courtyard. Gus gripped his bag tight to his chest and moved with his head down, even though he wasn't an especially tall man. Average height, and yet; he made himself smaller, and Britt could not be sure if it was because he was intimidated or trying not to be intimidating.

The carriage was directly before the barracks; it was heavier-set than others, no doubt to prevent the risk of attack or interference. The stairs were bolted metal, discrete things that didn't stick out all that well; Britt needed to take quite the step to make them.

Gus almost tripped over them as he came to the door and misjudged where the door would be. It was like he could barely see at all –

"You'd see more in this light if you took those goggles off," said one of the guards, exasperated and brusque but not cruel, and Gus shook his head.

... Oh.

Britt bit her lip on asking, or offering, and after a moment Gus's groping hand found the edge of the door and he pulled himself inside. He was followed by one of the guards, who sat opposite them both, and although Britt desperately wanted to ask –

The situation was not conducive to conversation.

There was none as they were taken to the river, through the darkened city lit mainly by the strings of lights on the bridges. The clouds were a lighter grey over the river mouth by the time they reached the docks, the suggestion of dawn not quite seeing fruition. The docks themselves were well decked with activity, more so than the courtyard.

Theirs wasn't the only barge aiming to take advantage of the tide; but it had to be done at intervals to avoid collisions on the river. State business had precedence over all others. And loading Gus had precedence over any other cargo.

'Loading' made Britt frown when she heard it, but no one was speaking *to* them, only calling to each other. Nevertheless, she stayed firmly nearby and just in front, hoping that in the darkness her off-white coat might be enough for Gus to see.

The cabin interior was marked by individual rooms, as the last barge on which Britt travelled had not. There wasn't a lot of space for many guards, and perhaps expectedly Gus's room was at the end, where escape – as if he was thinking it! – was most difficult.

Britt's room was directly opposite. She suspected it too was intended to be a cell, given the strength of the jamb and the lock on it, but someone had thought to put some slightly overwatered blue flowers in a pot by the cot, as if to remark on the unusual nature of the circumstances. They were hale enough to lend the room some floral scent, at least.

Still, it wasn't worse than some places she'd slept before, and it was only for one night. And from the sounds of it, they had at least avoided the worst of the rain, which had gone before them.

Britt very nearly wondered why exactly the general was bothering to stay on the barge instead of riding ahead and camping, which sounded as though it might be vastly more preferable, or at least comfortable. It was a hard world for people who did not feel at ease on a boat.

There was no opportunity to speak to Gus in private, but Britt at least managed to make sure he was as comfortable as he was willing to truthfully tell her. Fascinatingly, he didn't seem altogether bothered by the movement of the ship as they cast off. Britt would have thought –

Well. Never mind. She didn't know much about skydwellers, after all. No one did. The scholars were those who knew the most, and that was for having had one stay with them for ... for ...

How long had it been for?

It was more difficult to ignore the fraught ridiculousness of the situation when Britt had very little to do save read her books, with the knowledge that Gus had absolutely nothing. She'd offer lessons, but the guards were nervous about opening Gus's door while they were on the water. Couldn't they see that the man was hardly a flight risk? More and more all of this seemed a little bit silly.

... Somewhat less so when General Burnstone sent her aide to call Britt to dine with the general for lunch.

Fairly nervously Britt patted down her coat, considered changing, decided – if the general had meant for this to be supremely formal, she would not have waited until they were on the barge, with fewer utilities. And besides, the aide was waiting for a response, and seemed to expect her to come along immediately.

So Britt went. What else did she have to do? Her stomach rumbled, and her remaining snacks must be held for the afternoon; and surely the food at the general's table would be better than the fare Britt would receive in her room.

... The fact that it meant Gus would have to settle for whatever he was given gave her a pang of guilt, but it would have been so regardless of Britt's choice.

The general's cabin was close to the deck, and larger; Britt suspected it was ordinarily the captain's cabin. She entered from the hall on which all the cabins seemed to be situated, and had to pause to orient herself. The space was filled with a bookcase, a table, a trunk, a globe – all brass-fitted, all a trifle too pretentious for a barge which never went anywhere but the same route up and down the same river.

Overall it was the vestiges of a study-and-bedroom in one, with some books crammed into the shelves in a fashion which suggested they had, recently, been stacked elsewhere in the room and their owner did not realise how little space was actually available.

The leather roll laid out on the trunk beside the bed was incongruously utilitarian, clothes strapped into its pockets. Britt averted her gaze as soon as she realised what she was looking at, for the sake of the general's privacy if nothing else.

As she did so her gaze met General Burnstone's, seated as near to the window as she could get, with a chair opposite her.

The general's mouth tugged ruefully. The cast of her face was rather green, but her voice was strong enough as she said: "Come in and sit down, Mistress Birdie."

It was a narrow table for them both, though in this case the size of Britt's general area made the situation rather less awkward than it could have been. Her seat faced downriver, opposite the way they were travelling with the tide, but fortunately she'd never much been one for seasickness. Unlike the general, it seemed; the window was open, the morning breeze cool, and the boundaries of the river well visible. The scent of salt had long receded, leaving instead freshwater and reeds.

"Are you quite well?" Britt asked as she sat, grateful for the forethought of the cushion that raised her to a more convenient height. The way the corner of the general's mouth deepened was more rueful still.

"I'll manage," said General Burnstone, which was neither a 'yes' nor a desire to bend Britt's ear about it. Fair enough. "Mistress Birdie, I was hoping you might enlighten me as to Schecheya's intent here."

Well, Britt did expect to be caught in the middle, though doing so before the meal had even been served was either more eager or more impolite than she'd thought. Then again, General Burnstone was known to be brusque.

"I'm afraid I genuinely don't know," Britt answered honestly and while meeting the general's gaze. "Whatever it is, it's quite private. Master Cheya refused to confide in me several times, though I rather think he wished to. I do beg you not to think too poorly of him, General. I've known him for a while now and he's simply trying to do his job with, I suspect, barely more information than we have."

"That's not much more reassuring than if you'd admitted malice," the general answered grimly. "What *are* those people thinking about?"

Britt shrugged with a spread of her hands. "I do not know from whom Master Cheya's instructions come. Either way, I do believe he is only the messenger, as it were."

All of which was wholly true, and none of which yielded anything about Gus's real origins, or how much Master Cheya may or may not know about them. Let alone how much *Britt* did.

General Burnstone grunted something possibly disbelieving, possibly not, and then said nothing as lunch was served. It was not nearly so sumptuous as meals at the annex, but a good deal more so than Britt expected of a simple barge, being comprised of a rich fish stew with sourdough so freshly baked it was still warm.

Her stomach rumbled. General Burnstone didn't laugh, but the crook of her mouth upward seemed a little more amused.

"You're familiar with the three scholars your Master Cheya was so concerned about," she said. "Tell me about them. We haven't seen hide or hair since they left the fort the day before yesterday and I want to know how foolish they are."

Maybe it shouldn't be a surprise that General Burnstone viewed scholars as being inherently foolish, but it did cut a little.

"I wouldn't classify them as all that foolish, personally," answered Britt more tartly than she meant, and proceeded to butter her bread. "Passion might be a dreamer, but he's not the sort who's so busy looking at the clouds he'd walk into a pole. Ryan and Yoch are both eminently practical. All three of them did venture into the bog for five years, after all; I should hardly think someone simply *foolish* could manage that and live."

General Burnstone raised her hands. "A fair point," she acknowledged, and reached for the butter. "There are prospectors who set foot in the bog once and swore never again. When I heard some Schecheyan scholars were living there I thought it was a jest at first."

"Just so." With some effort, Britt relaxed her shoulders and exhaled. "None of them would ignore someone in need, but it beggars my belief to think either Ryan or Yoch would obey any request from a stranger without question."

"Such as a killer trying to hide his crime," said the general, now giving all the appearance of focussing only on her meal.

"Such as, yes." Or a skydweller trying to hide his eyes ... but that can't have been his idea. He would have had to know more of the world beneath the clouds to think that far ahead. "If you ask me –"

"I did."

Britt nodded and picked up her spoon. "Other scholars I might agree with you," she said. "But when I heard it was those three, my first thought was, *what don't I know*? If I saw them jump off a cliff, I'd look around to see what they're running from, if you take my meaning."

"Not the sorts taken by flights of fancy, then," murmured the general thoughtfully, and Britt couldn't help but smile, swift and small.

"Not unless the flight could be grounded and the fancy defined in every conceivable fashion."

As far as Britt knew, Yoch in particular didn't even believe in legends, save as the exaggerated fantasy surrounding a kernel of truth.

"And your Master Cheya was so willing to throw them to we hounds," said General Burnstone with a twisted kind of smile. "His own people."

Britt hesitated. "I can't speak for their current citizenship, but only Passion is Schecheyan by birth, in fact. Ryan originally hails from the Thalassocracy –" The general's eyebrows shot skyward. "– and Yoch from one of the southern alps."

Which Britt only knew because of the letters that came to the annex for the three while they were in the bog. Passion's seemed to come from all over, but all of them were postmarked through Schecheya; Ryan's seemed to have a narrower spread and primarily came by ship, but were far more abundant; while Yoch received far fewer than either. One or two a year, if that.

There'd been a time Britt wondered if Yoch *had* anyone beyond her fellow scholars, she received so few letters. When one of them finally arrived, the courier had practically treated it with the reverence owed to a holy artefact due to the far-off heights from which it had come. Yhedilitt might be further by league, but the alps were so isolated that to hear even a whisper from there was almost akin to a fancy, and the notion of a people so landlocked they might never have seen the sea simply fantastical.

The few goods that could be traded from there were near universally something only the wealthy could afford. There was a rug in Master Cheya's private office, a gorgeous piece woven of the softest wool Britt had ever touched, which cost more than Britt could likely make in a lifetime. It was hung on the wall, unused, to be ogled and lusted after.

"An asset," Master Cheya had laughed, "belonging to the annex in case of great need."

To be sold, Britt had interpreted, in the worst case of the annex being cut off from Schecheya at large and losing any other means of funding itself.

"That explains a lot," said General Burnstone, sounding thoughtful but also almost approving. Britt almost regretted saying anything at all, if the clarification only compounded the general's belief that Schecheyans were to a one too much with their heads in the sky for the pragmatic business of living. "I can't say I know much about the people from the alps, but I've heard things. Everyone has."

About life so high on a peak that winters might well freeze a village over, yes. It took the hardy sort to make a living up there.

Then again, from what Britt had read, sea-level had been much lower centuries ago. Perhaps modern elevation was considered equally silly to ancient peoples.

"Either way, you understand, I hope, why I'm disinclined to assume the scholars might have done any wrong," said Britt steadily.

General Burnstone's smile was a funny little thing, not quite wry. There was something – victorious about it.

"If anything, Mistress, you've validated my choice not to turn our man over to the annex." She snorted. "A killer from another state, my ass – someone is lying about something, and the character of the people involved is all I have to go on. If your scholars are as you say, they aren't about to be easily drawn into some conspiracy; and thus far I've been denied knowledge as to who, exactly, is levelling the accusation. But you've been honest and forthright enough, and so it's your opinion to which I lend the most weight."

"And because I'm not Schecheyan, I have to assume," said Britt, and forced a smile, patting her chest as though her heart were not *pounding*. "Since we're being *brutally* honest, General – you don't really trust Schecheya, do you?"

"No," said General Burnstone bluntly. "I don't. I'll not deny the treaties they forged stopped a war the world could ill afford, but that was decades ago. What have they done since then beyond chain us to those same walls? For a nation that prides itself on knowledge, it seems to have few answers."

Britt's stomach twisted, the same old old grief knitting up under her sternum. It wasn't like it was; no longer sharp, just blunted, and tired, and accepting. "They tried to save us at Cantlond," she said softly. "We're the ones who didn't listen."

General Burnstone's glance was nearly sharp, and she drew a breath as if about to say something – closed it. Drew again. "I suppose that's why you picked the annex."

"One of them," admitted Britt. "Why?"

For a long, long moment the general said nothing, only looked at her with piercing eyes. Finally she shook her head and sat back in her chair, picking up her spoon. "Never mind. I didn't bring you here to pain your heart with old wounds. I appreciate your candour, in any case, and hope it will continue come Aulerin."

What was that all about?

Britt waited a moment, but the general said nothing more: only resumed the meal with the grim tenacity of someone hoping putting food in her stomach might help it settle; and after a moment Britt followed suit, *wondering*.

CHAPTER TWELVE
Dammed

The barge was easier to sleep on. Erasmus barely realised that he did, from moment to moment; only that he was woken to be fed, and then woke again with the thud of the barge coming to a halt and the deep clunk of something unwinding somewhere nadir of its hull. The noises were different, and where they came from, but it was close *enough* to that of a berthing that Erasmus pushed himself upright before he realised why.

He was still grinding the sleep away when a footfall thudded outside the door, and hastily Erasmus fumbled the goggles back over his eyes. His collarbone ached where he'd slept on them.

The sound of the lock turning still seemed strange for not coming with the breaking hum of wards reweaving.

"Good even," said the guard, gruff but not unkind, if not wholly friendly. "We've arrived in Aulerin. Go on and pick up your things and we'll be moving on out, eh?"

There wasn't much to pick up, because there hadn't been much to unpack; and that which he did, he'd repacked immediately. So without a word, still a little groggy, Erasmus hauled himself off the cot and picked up Ryan's bag, trailing past the guard as she stepped aside. There was another in the hall whom Erasmus saw primarily as movement and silhouette, but it wasn't as though there were many places for him to go. The walls were indicated well enough by the dim lights on the floor.

A door just down the hall opened and Mistress Birdie emerged, looking far less ruffled than Erasmus felt. Composed, even.

Erasmus envied her a little, at the same time as he felt –

'Guilt' wasn't the right word, but it was the nearest one he could think of. This woman owed him nothing, and even less; but she was here, for seemingly no reason but to help. At – in the Empire the accused were always provided with liaisons. Somehow Erasmus hadn't expected it here, and didn't know if it was because he assumed they were less compassionate or because it was him.

... *Usually* in the Empire the accused would have liaisons.

Not if they were heretics.

Not if they were *royal* heretics.

So there was no way Mistress Birdie could have known how deeply and thoroughly a simple kindness lanced him. Erasmus spent more time weeping that night than sleeping. The cookies themselves had been alien, and yet

–

And yet they still reminded him of thieving Alexander's kitchen, of the early mornings in which they might collide in their individual clandestine missions of baking something for the day. Once Alexander stayed up all night just to beat him to the oven, and Christopher flatly refused to mediate whether that counted as 'last night' or 'that morning', and therefore whether Erasmus had won or lost …

"Alright, Gus?" asked Mistress Birdie.

Erasmus nodded again, still wordless, but this time because his throat was too closed for words to find their way – if he even knew which ones he'd use. Everything he'd learned of this language had deserted him.

Mistress Birdie patted his hand with a smile, and then walked ahead; behind the guard, in front of Erasmus. Her coat was a kind of immensely pale brown that made her more visible than not, and easy for Erasmus to follow with his brain turned off. As a bonus, her height made it obvious when she reached the stairs. He actually managed to get up them without tripping on anything.

Coming out on deck was simultaneously a revelation how stuffy the cabin had felt and slamming into a discordant shriek. Erasmus stumbled, righted himself; fixed his gaze to the back of Mistress Birdie's coat and kept walking. The air was fresh and cool, but the lodes –

There was so much happening here. So many lodes clanging together with an unruly din until his head throbbed. He almost didn't notice Mistress Birdie stopped until he stumbled into her, there at the rail, where the water washed against the side of the barge and shaped the gangplank by its absence in his vision.

"Are you alright?" Mistress Birdie asked with vastly more concern in her tone.

Frankly, Erasmus was afraid if he opened his mouth something other than words might come out. He swallowed hard and took a deep breath. Counted. Let it out slowly.

One had to remember to breathe. When in fall. When in float. When so close against the cusp of the world's curve that air itself threatened to yield and all that remained was pulled together by oneself.

He hadn't realised it would be so vital here on the ragged earth.

... Then again, he'd been sick for weeks after landing because of it. The air was so much denser here.

Mistress Birdie's fingers hooked around his, and the flinch came before Erasmus could stop it. "You're quite alright," said Mistress Birdie firmly, as if by saying it she'd make it real. "Come on, now."

Gently she tugged him forward, and Erasmus's feet went. Automatically, dazedly, and thank Light for that. He didn't feel distant the way he had on the beach, under the inexorable throb of water that extended for miles and miles – this was more a too-close setting in. His head ached.

Getting his feet on solid stone – helped. There was something about the solidity underfoot, something grounding that Erasmus had never quite felt in the Empire. All the islands were perfectly stable, but this –

He hadn't realised, with so much water around him of late, how much stone itself could be constant. Even as its very presence made the lodes difficult to parse, it was at the same time *rooting*. Had it always been like this, and he just hadn't noticed? Or was it *because* of the weight of the fundament unyielding beneath him?

There was too much around to really find lodes with it, and yet: the jangle seemed less like this.

"What's the trouble?" asked the general with the brusque manner, already on the dock. There seemed to be an awful lot of people in the area, cordoned by guards to give them space, and the ship crew grumbling about it. *That* was a shape and murmur Erasmus knew well.

"No trouble," said Mistress Birdie cheerfully, squeezing Erasmus's hand and guiding him in the direction of the general's party. "Just a lot of people all at once, I think."

It wasn't remotely it, but if she thought so, it was probably just as well.

"Very well," said the general briskly. "We'll take carriages. You'll be riding with him again, Mistress?"

"Yes," said Mistress Birdie very firmly, and did not take her hand from Erasmus's even as they were guided to a carriage. Like the last, this one's windows were drawn and pinned down with only a slit for air; and the carriage weighed with so much ferrum Erasmus was fairly sure he could have torn it apart if he needed. Unlike the carriages in Lammandan, with their heavy bases made of something Erasmus couldn't identify but certainly wasn't conducive to lodes.

But doing so would *definitely* label him as both a user of magic and extremely dangerous. And Erasmus was fairly sure he didn't want to find out what the people here would do if they thought him genuinely a threat.

(*Wasn't* he, though? The only reason the Empire imprisoned him was the fallout should anyone realise a member of the royal family had been executed, and *why*.)

There wasn't anything to say. Erasmus wasn't altogether too certain it was a good thing, the way time kept slipping away from him; but he was fairly sure it also wasn't related to his – problem. Time had been slipping for him for the last year, both too fast and unbearably slow. It had been the same when his mother died. A kind of grief, warping the world, until it was hard to tell whether time was even real.

But it was impossible not to hear the fractured, discordant hum and know – this was all too real. With his feet off the ground ...

Erasmus bent over his lap and breathed, fingers tapping his knee in a way he hadn't needed since he was ten; and he was conscious of the small hand that rested on his shoulder.

The scholars had told him that cities were powered by levin, like the bricks and generators they used. It had been a novel idea, in as far as Erasmus could find anything novel, that way of bringing light and flame to a place which had so little. The levinbricks had even been soothing, in an odd way, like the constant flow of water; alien at first but then companionable, the pattern of the lode a reassuring constancy.

He hadn't thought what that might mean for the cities.

He hadn't realised it would *clash* with itself. Lammandan had been tolerable, but this –

It was almost a surprise when the carriage came to a stop, jerky and inelegant. Erasmus pushed himself upright, taking one last deep breath, slow in and slower out, in the hope it might unknit the knot in his chest and keep his stomach down both.

"We'll be somewhere you can rest soon," said Mistress Birdie soothingly. Erasmus bit his tongue on a hysterical laugh, the thought of what, exactly, she must believe. Seasickness? Anxiety? A surfeit of people, truly?

The buildings in Lammandan had been made of stone. Maybe, *surely*, it would be safer inside.

And it was, at first. He didn't pay any mind to his surroundings save to focus on Mistress Birdie's light-brown coat, but their footsteps came duller, the sounds around them the same. The heavy stone of this building felt almost as solid as that under him, such that Erasmus's shoulders actually began to unwind some.

There was levin in – on? – the walls, but that didn't strike him poorly with the distance created between what was outside and what was in. Inside was enclosed; but it also concealed him from the rest of the city. It was fine. That was fine.

Until the guard opened a heavy door and stepped aside, motioning. Erasmus followed the gesture meekly –

He stopped short on the threshold, his heart pounding, his skin abruptly drenched in sweat. His breath rattled in his chest. It was a room. Just a room. But it was a room meant to contain, and the sound of the levin in the walls –

(wards like an ever-present rasp against his skin, humming and humming until all that was left was the rattling throb of weight bearing down *insufferably how long must he –*)

"Gus?"

Unthinkingly Erasmus backed up, his nerves suddenly jangling as loudly as the lodes; the long distance expanding like the yaw of the world beneath, the expanse of a float yielding to gravity and the sure knowledge that he was on the cusp of a fall.

He backed *into* someone; he heard the grunt; but he couldn't. He couldn't stop until his back was against the wall, grounding and solid, until there was *something* there that wouldn't let him simply. Fly off the world. His knees felt like jelly; he slid down the wall to the floor, breathing as deeply as he could manage with his knees drawn up.

Mistress Birdie's hand landed on his arm and he flinched.

"I can't go in there," tumbled out shaking and petrified. He couldn't. He couldn't. Three months in the same cell with naught but wards between him and freedom and the never-ending thrum of levin seesawing him between reason and reflection.

Not for nothing did they say eidols captured the soul.

Mistress Birdie's face was too much in shadow for him to see her expression, but she might have frowned. "I'm sorry," she said carefully, "I didn't quite understand that. Can you please repeat it?"

– He'd been speaking Imperial. Terror struck a blow far more sharply, and not even the grounding sort. The sort that made his stomach rise and his head ring dizzy flush instead.

"I can't –" He fished wildly for the right words, the right *language*. "– I can't."

Mistress Birdie kneeled beside him, taking his trembling hand in hers. "Alright," she said calmly. "Are you able to tell me why?"

"The sound," Erasmus whispered. "The sound in the walls."

The wards had never bothered him in development, though they'd always had that low hum. He'd walked through the test halls a few times, then dragged Christopher down to see them; they'd almost been soothing, really. What resources could be reclaimed if their highest-security prisons, needful but costly, did not need heavy doors and containment? What if all that could be used to contain a person was the right kind of lode, a gentle kind of aversion, one that prevented escape without weighing on the island or causing harm?

It hadn't bothered him then.

Not until he'd been put in one of the cells he'd helped design.

Tell me your name.

"It's just the levin grid," said the guard, sounding rattled and wary. "It powers the lights and things, see?"

He reached inside and Erasmus heard a click, and the whole room beyond the door plunged into darkness. What seemed to be *absolute* darkness. As absolute as the bunker beneath the cliff, which he'd never been forced to suffer for more than a few days at a time.

Oh, Light, if he had to live in *that* –

It took him a moment to realise the echo was not his heart in his ears but the sound of further footsteps approaching much more swiftly than they'd come down the hall to begin with.

"What's wrong?" demanded the general. "Do *not* say nothing, Mistress; you've been forthright so far. Don't ruin it."

"I think it's the sound of the levin grid in an enclosed space," said Mistress Birdie matter-of-factly, patting Erasmus's hand. All of a sudden he felt both pathetic and pathetically grateful that it made him feel even marginally less alone. "The room he stayed at Lammandan was used because its utilities were under repair; handheld lamps only. That's why you weren't afraid of it, isn't that right?"

She smiled up at Erasmus, but he didn't have an answer. It could well be. He didn't know what was normal and what wasn't. It hadn't occurred to him that the room was unusual in any way.

"The sound of the levin grid," repeated the general more slowly. Erasmus twitched as she crouched, her face even more shadowed than Mistress Birdie's thanks to the angle; but unexpectedly, although her voice was not gentle, it came kinder than before. "I was told you escaped from a prison." Erasmus flinched. "Did they do anything to you before they put you in there?"

Do anything? Erasmus choked on a strangled laugh. What was *she* expecting, now, what was she *thinking* had been done to him? What was he supposed to say, about his best friend arresting him, seeing something alien looking through his eyes and seeking to upturn it to

Light while Erasmus was strapped down and blinded as a consequence?

Tell me your name *and we can both* end this.

"There was ... a chair ... and ..."

Even those words took effort to push through the closeness of his throat. He *meant* to explain an interrogation – such as it was – but Mistress Birdie's breath drew sharp and the general nodded as though Erasmus had said something insightful in truth.

"A chair and levin," repeated the general, and then muttered: "A killer my *ass*." Erasmus flinched again, but she was already pushing out of her crouch, her words directed over his head toward someone in her escort. "Is there a barracks?"

"Yes, General."

"Shut off the grid in that part of the facility and arrange an appropriate guard, and lighting," said the general. "We'll keep him there until I've decided what's next. I'm not going to help – *whoever* is targeting this man – torture him further."

She strode away before Erasmus really even processed her words so much as the bitter disgust in them, and when he *had* –

His heart jolted uncomfortably against his ribs and down into his gut.

"I wasn't tortured," he whispered to Mistress Birdie, but her smile was crimped and she patted the back of his hand. "I ... I wasn't ..."

He can't have been. That would mean Christopher –

No. No, he hadn't been. Christopher had every reason to believe it wasn't him, and there hadn't been levin involved the way the general was assuming. It had just been ... a chair. And too much light.

He hadn't been *tortured*.

He *hadn't*.

Chapter Thirteen
The cold fingers of fate

Tyrian found them a room at one of the inns within streets of the bunker, with their target just visible from the window. The street curved such that the slope of the bunker's hulking stone exterior was visible above the eaves of the building across, built into the wall of the next ring up – and the stone beneath it thereby. More helpfully, any carriage by which Gus was bought would have to pass directly past the inn. They would know when he arrived.

And they did, alerted by the clatter of wheels on cobbles and the heavy grind of the prison carriage's engine as it passed. Through the window Yahvanna saw the pedestrians staring after and chattering; aligned around the edges of the street, partly to get out of the way and partly due to the looming greyness of the clouds. Tyrian told them it wasn't common for vehicles like this to come by this road, let alone with engines; and the only thing *here* was ...

Well, the bunker.

"If nobody knew it before, everyone's going to suspect a magician now," said Tyrian grimly, and leaned away from the window, crossing his arms. "How are we playing this?"

"Are we actually breaking him out?" Yahvanna asked, still close enough to the window to watch through it. The carriage was well out of sight now, but there were still people lingering; rubbernecking, trying to see whether there was indeed a magician. A line of guards had pushed onlookers back to the street's end, so Prittuni was taking this seriously – and the very act of it drew attention despite the humidity in the air and the scents of rain and ozone threatening. "The way Birdie described it, General Burnstone seems sympathetic enough."

"Indeed," Vespasien agreed, seated on the tattered bed further into the room. "Could we not convince General Burnstone to release Gus as non-threatening? Gus has, after all, committed no crimes on Prittune soil."

"And neither have we," Yahvanna added. The alien fabric in Vespasien's luggage might be counted as something he ought to have turned over to a prospector, but if anyone recognised it as alien there'd be other questions to answer. Perhaps they'd be fortunate and whoever examined their possessions would not recognise it as such.

"Gus's existence might be a crime," Tyrian pointed out. "I'm worried the longer he's in their hands the more likely someone will find out he's a skydweller."

"Not if Birdie has anything to say about it," Yahvanna murmured. "Right now, Prittuni seems positively inclined. Breaking him out would ruin that. If we somehow have more allowance from them than Academe does ..."

She spread her hands and shrugged. It was unlooked-for capital, but they had it. Schecheya had thrown its weight around a little too much without enough in the way of recompense to make the presumption palatable. Even if they were only higher in the general's esteem because Schecheya was just that low, it was leverage to work with.

"Do you know the layout of the bunker well enough to enact a prison break?" Vespasien asked with every evidence of curiosity and none of either judgement or sarcasm.

Tyrian sighed a long sigh that made his shoulders relax, and he slumped against the wall. "No. I could probably get the information, but it would take just as long as a negotiation." He jerked his head irritably toward the window. "What are we to do, then? Present ourselves to the bunker, after all this time trying to stay out of custody?"

"One of us, perhaps," said Yoch, and turned from the window toward Vespasien, who clasped his hands and unclasped them not quite anxiously. "I think it must be you, Passion. You're the one with any amount of expertise in possession, and that's the crux of the fear. Convince them Gus isn't be possessed – and Gus as well –"

"Indeed," agreed Vespasien thoughtfully, and clasped his hands again, despite there was no sign of anxiety in his voice. "Perhaps to have Gus released under medical auspices. If we delivered Gus safely to the Owls, it would fulfil just such a promise as I could make to the general."

"It might work," said Tyrian, and his slump became more of a slouch as his shoulders relaxed further. "Passion's pretty convinc–"

The world shook with the sound of something *tearing*. Yahvanna's ears rang, waxing between the throb of her pulse and a high-pitched keen. She pushed herself to her knees using the wall and didn't know when, exactly, she'd fallen; she saw Tyrian haul himself up on the windowsill, and the blood drain from his face.

Flood, he breathed, a word more in the shape of his lips than in Yahvanna's ears. Grimly she gripped his arm and pulled herself upright, found herself panting with the effort and the ringing.

People on the street were screaming, waning in and out of her hearing, but Yahvanna didn't look there. Tyrian's gaze was not directed *below*. Even so, it seemed to take forever before her mind wanted to see what her eyes were.

The distant horizon, the mountains, had become a seething mess of mist and rain. Lightning split the sky again and again with reaching purple claws; one cracked so near that Yahvanna's ears throbbed almost in the same instant.

"That's very close," she said through numbed lips, and was gratified that at least she could hear herself in *some* measure.

"The dam," said Tyrian shakily. "Yahvanna, *the dam*."

– It wasn't rain. It wasn't just rain or mist that obscured the horizon it was –

– *flood* –

– the thunderous force of a million tonnes of water and debris crashing toward the plains and the city's half-built wall.

Something wrenched her from the window and Yahvanna tore herself away, snarling; but it was Vespasien behind her, Vespasien with his hands on her arms, his eyes wide and face ashen.

"We must go," he said urgently, his voice clearer in her ears now, backdropped by the sound of citizens screaming.

Klaxons began to peal; someone's voice came barking and vaguely distorted through the district intercom. Yahvanna couldn't tell if she failed to understand the words because of the intercom itself or because her mind felt so *frozen*.

She did not resist Vespasien pulling her toward the door.

"Not that way," said Tyrian sharply, and thrust Yahvanna's bag into her hands, which mercifully she was capable of accepting. "Listen – out in the halls."

The thudding was not only in her ears, Yahvanna realised dimly, but the sound of footsteps and bodies crowding the passage despite the strained voice – likely someone owning the business – trying to keep some semblance of order.

People could be their own flood, and just as liable to crush as water.

"Out the window, then," she said, and was startled by the steadiness of her voice.

"I'll go first," said Tyrian, buckling his bag across his chest and peering at the window as he did. "Passion, come next so I can spot you. Yoch, come last. We'll aim for the bunker. Try and stay together. We might be able to make it to the street-end on the eaves, but if we have to hit the ground we'll stick to the side of the street."

Yahvanna bit her tongue on pointing out they'd have to cross the street to *reach* the bunker, but first things first.

"Very well," said Vespasien, his face even greyer than before and fingers trembling so hard on the buckle of his bag that Yahvanna pushed his hands away and yanked it taut for him. "Thank you."

Tyrian was already half out the window, easing carefully but quickly onto the eaves of the storey below. Yahvanna watched where he stepped as he hopped to the next building over, and kept her hand on Vespasien's elbow as he clambered gracelessly out.

A few people looked out their own windows, faces as white and eyes as wide as the rest of them; but although some of them made movements to exit, no one else had taken the risk by the time Yahvanna climbed over the windowsill. She did not dare glance down, but in the corner of her eyes caught the writhing mass of people rushing into the streets, threatening to become a crush.

She followed Vespasian's back, keeping an eye in case he stumbled – though if she tried to help they were both likely to go over. He was clumsy on the roof-tiles, but did not fall, though her heart leapt every time he lurched, and when the lightning cracked overhead –

She almost fell herself.

But only almost, and in short order and an eternity they reached the end of the eaves.

At the end of the street the guards had broadened the circle to maintain order around the intersection overlooked by the bunker's door. One of the officers climbed onto a levin carriage, her voice tinny over the loudspeaker in her hands. The sound of her voice authoritative seemed to be keeping people down that end of the street calmer, at least, and there was some movement from the centre of the guards letting people through and directing them somewhere further uphill.

"They'll be sending people toward the locks to the upper rings," said Tyrian from the edge of the roof, voice raised and terse. "There's levees quarantining the districts. If the outer wall holds long enough they can quarantine the outermost districts to give them time to evacuate those inside."

Yahvanna did not ask how long the outer wall would hold. She had lived too long on a waterfall's edge to ask foolish questions. They had some time – but urgency and fear would lengthen the time they *needed*.

"Have you a way down?" she asked instead, because although they were now at the edge of the eaves, they had not quite made the end of the street.

"I think we'll have to go up first," said Tyrian, and pointed to the edge of the roof above them. It extended along the rest of the block, a long line of unbroken building for multiple dwellings; a barricade against flooding between one street and another. Prittuni's roofs were constructed with a wavy kind of tile providing natural gutters, which made them unnerving to walk on even dry. For a mercy the rain had eased enough earlier that they weren't wet, but if they didn't hurry, it might begin again. "You first, Yoch."

Tyrian laced his fingers together and heaved her up when she stepped in the hold. Yahvanna gripped the side and hauled herself over the edge; a little far, for her. It'll be easier for Vespasien – he was almost as tall as the roof here – but it still took him a minute, a lot of scrambling, and Tyrian and Yahvanna on either side as a lift and a counterweight. Climbing simply was not among Vespasien's strengths.

Some of the panic had calmed in the street, enough that the risk of a crush might have subsided. When Yahvanna glanced it was to see a seething mass of people, the slow-moving worms of the lines slowly becoming visible in contrast to the parts of the crowd which did not move at all.

Soon enough, neither did they. The street-end of the roof peaked, and when Yahvanna peered down the wall she saw the brick-and-mortar of what had once been a balcony and was now outside storage.

"How do you mean to get down?" she asked again, without turning. "There's a ledge here, but nothing under that."

There had been a ladder once, judging by the rusted hooks in the brickwork, but there was no longer.

"With a little help," said Tyrian, standing lower on the roof, close to the gutter and at angles that looked alarmingly perched. "Look."

Yahvanna looked. The bunker's heavy steel doors had been hauled open and other carriages brought around, returned almost before they'd even fully been garaged. There was a hustle of people emerging – the rest of the relatively small detachment of guards – and the general herself, along with Birdie and Gus, the former hunched around the bag clutched to his chest.

Tyrian whistled long and piercing, cutting past even the tinny ring of the intercom before being lost in the not-distant-enough crack of lightning. People craned their heads; Birdie looked up, visibly searching until her gaze caught on Tyrian's waving arm. She hastened forward to the general's much lankier frame, and they all saw the pause as Birdie caught her attention and pointed toward them.

The general looked, her eyes narrowed, and then turned her head and spoke to one of her aides.

"Let's get on the balcony," said Tyrian, and offered his hand to Yahvanna to lower her down first. Some of the crates were moveable; she stacked them higher so Vespasien could reach them if he stretched, steadying them such as she could with what little weight she had. For a mercy he was so tall; with Tyrian's counterweight gripping his arm from above, Vespasien lowered himself gingerly without having to drop or hold himself upright too long.

Beneath them the crowd shuffled. The carriage on which the officer was perched came alive with a rumble, approaching the wall at a crawl while the rest of the guards stopped the lines around the perimeter. The crowd muttered anxiously as exodus slowed to nothing.

Tyrian dropped down beside them. As soon as the carriage was near enough Yahvanna climbed over the rail, her hand sweaty in Tyrian's as he lowered her to the carriage roof. The officer helped steady her, then Vespasien; in moments they were down, or as down as they were going to get, and the carriage backed up without turning.

It only took a few minutes, and yet the air of taut anxiety reeked sour before the carriage was clear and the perimeter guard allowed the lines to start moving again.

As soon as the carriage came to a halt Tyrian vaulted off it, while Vespasien and Yahvanna climbed down the driver's seat and into a circle of guards who hustled them toward the bunker. Toward the general's entourage, rather. It was difficult to tell whether they were being protected or arrested, at least until General Burnstone motioned the guards away impatiently.

"You're alright," said Birdie, relief in her tone and written across her face. Gus was – squinting, again; worse for the goggles no doubt, but at least *wearing* them, and holding back as if he was afraid to let on he knew them at all. His face was ashen, but there were too many reasons for that to guess the cause.

"We're moving out," said the general brusquely over the loudspeaker and the soft rumble of the prison carriage engines. "Two of you in one carriage, the third with Gus and Mistress Birdie. We'll sort out your status when the crisis is over, but rest assured I do not assume –"

The ground rocked. Yahvanna's ears rang. She didn't fall, not this time, but only by catching herself on Vespasien. She tasted bloody acrid fear in the back of her throat, heard the sound of the world groaning; looked up, and saw the next ring's stonework crumble. The levin-bole atop it toppled, seemingly slowly, with the metallic snap of cables breaking and levin sparking.

People screamed, scattering from the bunker. Someone – Vespasien – yanked Yahvanna backward and her heel caught on either someone else's foot or simply – nothing.

The bole collided with the ground with a crunch of stone and metal. Levin arced across the intersection. Yahvanna saw a moment of clarity, that there was no way for so many to escape such a large discharge. Not only the lightning-strike, but the levin still powered through the cables.

This *was* how people died, Yahvanna thought clinically. Suddenly and without fanfare, lost to nothing but poor fortune and the travails of the world around them.

Levin bent away from them, jagged reaching fingers fitfully in motion turned toward the point of their emission. Gus strode forward step by step, his hands outstretched, fingers pointing as if to indicate – or command – or perhaps pin. It was as though there was a void space around him where the levin dared not spark; and where he shifted his direction, the levin followed.

Dark as his clothes were, he was framed by the light: an aurora of blue levin surrounding him and setting his tellingly alien hair ablaze. Behind her, Yahvanna heard the dull sound of someone – multiple someones – cursing.

"Is everyone alright?"

The voice came strong, warped by the throb in Yahvanna's ears; so authoritative that at first Yahvanna didn't recognise it was *Gus*. He didn't turn toward them, his attention wholly focussed on whatever he was doing.

Controlling the levin; reducing it. The bole was a crumpled wreck on the ground, crushing one of the carriages and partially blocking the far end of the intersection. The live cables sparked, the discharge feeding back into the bole until the whole thing whined so highly pitched that Yahvanna felt it in the back of her teeth. She inhaled and smelled burning flesh, so someone hadn't escaped unscathed across the intersection – but it was not *all of them*, at least.

Yahvanna pushed herself upright, gravel and bits of debris clattering off her sleeves as she shook off her arms.

"We need to shut that off," said Tyrian, too loud, too throbbing, and Yahvanna couldn't tell if that was his fault or not. The general's voice, nearly on his heels, was not much better.

"Where's a *damned radio* – thank you."

"Before you do that," said Gus, not terse but very definitely concentrating, and the general's brusque voice cut off from giving instructions. "I need a –" Gus said something then in his native language.

"A female?" asked Vespasien nearby Yahvanna's shoulder with a baffled kind of daze. Too close – on the ground, not standing. "A – forgive me, I cannot –"

Yahvanna groped for his shoulder, then the back of his neck, and pressed his head firmly down between his knees. His back rose shudderingly as he took deep breaths.

"A – female, yes," said Gus, and his head turned slightly, followed by something that had the tenor of a curse in his own tongue. "The – the other side, the other end, *somewhere to put it.*"

"You want a grounding rod," said Tyrian, and Yahvanna looked up at him as he came closer – not to Gus's shoulder, but nearer than anyone else was daring, his head turned as he looked along the shattered bole. "There's too much charge. If we shut it off now the rest of it still has to go somewhere."

"Yes," said Gus with relief suffusing his voice. "I'm directing the – the charge into itself."

"Correct me if I'm wrong," said Tyrian with that conversational kind of calm he only used when things were *incredibly* dire, "but that sounds like an explosion waiting to happen if we let it continue for too long."

"Yes," said Gus simply, and still his stance did not falter. The whining took a greater pitch, but Yahvanna couldn't tell if that was because it actually had, or because she simply understood its implications better.

She pushed herself to her feet off Vespasien's shoulder. He quivered under her weight but did not collapse. Yahvanna took what seemed like her first deep breath in hours and turned toward the general, but spoke to anyone in the vicinity who knew the answer. "Where's the nearest lightning rod?"

"On top of the bunker," said General Burnstone grimly, and they *all* looked. The top of it was still smoking. It had done its job; either there had been more than one strike or it just hadn't been enough. Sometimes it wasn't.

"How are you going to let it go?" asked Yahvanna. "A constant direct current surely can't be good for the soil beneath." The charge that was building – *could* the ground itself ignite, if enough of a charge? Surely it was too much to risk it all at once, now.

"Better than exploding," Tyrian answered, and went to stand directly behind Gus. "I'm behind you. We're facing northeast. The bunker's to the southeast. Got that?"

"What –" General Burnstone began, sounding very nearly rattled, and Yahvanna cut in.

"He can't see in this light."

Gus's head had turned, but not to look; it looked almost as though he was –

"I hear it," he said more calmly than Yahvanna felt was strictly appropriate. "Excuse me."

He pivoted then, smooth on his balance, and Tyrian hurriedly stepped back. Gus's near hand pointed toward the bunker's roof, and the levin – *cascaded*, almost. Like a bulging rope attached to a pulley it arched over their heads and into the bunker's lightning rod, drawn there by something none of them could see. Cables sparked on the bunker's exterior, levin crackled as it earthed itself; the acrid scent of burned stone filled the air. But nothing exploded, and the only other sound was General Burnstone talking to the person on the other side of her radio.

"Alright," said Gus, and he sounded almost cheerful. "It should be safe to turn off now."

"Shut it off," General Burnstone ordered.

The district in the ring immediately above them went dark, and the power pushed through the bole suddenly cut off. The absence of the high-pitched whine left a throb in Yahvanna's ears. The last of the levin was drawn to the lightning rod like static, and Gus lowered his hands.

Almost at once there were a dozen rifles pointed toward him – toward all of them. Yahvanna froze, her hand on Vespasien's shoulder. Tyrian went very still, considering the gun in front of him and then the woman behind it. His hand was loose at his side, not nearly close enough to the pommel of the knife strapped to his thigh to be of any aid, as if *drawing it* would be.

"Wait –" began Mistress Birdie, sounding tersely distraught.

Gus turned toward the noise, *stepped* uncomprehending toward the noise, almost directly into the barrel of one of the rifles nearest him. Yahvanna exhaled slowly and *hoped* its owner did not put their finger on the trigger.

"What was that?" Gus asked, suddenly vastly terser than he'd been with levin practically in his hands. His hair was still too, too bright; fading by degrees, but still so obviously alien in its crimson highlights.

"You really can't see," said General Burnstone, too grim herself to be marvelling. "No wonder you've been tripping over everything."

Could he truly not even see what was *right in front of him*? Was that due to the dazzle of the levin, or because he'd been concealing the extent of his blindness all this time?

"They have rifles on us," said Yahvanna low, and the sound Gus made –

Impatient incredulity, but not quite a laugh but not a snarl. He stepped forward again, almost in the general's direction. The barrel of that rifle thudded into his chest, though he didn't seem to realise what it was, or the threat. His hand swiped the air.

"*Your people are in danger*. Is your hatred of magic so absolute you'd hew to principle at the expense of *their lives*?!"

"General," whispered Mistress Birdie, and Yahvanna dared to look.

Unexpectedly, the expression on the general's face was an incredulously reluctant grin. "Stand down," she said, and didn't look away from Gus as a dozen rifles were, in some cases with vast reluctance, uncocked and lowered. "I'm not going to ask where you're *from*."

Thank the Spire for that. It was not an answer best given in a crowd of rattled people.

"That's probably for the best," Gus agreed, and spread his hands. It made the nearest guard flinch. "Can we help?"

Yahvanna exhaled, and it was almost a sigh. Tyrian shook his head with a crooked smile. Vespasien raised his head with a bracing in-drawn breath.

None of them argued about the 'we'.

"After all this –" began the general and then cut herself off with a sharp shake of her head. "There's been lightning strikes all over the city. Some of the outer ring's levees have lost power. Without them we can't close all the gates."

"The flood will get in and drown the unprotected districts before they can be properly evacuated," Yahvanna clarified for Gus's sake, and Gus's face lost what little of its colour it had regained.

"Every district that's breached will make it that much harder to contain the flood in the other districts too," Tyrian added, and crossed his arms, his gaze intensely unblinking and voice *almost* jovial. "If, on the other hand, someone could provide levin to the machines in question …"

Could Gus provide levin? He had only directed it –

"Get me there and I can do that," said Gus immediately. "Better if I can draw from the – the levin grid, but if that's not an option I can draw a strike and use that."

There was an *immensely* wrought pause filled only by the orders of the terse-sounding officers around the perimeter, the sounds of people sobbing, the distant boom of thunder.

"You can?" asked Mistress Birdie, sounding small and strained, and Gus's smile toward her was sympathetic.

"Yes," he said gently, "I can."

"Without killing anyone," General Burnstone muttered.

It didn't *sound* like it was a question, but Gus's head turned toward her and he said, "Yes. Without killing anyone."

The general pressed her fingers to her face and mouthed a curse toward the overcast sky; and then she looked sideways at her pale aide and ordered: "Get me a map."

Chapter Fourteen

Blitzing

Aulerin wasn't ordered in any way Erasmus had seen before, if seeing was what he was doing with it. The sky was so dark that there wasn't even a point in taking off his goggles; the lightning was infrequent enough that he couldn't see the maps much better in the moment he had, and he didn't dare draw a light of his own to see by.

But he could *hear* it. The discordant jangling of the levin grids. The blessed, dangerous silence where the grids had failed.

The city was done in rings, Yoch said, taking his hand to draw his finger around the shape on the map. It didn't seem like a perfect circle, and everything inside the rings was disordered. *Unplanned*, rather – a mishmash about which Erasmus bit his tongue. General Burnstone wasn't asking, and *saying things* about where he'd come from was a bad idea.

His heart still pounded with adrenaline, but it was scouring. The last year was a fog of malaise and grief, and now *finally* there was something he could do – something *only* he could do, which wasn't his favourite, but there it was.

Mistress Birdie's small *Can you*? still rang in his head, a shaken expletive of fear more than disbelief. He'd never told even the scholars what he *could* do. They hadn't asked, not even for how he'd survived the fall.

But at least for now, he had a *purpose*.

The city was done in rings, and they were on the naddiest, the one just below sea-level and first to be drowned. The sound of the thunder matched Erasmus's memory of the waterfalls colliding with the mangroves, and all he could think about was the debris in the floods' wake, the brokenness of the bodies he and Ryan recovered.

How much *worse* for it to be a *city* –

There wasn't time for him to panic.

There were four levees in the outer ring affected by outages. One of them was close by a lock leading zenith to the next ring. General Burnstone moved her command there to oversee evacuations and repairs by their own people. One of the others was close-by a generator of some kind and already being attended by engineers. The other two needed to be dealt with.

"The problem is getting there," said Ryan grimly. "If the other engineers could do that in a hurry, you might not need Gus. The evacuation is blocking all the roads."

"And it's too dangerous to have skyrides in the air with this much lightning," answered the general, her fingers tapping impatiently on the map. It was a different staccato than Christopher's but it still made Erasmus's chest ache and his mouth twitch at once.

"Why?" Erasmus asked, patient because – because even if she wasn't *Christopher*, the urge to frustrate by being contrary was still there. "I'll be on it."

"You might get hit –" the general began, and then stopped. Erasmus smiled at her – or at least at her silhouette. "Shit," she muttered, sounding halfway between resigned and incredulous. "I'm not asking one of my guards to fly a damned ride in a storm on the basis a *magician* can *shield* them."

"Then I'll fly it," said Ryan immediately. "What's next?"

At this rate, Erasmus might start to assume Ryan could do nearly anything.

"You might need an engineer," warned the general. "One of the levees was just shut down, but the other might have taken damage in the strike."

"I repaired my own generator out in the bog," said Yoch. "I shan't claim to be an expert, but I dare say I could follow instructions through a radio."

"So could I, in a pinch," Ryan added. "Where's the nearest landing pad? We should get going before the rain starts."

Because it was impending. The smell of it was everywhere – different to that of the bog or the mangroves or even the ocean. Closest to the last, with its sharpness, and yet more comforting for the fact that the sharpness came from ozone.

The nearest landing pad wasn't much more than an intersection cordoned to give the rides room to land, and the streets on this side were more orderly than the original panic had sounded. Or at least, it seemed to be; the voices of the state's officers were a steady, regular occurrence, bidding people to leave behind their largest possessions and processing them through the lock as swiftly as possible. The three of them got to the landing pad without trouble, at least, and one of the rides had already been prepared for them.

Erasmus didn't know if that meant *loaded* or *unloaded*.

He did know that were he – above the firmament, he'd at least have a spotter who was also a lodeshaper. That didn't always happen in an emergency, but it was good preparation.

The hold, when they climbed in through the side, felt bigger than it would have been if they were sending supplies, so it seemed they were given naught but an empty vessel. The moment the door was drawn shut behind them Erasmus peeled the goggles off and rubbed his aching eyes. He'd been wearing them for so long he felt as though the edges had cut permanent lines into his skin, only throbbing now his face was set free.

Things were still entirely too dark, but at least it wasn't also made worse by grime and smudges and the enclosed vision. He could actually *have* peripheral vision.

"Can you turn her on?" Erasmus asked Ryan, who was already in the pilot's seat but with the door between him and the hold open, the metal floor faintly shiny from the light of the controls. "But don't take off. I need to know how she feels first."

Imperial vessels weren't wholly common the way machines seemed to be here, but Erasmus was in the business where the use of them was. He'd know how to lodeshape around something Imperial – Light, he knew that *intimately* – but he wasn't sure exactly how the levin charge the people here relied on would interact with a lode.

"Well, you know how to talk about a ship, so there's that," said Ryan, sounding amused, and the metal floor under Erasmus's feet vibrated with a faint hum. The powering lode, the generation – the engine? – was on top, to either side; two cartridges, slung under hoods like one of those gargantuan armoured beetles from the bog.

Erasmus almost laughed when he realised it. Didn't they *know* what their own equipment was doing? "Oh, that's so easy."

He stretched his hand toward the ceiling, too high for him to reach; but he didn't need to touch, or even to see. It was a bad habit of his, that was all. *Overdramatic*, he'd been told. His cousin used to snidely tell him he should've gone into theatre –

Erasmus exhaled away the knitting shock and gently nudged the lodes to shape a third – slightly above them and the ride's outer shell, formed by the power in the space between them and their current. It was so, so easy; a blossoming drape, a gentle blanket across the ride's metal exterior that would ensure the lightning wouldn't want anything to *do* with them.

The hard part was remembering to shape it as neg and not poz. Half the things on the fundament were the opposite of what he'd known.

"Alright, go ahead."

Yoch took Erasmus's hand and he twitched for the unexpectedness, but she only led him over to a row of seats affixed to the wall, something he only realised was there when his shins bumped the edge. There were straps, but Erasmus didn't bother to use any; the last thing he needed, if something was to go wrong, was to be chained to something that would make lodeshaping more difficult.

He was confident in his lode – but this wouldn't be the first time something he expected to be poz was neg. Or vice versa, in this case.

The rumble heightened and the ride lifted off, heavy and inelegant and loud, and yet soothingly familiar for all that.

"Do you have ships like this above the firmament?" Yoch asked, and Erasmus's mouth twisted wryly.

"Of course," he said softly, and then nothing more, in the hope that the lump growing in his throat might ease if he didn't try to force words through it. For a mercy, Yoch didn't press, and the silence was not uncomfortable. In as far as it was silence, between the ride's rumble and the splitting crack of lightning outside –

But Erasmus heard the prelude. Up here, above the city, lodes were a little clearer, less erratic; the shape of them moulding more obvious to him. They weren't going so fast that he couldn't predict the lightning strikes. They were loud, but none of them came near to the ride.

"Coming up on the first one," said Ryan through the ship's speakers. There was so much *noise* in this kind of vessel – no wonder they needed machines to speak for them. "It's right next to the adjacent district, with a working levin grid. We'll be able to tap into this one, easily."

"Just give me something to draw from and put into," said Erasmus. It was so – clumsy. He didn't have these words. He didn't *ask* about them enough, he didn't ask enough about the generator, how it *worked*. Maybe they wouldn't have understood even if he had. Maybe they would, if he could only explain it.

"I can open a wire on either end," said Yoch. "That should be simple enough, at least where the power's out. If you can draw from the live end without sending the entire district's grid down, that would be useful."

"Show me a wire that won't do that and I'll see."

He'd try – but he wasn't wholly certain how the grid worked, save the constancy of the current through it and the myriad directions it coursed. It was familiar and alien at the same time. If the wire she showed him wouldn't overtax the grid for being abused in such a way, then he should be able to manage.

"I'm putting us down right on the street," said Ryan, and Erasmus felt the gentle lift of something descending faster than he was, without bothering a lode to anchor him to its surface. Nearest thing to float some people could get.

... Probably the nearest thing to float *these* people could get.

The first levee went as smoothly as they could hope. The street was deserted, but there was debris Erasmus nearly tripped over, the remnants of households dragged from buildings and then abandoned. Someone had spilled something: he smelled the sweetness, pungent in the way of fruit out for too long.

Ryan stayed in the ride in case of an emergency escape. Erasmus barely needed Yoch's guidance to find the district without its grid active, but he heard her kicking debris out of his path after the first stumble. She bared a wire on that side for him to pin with a small, innocuous lode he could make stronger later, and isolated one on the other side of the street, still with charge through it.

"What exactly are we using here?" Erasmus asked as he held that narrow wire between his finger and thumb, regarding the rest of the lodes inherent in the small space. He just needed one, but it had to hold. The rest would shatter as soon as he drew charge. "Whatever it is, it's about to be broken."

Everything was just silhouette and shades of grey, and with no movement in the street – he could barely see the ride, save as a hulking blackness behind them. Far easier to determine its location by the shape of it contrast to its lodes. It helped that it was still shrouded in one of his own.

"A streetlamp," said Yoch. "It shouldn't impact anything else."

Alright, that would do it. As strange as it was to need an entire contraption just for light.

"The ferrum in the wire itself is going to be bared afterward," Erasmus added. It was coated in a kind of rubber – something insulating, something that felt almost numb against his fingers. Just his imagination, almost certainly. "Do you have something I can put over it after?"

She did, taking his off hand to put something equally rubbery in it, but malleable enough to close over the end of a cable.

"Stand back."

The rest of the lodes in the box went out when the levin pulled from it, drawn inexorably by the enlarging of the lode on the other side of the street. Making levin go from one place to another – it was easy. Making it go from one place to another without manifesting as lightning was much, much harder than this.

Diverting the sparks from harming *him* was harder than this.

And he didn't have to hold it for long. He heard the rumbling hum of the machinery on the other side of the street coming to life, and the faint banging as Yoch found the controls and followed the instructions given to her over the radio. The gate groaned with a long scrape of metal, but it closed, then thudded as Yoch locked it to stop the emergency system from opening once the power was out.

She called down: "That's enough," and Erasmus dissipated the lodes. The streetlamp was still sparking in places, but nowhere that should be immediately harmful once he grounded the live wire in his hand.

They met at the ride, Erasmus's boots scraping against and kicking over debris he couldn't see on the way there. At least he could *get there* without having to wait for Yoch to guide him, even if he needed her help not to crash wholesale into the side of the vessel while trying to get in it.

They rose almost as soon as they were in, before they'd even taken seats, and unthinkingly Erasmus anchored himself to the floor to catch Yoch as she stumbled.

"Are we suddenly in more of a rush?" she demanded as she straightened with her hand warm on Erasmus's shoulder, her voice loud to surmount the rumble of machinery working, the rush of wind howling outside the open door.

"One of the plains stations just went down," said Ryan grimly through the radio. "The flood's moving faster than we thought – and with more tonnage."

"What does that mean?" Erasmus asked, not *intending* to whisper, and yet – quieter than he meant, as if an aside.

"The main dam in the mountains should only contain so much volume," Yoch answered, not exactly *quietly*, but low. Thoughtful. "Prittuni's estimates would have assumed that as an upper limit. If it's incorrect that suggests other dams failed at the same time."

"It's not impossible, given the proximity of some of them to one another," said Ryan with a crackle through the radio. "A landslide in the wrong place. We can think about it later."

"Sometimes the unlikely happens," said Erasmus, and walked Yoch toward the wall, his hand outstretched so he didn't collide with it. The soles of his boots felt as though they sucked at the metal floor, the thick rubber resisting the lode's demand to adhere.

"That sounds like the voice of experience," observed Yoch as Erasmus's shins hit the edge of the seats and she let him go.

"We have vessels like this in the Empire," Erasmus said, trying not to *think* too much about it. He leaned against the wall to find the seat and lower himself into it. "I was one of the lodeshapers on a research trip to study the surface of the ... the cloud sea, once. Usually the surface is reliably –"

How did he – how *does* he –? How could he have been here for a year and his words still so *lacking*.

"It's like how the lightning finds the fundament," he said lamely, fishing. "The – the difference that causes them to attract."

"The positive and negative charges," said Yoch, and the frustrated tension in Erasmus's chest unwound all at once and with a sigh. "The underside of stormclouds are usually negatively charged. Scientists have presumed that means the top is usually positively so, based on the evidence we possess."

"It's usually reliable," Erasmus agreed, and gave up on trying too hard to find the right words. His own were surely enough context. Surely. "And it's a simple – shape. To make a skimmer float just above the cloud sea's surface. A lodeshaper doesn't even have to do it; it's built into the ship. There's always a lodeshaper on board, though. Just in case." His smile *felt* weak. "We ran over a patch of neg. That's *rare*. So rare it's barely even in the risk assessment. The lightning sheared through the lode and the cockpit before anyone could do anything about it."

"You're alive, I note," Yoch pointed out.

"I held the skimmer in float until the main research vessel realised we were overdue and came looking."

His voice came grim. They'd been expected out there for hours, so it took six before rescue showed up. He barely even remembered the tail end of it, exhausted fighting the levinfield's inexorable draw and holding the remains of the skimmer together so everyone had something to stand on and sufficient air to breathe.

"In …?" Yoch asked promptly, and Erasmus rubbed his forehead.

"Like in water," he said finally. "When you're – not on the surface. Not on the bottom. Drifting."

"Floating." Yoch's head turned toward him. "You kept your ship floating, *midair*, until help arrived."

"It's easier when you have something to stand on," said Erasmus, because otherwise he'd have to acknowledge the faint trace of awe in her tone. It wasn't … much. It wasn't even discombobulated, like the general's had been, like Mistress Birdie's had been. There was something – hungry about it. As hungry as Passion when he asked Erasmus questions about the stars. "A good lodeshaper can keep themselves in float, but it's hard. Exhausting. You can't do it for long. Something under you that responds to lodeshaping – that's easier. And it's easier to hold air together that way too. There were three researchers on that vessel, and me, and the pilot. Only the pilot died."

Despite everything, despite that the memory was one of the worst moments of his career, Erasmus couldn't help the tired satisfaction. There were times in the aftermath he'd wondered if he could have done more, better; times he wondered whether he should have told the pilot to move slower so he could assess the cloudsea's surface.

But neg in the cloudsea – that side of it, at least – was rare. No one actually considered it anything more than a fluke accident. If the risk had been great enough to warrant speed restrictions, it would have been flagged at multiple stages through the application.

... It was considered a little more seriously now than it had been back then. Erasmus had heard of a few more incidents since his. Neg suddenly wasn't quite as rare as they'd thought. Not nearly rare *enough*, given –

I'm sorry, Erasmus. There wasn't enough to bring back.

"That's how you survived the fall," Yoch murmured.

Erasmus's heart lurched from one old incomprehensible grief to a more recent one. "Yes," he said, in lieu of anything else, because the truth was –

He barely remembered falling. Let alone *landing*. He couldn't have kept himself in float forever without an aid; but curtail his speed enough to live without injury, yes. That's ... almost certainly what happened. Almost certainly.

The radio clicked. "And why you're not all that concerned about the ride."

Erasmus snorted before he could help it. "You've got all sorts of things on the ride to spare the people inside from being injured," he said. "The worst thing that happens is I have to slow our descent, unless one of you decides to fling yourself out of it."

Keeping himself in float without a tool was difficult enough. He could manage someone else – more than a couple, even – but not for long, and they'd have to be close. The ride itself? Easy.

"Do not fling myself from the falling ride," said Yoch very dryly. "Duly noted."

"We're coming up on the next levee," said Ryan, and the ride's internals clunked the same way it had when they were about to land the last time. "Don't dawdle too much, and good luck."

Erasmus exhaled as long as he could manage; inhaled cleaner. He didn't wait for the moment the ride grounded, but pushed himself to his feet, resetting the anchor more firmly, and held out his hand to Yoch to guide her toward the open door so they could exit as soon as they were stable.

CHAPTER FIFTEEN

How many lives?

Britt did not remember ever being so *useless*. She'd only ever been an administrator of one sort or another. Managing people, finance; culminating in an organisation, at least where Prittuni's annex was concerned. A physical crisis like this?

Her ears kept ringing in and out, alternating between thunder and shouts. The worst part was that the sounds here were just the same as they'd been *back then*. The earth was still beneath their feet, it hadn't crumbled into water; but that wasn't much help if the water was coming to them, was it? At least the smell here was honest rain and not salt. It helped, almost.

She climbed up beside Passion on his crate, her legs and body entirely too short to quite touch the ground on something tall enough to allow Passion to sit properly.

"How are you feeling?" Britt asked. Passion still had his head in his hands, his elbows on his knees. His bag he'd unbuckled, but it still sat curved around his back.

Ryan's and Yoch's were currently stowed behind his ankles, tucked against the crate. And Gus's, of course.

Passion raised his head with a weak smile, the corners of his eyes creased. His face was still pale, especially with the bandages taped to his cheek. The cuts weren't large wounds, compared to what they could have been, but deep enough that between exertion and shock he'd almost passed out. Passion, Britt recalled from his file, reacted poorly to blood-loss.

"I feel better than previously, thank you," he said, and at least his voice was calm and steady enough. "Are you as well as could be, Mistress Birdie?"

Britt looked around. The intersection here was something of a half-star, streets radiating from the lock. The general's pavilion was to the side of it, and Britt and Passion ensconced in a corner of that, close by the garden at the base of the next ring up. The lock was down one way, a babble of anxious people being processed. There had been one or two scuffles as someone tried to push forward – but the guard had things well in hand, General Burnstone's initial small entourage supplemented by guard mobilised from the upper rings of the city.

The lock itself was something of a private reservoir, drawn from the underground moat fed by the water runoff that came from – just about everywhere. Such recent rains ensured that it was well-supplied, as were the hydropumps which powered the city's levin grids.

The locks were built to expect the lower rings flooding, but until that point the floor was a massive flat buoy; an elevator driven by the influx and drainage of water, managed by the state and ordinarily used for moving cargo delivered from the docks.

Birdie wondered whether it was ever as packed as it was now – but with people, instead of cargo. Just as slow-moving, she dared say.

Most of the fast activity was close to them, around the general's unfolded table and the radio operators managing the flow of information. Britt looked at that mess and didn't have a clue what was going on in it, or how to penetrate it.

She ought to be better than this. Managing a state's crisis couldn't be *that* different from managing any other crisis, surely.

And yet when Britt looked, the activity flowed over her head, a heedless babble she could not quite grasp.

"Mistress Birdie?" asked Passion kindly, and Britt smiled weakly up at him.

"As well as could be," she answered him finally. If nothing else, their immediate surrounds were different enough to Cantlond to keep her here and there, however tight her chest.

"You didn't accept the offer to be taken to a higher ring," Passion said.

"Neither did you."

For all the good that either of them were. Passion especially looked a special kind of bedraggled, and it hadn't even started raining yet. Imminent, but in the way of 'never quite', and making them all more anxious for the holding.

Britt simply –

She simply did not want to be somewhere else. She was supposed to be watching after Gus, despite that Gus very suddenly did not appear to need watching-over. So despite the risk –

Well, there were a dozen levees between her and the flood, at any rate. Especially if they fixed the one just down the way. Despite how the activity had grown more frenetic in the very recent past. Despite that everyone in the state's livery had looked increasingly strained.

"What happened?" Britt asked. "I didn't hear."

She'd volunteered to deliver some coffee to the guards stationed at the lock, which had been well appreciated, and also left Britt feeling vaguely as though she'd just escaped a storm someone else had to deal with.

"The flood is moving faster than the forecasters expected," said Passion quietly, and Britt's heart lurched.

"But the others will be –"

A shaft of lightning lit the grey sky, tendrils sprayed off it as though a crashing wave; but it was oddly. *Narrow.* And … lingering. It seemed to stay for seconds on seconds, splitting the horizon like a mural of one landscape divided between two panels. The eerie silence made Britt's ears throb, even as she rose to her feet on the crate, her hand on Passion's shoulder for stability.

"That's in the outer –" she began, and the lightning cut out, as if ... *turned off*. Clouds pulled together and thunder roared overhead, seemingly all the louder for having been delayed; and then –

And then lightning erupted from the *ground* and reached toward the *sky*, even narrower than the first had been; needle-point thin, almost, and yet impossible to miss. Everything shuddered; the crate rattled so hard underfoot it made Britt's soles itch. Her heart thudded so hard her chest ached with it.

It wasn't – impossible for that to happen, she'd heard. For lightning to come from the earth instead of the cloud. But she'd never seen it herself, and very suddenly she remembered Gus saying –

You can do that?

Yes. I can.

... Where *had* he planned to put the excess charge, if there hadn't been a lightning rod in easy distance?

Passion rose, taller than her while she was standing on the crate; so sudden that Britt jumped. And then jumped down, scrambling as she did so, to follow him as he hastened toward the general's pavilion. The radios crackled static.

"No damage," said the operator, hand to his ear while glancing distractedly toward General Burnstone. "Reading the, uh, away team now."

"It's fine," said Ryan, staticky through the radio, and Britt released the breath she hadn't realised she was holding. "We couldn't find a good place to tap into the grid. Gus called down a strike and sent the excess back up. No one's hurt. A bit of percussive damage on the street and the ride's chassis. Everything else is fine."

... He almost sounded as though he was trying to convince *himself*.

"The levee?" asked General Burnstone impatiently, but when Britt glanced up her face was grey. Determined, but grey.

"Yoch's got it closed and locked. We're coming back now."

The snap of the radio turning off made Britt's ears throb once harder than the rest, and she rubbed them with a shiver that went through her from head to toe. She dug the ball of her foot into the ground, as if that would stop her soles from itching. General Burnstone glanced over, almost distractedly – and then with more intensity when she realised they were there.

"Did you know he could do that?" she demanded.

"No," said Passion. *His* colour hadn't improved any, but he was steadier on his feet than the rest of them.

If hunched, perpetually; he was taller than General Burnstone, but didn't seem it.

"But you knew he could do magic," accused the general.

"We did not ask about Gus's capabilities or lack thereof regarding magic," answered Passion, and the general let out a soft growl. "Gus is offering his aid to you, General."

"He's *Surge-sodden dangerous*," the general snapped, wheeling on him. Britt flinched.

Passion spread his hands. "A man with a rifle is dangerous," he said simply. "And yet you do not outlaw guns: only limit where and how and by whom they might be used, because you recognise they are a tool." General Burnstone pinched the bridge of her nose. "*Is* your hatred of magic so absolute, General?"

Somehow, Britt couldn't have done it, Passion made the question unpointed, a genuine curiosity instead of an accusation. Nevertheless, General Burnstone lowered her hand and shot him an impatient glare.

"Evidently not," she said grimly, and her smile was humourless. "But I can't help but wonder if that was the same for the people of the ancient past, when they caused the Storm Surge that drowned the entire sodden world."

"I quite strenuously doubt that allowing a magician to save the lives of your people would cause a calamity," said Passion gently.

"The road floods by good intentions, as they say," said the general.

"And the same road is dried, thereby, through good action," Passion countered, and the general's mouth tipped up a little more honestly, a little less bitterly.

"You're not what I thought you'd be," she remarked almost conversationally, and Britt pressed her hand to her mouth so she didn't break into hysterical laughter.

But that was the last of the conversation; the radios chirped then, and General Burnstone turned away; and there came a rumble as a ride sailed overhead, aimed for the bit of intersection between the pavilion and the open levee gates. It was the clearest point, and the nearest, if anyone needed the ride in a hurry.

"That must be them," said Britt, relief spilling into her voice as the tension in her chest unravelled some. The part related to three of them being out of sight, at least, because Britt could hardly say it was any more dangerous out there than here, near the city's westernmost lock.

Behind her General Burnstone ordered: "Close the rest of the levees. Send a broadcast to anyone remaining in a district without a lock that they should get on their roof and wait for rescue by air."

And almost at once, Britt's gut shrivelled. She hadn't been imagining the faint tremor underfoot, then. The vibration of a million tonnes of water bearing down, close enough now to make her soles itch. She hadn't been imagining the distant roar, only pretending it belonged to ride and to people.

"General," said one of the officers tersely, "we haven't been able to repair this one yet. The engineers need more time."

"Then stop *wasting it*," snarled General Burnstone, and pressed her fingers to the bridge of her nose again. "*Shit*. How long?"

Britt didn't hear the response. The world lurched; stone boomed. Britt staggered against Passion and found his hand on her shoulder. She looked, they all looked, westward to the most complete part of the wall –

Frothing water bulged at the wall's height, an inexorable wave suspended for heartbeats, for an eternity. Stone shattered in slow motion, cracks becoming spurts between one breath and another, and the wall crumbled. Water sheeted down, stalled but not stoppered – crashing into the moat and the lowest ring, deluging the outermost buildings entire.

"Surge," someone breathed, her voice choked with terror.

"It's flooding over the outermost levees!" shouted one of the radio operators. "Three districts flooded. Four. The middle levees are holding, but – *shit*."

He jumped to his feet and spun toward the levee. They all spun toward the levee.

Britt's feet didn't want to move. She heard what might have been screaming behind her, but her *feet* didn't want to move. She looked, though – looked the way everyone else looked. It was funny, how silent it was, how she couldn't hear anything as the people around the levee dropped everything they held and *ran*.

Not anything, save the thunder of water tearing through streets toward them.

"GET DOWN."

And a strangely fizzling sound of stone and metal breaking.

The ride, the streetlamps, carriages – anything made of metal between here and the levee gouged long divots in the street as they – *lunged* – toward the oncoming flood. Metal clanged; water jetted skyward in a sudden burst and washed across the tops of the nearest buildings. The entire mess of debris shrieked as it barrelled toward them, and then suddenly –

Stopped.

With a jolt in the earth and the groan of metal complaining, the wall of debris stopped. The flood moaned over the tops of buildings, a thin rolling sheet that drained off, sluicing between crevices and eaves until finally the water-level subsided to something less than standard roof-height. Water gurgled across newly-made potholes and into drains, washing toward the pavilion and around their ankles.

Gus stood between them and the tangle of metal, breathing hard, his hands outstretched as if pushing. He shifted his weight, carefully as if to reorient himself; stood upright, and raised his hand. Something twanged as the debris groaned, and water cascaded between the cracks. Gus grunted and set himself, as if it was his whole body braced against the wall. Britt saw the debris re-settle more tightly, cutting off the rivulets seeking access past the debris.

"Okay," Gus said, his voice oddly ringing in Britt's ears, oddly *calm*. He exhaled. Resettled his weight. Rolled his shoulders as if to get comfortable. "Alright."

Britt took what seemed like her first breath in an hour and almost choked on it. The silence was – deafening – and not really silence. Just her ears, not wanting to work; turning everything throbbingly distant, half-dazed, as if not quite real.

"Shit," said General Burnstone again, her voice trembling; and her first step seemed like an automatic thing, like someone just learning how to walk again.

But it snapped everyone's dizzy paralysis. Radio operators turned back to their equipment. Guards went to help control the shouting crowd behind them. Dozens of engineers and guards picked themselves up from the street, soaked from the shallow dousing. Dazed. Terrified. Some were bleeding, some moved too gingerly to be anything other than injured – but medics were already rushing toward them.

It was an odd kind of arrangement. The scattered way people were seated – it looked almost as though they'd been flung.

General Burnstone passed and unthinkingly Britt matched pace, her own knees so rubbery she wondered if she should sit – but her fingers were gripping Passion's sleeve, she hadn't realised he was walking with them, and Britt wasn't sure she'd be able to make them let go.

Ryan climbed to his feet, wet-through, and held his shaking hand out to Yoch. Static sparked between them and Yoch grimaced, removing her hand and shaking it as soon as she was up.

"Well, we're not dead yet," Ryan said with an unnerving kind of calm, his gaze on the groaning wall of debris. "How long can you keep that up, do you think?"

"Oh, at least six hours," said Gus, with *vastly* inappropriate cheer despite the thread of tension in his voice.

Laughter bubbled up hard and fast until Britt leaned giggling on Passion's arm, trying to smother the sound while also not to fall. Wordlessly he kneeled, his knees immediately rendered sodden by lingering water, and let her lean against his shoulder.

"Shit," said the general again, and turned toward her officer in charge of the engineers. "Can we still close the levee?"

"We'd have to do it against water pressure," said the engineer with a rattled kind of calm. "But – maybe."

"I don't think that matters," said Gus, and raised his head with a breath to look toward what he'd ... made. "I think I grabbed it trying to anchor all this."

Britt's bucking laughter cut off so hard she hiccupped instead, pathetically grateful for Passion's hand rubbing her back.

"You *grabbed* several tonnes of solid steel anchored in concrete," said the engineer, sounding rather less calm and rather more rattled.

"In my defence," said Gus, sounding very defensive actually, "I'm not used to this much *water* and I didn't know how much *mass* I'd need to *block it*."

Somehow Britt *severely* doubted Gus's apparent lack was what the engineer was remarking on.

"*Fuck*," muttered General Burnstone, and turned toward the aide with the radio headset in her ear. "Get me the spotter on the next ring. What does she see?"

"Debris, General," the operator reported, her face extraordinarily pale and her eyes wide. "It looks like half the street's been torn up. The levee, it's – it's gone." She looked toward the debris. "Into ... that."

Silently they all followed her gaze. The wall was such a mess that at first it was hard to see it as anything other than a massive cluster of *things*, but after a moment Britt's eyes started picking out objects. A streetlight stuck out here and there, the ride and several carriages mostly visible by their size. There was an unexpectedly flat surface which had to be one of the levee gates.

The wall was still groaning, which Britt thought at first was the water, and then realised that some of the metal was ... moving. Oil dripped out the bottom of one of the carriages as it collapsed with a high-pitched squeal. Other bits seemed to be doing the same; getting flatter, moving *closer* to each other. Something in the ride sparked as its chassis sank in.

"The debris is compressing," said Yoch, alarmingly clinical. "You're doing that?"

"Yes," said Gus. "I've got a –" He said a word Britt in no way knew. "– holding it all together. It's strong enough to collapse the debris. It has to be."

"That sounds almost like the word you were using during transit," said Yoch. "The one I presume referred to ... people like you. Who can do ... this."

Gus said another word, and it *did* sound almost similar. Almost, in the way of one word leading to a relation. There was frustration in his voice as he added: "Like a – like the compass Ryan gave me. The thing which – which shows the way to north."

"You refer, perhaps, to a lode," said Passion suddenly, almost too loud when he was so near, still cradling Britt in his arms. "In the ancient past, the very first compasses were called lodestones. They were comprised of magnetised minerals which oriented north. The etymology of the word 'lode' refers to a way, a course, a journey. That word you just said could perhaps be translated as *wayfinder*, except that we already have this word, and it is very clearly *not* what you're doing."

"You said something about shaping, earlier," said Yoch to Gus. "The way you speak of it, as though you're – *manipulating* something. Magnetic fields, perhaps. I don't believe you're manipulating the levin itself, so much as what defines its behaviour."

The engineering officer let out a strangled noise which could have either been a whimper or something more awed. Perhaps both.

"If you say so," Gus answered dryly.

"Lodeshaping, then," said Ryan impatiently, "and now that we've got what we're *calling it* out of the way – is there anything you can do to make that more permanent, the way you protected the ride?"

His head jerked to the wall of debris.

Gus exhaled. "No. I mean – yes, it's possible, and no, I can't do it. I can't keep the wall up and make the – the lodes to pin it at once. It's one or the other."

"That's what you were trying to do earlier," Britt blurted. When the debris started to shift.

"Trying," said Gus grimly. "Failing. By rights I shouldn't even be able to do *this*."

"Then how are you?" Yoch demanded, crossing her arms over her chest and examining Gus instead of the wall.

"The fundament," said Gus simply. "You can – tether. Lodes to one another. Something with a naturally large lode will take the strain of the smaller one, like an anchor. You can build lodes on top of each other that way, and depend on the leverage to hold them together." He shifted his weight, and there was something – marvelling in it. Something about the way he planted his feet. "This earth, the – *ground* – it's taking nearly all of the strain. I've never – there *aren't* lodes this powerful. Usually." He went quiet for a moment, and then said with a breathless kind of awe: "I didn't *know*."

Know – how big the earth, that it had its own magnetic field; didn't know how powerful it would be? Britt didn't know what he meant by that, and didn't dare to ask in case it revealed something they were only *barely* skirting around as it was.

But it was hard not to be endeared by the near-childish wonder in his voice. How *could* he have known, if he'd spent his life so far above the firmament?

General Burnstone rubbed her face. Britt realised suddenly how *tired* she looked. How tired they all looked, probably, but the general was so focussed it was a shock to see how her greying hair was coming loose from its braid, how lined her face had become.

"Six hours, you said," said the general briskly. "Is that a guarantee?"

It wasn't *much* time for an evacuation, but – perhaps.

"Actually, probably longer," said Gus. "The last time I did anything like this it was a lot more taxing. The ground's taking most of it; I just need to keep the lode together, and that's not hard now I've got it up." He turned his head just enough for them to see the quirk of his mouth and a flash of his eyes, his pupils so large he looked vaguely drunk on whatever power he'd wrought. "Just bring me something to eat now and then. And maybe talk to me. I hate getting bored."

Hysterical laughter punched the underside of Britt's diaphragm, and Passion steadied her as she dissolved into such helpless mirth it came with choking tears.

Chapter Sixteen

A settling of priorities

Someone brought over some foldable chairs for them to use. For Birdie, most particularly. The fits of crying laughter were alarming, though Birdie at least seemed aware that they were, and one of the medics stopped briefly to make sure she wasn't going into shock.

Or that any of them were.

Yahvanna sat in her chair and watched Gus until the medics departed. The general and her aides had gone back to the pavilion to oversee the evacuation with as much alacrity as possible – which, in Yahvanna's estimation, could not be hastened any faster than it was. The storm's lightning had subsided to some degree, but thunder still rolled intermittently, and the scent of rain was more heightened still.

Combined with oil, wet metal, and the stench of lake water now filled with too many things to be even remotely called clean.

"Six hours," Yahvanna said finally, when it was only the five of them, those who *knew*, and the weight of curiosity had grown too much for silence to bear. "Is that how long it took before the research ship rescued you and the scientists you saved?"

Gus's mouth was lopsided, and he didn't glance around. "About that."

"While you held a ship in float."

Yahvanna could scarcely imagine. Such magicks as she'd dabbled in had always been small, to function without notice; an aversion to water to keep her things dry, a touch of healing to hasten recovery. The ability to map a person's leys, the ways in which flesh and blood knitted together to become a whole entity.

And that was the allure of understanding Gus's capabilities, was it not? A being made from cells was just as subject to the limitations, the boundaries, of similar principles. How far did Gus's power *go*? How deeply could it reach?

"You said you're hooked onto the planet's magnetic field," said Tyrian, and he turned away from what appeared to be a study of the wall to come closer, his arms folded across his chest. It was as closed as Yahvanna had ever seen him, and he made a pointed route that avoided placing him between Gus and the wall.

Probably it was wise. Though the science of magnetism was known to them, in this situation – it was difficult to tell what might be there, unseen, and what impact it might have.

In Tyrian's case, however, it bespoke the end of his tether. Tyrian had always only pretended at being more comfortable than he truly was.

"*Yoch* said that," Gus pointed out. "I don't know what some of those words mean except by inference."

"On an extraordinarily simple premise, magnetic fields define how levin behaves," Yahvanna said. "Drawing magnetic objects together, or repelling them." She glanced toward the clouds, greyer now than they were, nearly black. Would the rain make it more difficult for Gus to maintain this lode? "Causing lightning to form, due to the positive and negative charges from one place to another."

"Making it possible for technology to be powered by levin at all," Tyrian added.

"The levin grid," Mistress Birdie murmured, and raised her head from her knees, her arms tucked around them. It wasn't enough of a motion to disturb Vespasien's hand on her back, and Birdie's face was wan. "You can hear it, can't you? That's why you looked so faint when we came off the barge, and why you –"

She visibly bit her lip before ending that sentence.

"It's not particularly ordered," said Gus tersely. "Being on the water was soothing. Lammandan was on a cliff, and had fewer lodes inherent. But Aulerin is contained. Coming into the city was like – walking into a din. A cacophony of a thousand different tunes playing all at once. Any given one would have been – fine – but altogether ..." He shook his head. "And walking into an enclosed room like that, with that sound in the walls, *knowing* there was no way I could get out – I just. I couldn't put myself in there."

No wonder. There was a reason the deliberate constancy of noise was considered a form of torture. If this is how Gus interacted with the world – it might explain how he was managing to navigate with such poor sight, and also why he looked so constantly strained.

At least it sounded as though it could be mitigated. If Lammandan was not a trial, then it was simply a matter of infrastructure. Perhaps adjustment. He was not suffering just to *be* on the ground.

"Has it always been like this for you?" Yahvanna asked.

"In a way," said Gus vaguely, and his mouth quirked wryly. "My sense of north was always a bit off. It took me longer than most children to pin it down."

Tyrian snorted suddenly, caught his breath; let out a scattered bark of laughter. "The compass. The look on your face when I handed you the compass. As if I was handing you a toy."

"I haven't needed a lodestone since I was ten years old," Gus grumbled, and the way his mouth pulled seemed torn between humour and grimace. "But it's harder, down here. There's so much – in the way. Cliffs. Hills. Cities. *Things*. Like a massive clutter between me and north. I was so busy trying to find it that I never reached for –"

He shifted on his feet, a switching of balance as if he could feel the magnetic field beneath him through the soles of his boots. Maybe he could.

"... It's so *big*," he finished with that same wonder as before.

"I wonder that you didn't notice," said Tyrian with exasperation, and Gus glanced his way, his eyes wide. "How do you think we *find* north, anyway? It's all the earth's magnetic field, no matter how high up you go. You're just closer to it now, that's all."

"Such fields are more powerful in close proximity," Vespasien murmured.

"You don't reach deep for a lode, above the firmament," said Gus. "Reach too deep and you'll find the nexus lodes that keep the islands raised." Yahvanna closed her mouth on a thousand sudden bubbling questions. "They're too complicated for any one person to accidentally pull them apart just by touching them wrong, but still, you don't ever, *ever* try to reach beyond the surface anchors."

"Surely there's maintenance," Yahvanna pointed out, and still couldn't quite contain the vibrating curiosity in her voice even as she closed her mouth on demanding *more*.

They genuinely did live on islands above the clouds. There were stories, legends; hypotheses. Of course people must live up there *some*how.

But Gus had never said; and they had not asked. The most Vespasien and Yahvanna dared was to reason between themselves, trying to decide whether ships or land or something else; and *how*, if so, such terrain could be held so aloft without ever setting down to earth. They had concluded that great ships were the most likely.

That there could be *landmasses* above the firmament, secured by magnetic forces, only opened to the door to a dozen further questions. For one thing, what limits were there to altitude? How did they account for the thinness of the air? Judging by Gus's illness when he first fell, and his unexpected capacity for holding breath while underwater, they'd obviously have different physical requirements; but even so – he *did* breathe.

Yahvanna was glad of her restraint when a swift motion caught her eye, and out of the corner she saw General Burnstone coming toward them with a fast pace and purpose.

Vainly, because a moment later Mistress Birdie asked, unknowing: "Can every skydweller do what you do?"

General Burnstone stopped short, her back going rigid and her face – well, studiously blank. Perhaps it wasn't *so* much of a surprise, after all, given the alienness of Gus's colours. There was a reason the general had been deliberately not asking.

"Anyone could learn it," said Gus, as oblivious as Birdie given the general approached from behind him. Tyrian grimaced. "Everyone's got a good sense of direction, but not everyone learns to lodeshape."

"But *anyone* could learn how to –" Birdie reached out toward the wall, her brow furrowed more in thought than effort. "– just with a wave of their hand?"

Gus snorted again. "Gestures is amateur hour," he said self-deprecatingly. "I've just never been able to break the habit. A true professional won't. And most truly skilled lodeshapers often can't. The woman who taught me only had one functioning limb. She'd shape lodes without lifting a finger. She used to say –"

His voice changed then, a passable falsetto; an obvious quote with an impish tone. Yahvanna looked at Vespasien. They all looked at Vespasien, except Gus.

Vespasien looked blithely back. "I only possess one hand," he said. "I'd rather use it for more pleasurable activities."

Birdie choked, her hands covering her mouth.

"Is that a direct translation?" Yahvanna asked dryly.

"I would never be any more imprecise in my translations than can be avoided," said Vespasien gravely, and Birdie's coughing fit turned into helpless giggles thankfully less hysterical than the ones before.

"Then your teacher could shape without telegraphing at all," said Tyrian with that ironic tone of voice which suggested he was more amused than he wished to be. Given the topic –

Yahvanna glanced toward the general and her set jaw. Yes, between Burnstone and Tyrian, this was probably not a particularly *comforting* revelation, for all that Gus showed no sign of realising just how alarming it might be.

"Definitely," said Gus. "I've seen her shape across a room without even glancing up. My cousin used to –"

He cut himself off with a breath, as though he'd only realised what he said as it cut. The wall of debris groaned suddenly with a heavy twanging of steel, the distant drip of water turning into an abrupt gush. Gus hissed an unrecognisable curse, and the hair on Yahvanna's arms stood up as the debris groaned again –

Settled. Again.

There was a moment of dead quiet, not only from them but the suddenly pale-faced officers by the pavilion, and Gus exhaled slowly. "Alright. It's alright."

But there was a thread of wrought tension that hadn't been in his voice before, a crease to his eyes and a rictus downward pull to his mouth. The wall might be fine, but *he* was not.

"Perhaps we should discuss something else," Yahvanna suggested. Her heart pounded hard against her ribs, painfully so; her hands were suddenly itchy with sweat and adrenaline. Whatever he said about the lode being simple now it was raised, he clearly still needed to concentrate on it. And thinking of his cousin –

He had been accused of a murder, hadn't he?

General Burnstone kicked a piece of debris as she approached, perhaps by design. Mistress Birdie jumped under Vespasien's hand, and his thumb rubbed soothingly and most likely unthinkingly.

"I'm coming to give an update," said General Burnstone shortly, her eyes on Gus's back. "We've deployed as many skyrides as we have available and we're directing as many people as we can to other locks, but it's still going to be hours."

"And if you redirect too many, you'll only cause a blockage elsewhere and slow things down again," Tyrian observed. The general nodded at him, once and short. "How's the rest of the city?"

"The other levees are holding," said Burnstone. "The outermost districts to the west are flooded, but most people managed to get at least past the centre levees before they shut. Less than a fifth of the outer ring is flooded all told. The worst seems to be past so we're enacting shelter-in-place orders for the east and some districts in the north and south to make room for the displaced from the west."

Less than a fifth was still more than they'd hoped for. The flood had cracked the wall entire, and swamped the closest levees thereby. That did suggest more water than Prittuni calculated even in its assessment of the worst eventuality, and yet: between the promptness of the evacuation and the levees throughout the districts, the majority of lives had been spared.

And Gus's unique-to-the-fundament skill. The entire population of the western outer ring might have been killed in the process of evacuation if not for him. As well as themselves, and Prittuni's most accomplished military officer.

"Provisions are going to be scarce," Yahvanna murmured, and General Burnstone's nod to her was equally short. "The western farms must have been destroyed."

"Utterly," said Burnstone flatly. The way she stood was still absolutely rigid. "But none of that is your problem. This levee is."

"That's a generous description," Tyrian muttered. The general ignored him.

"How *long* do we *have*?" she demanded directly to Gus's back.

"I don't have an answer to give you," said Gus. "I truly don't."

"I'm moving the command post up to the next ring," said General Burnstone very nearly through gritted teeth. She exhaled long, and pressed her fingers to her eyes. "We've still got thousands of people waiting for evacuation through the lock here. We can't move them all out any faster than we are."

"I know," said Gus simply, and still did not turn. He leaned on thin air, on his lode, as if the debris and a million tonnes of water were held at bay by the weight of his body alone.

Perhaps it was, after a fashion. Yahvanna didn't know from where this lode of his was being sourced. Perhaps there *was* something there for him to lean on, something the rest of them couldn't hope to divine. Perhaps it was channelled *through* him entire, after all.

"We don't have the equipment to take the brunt of the water," said General Burnstone, in the tone of an argument; as though she'd come here expecting to have to – what? Convince Gus to stay where he was? If he wasn't prepared for that he'd never have started. "It's contained between here and the next levee, but since the district over is flooded, we have no way of draining it. And we can't bring in cranes or earthmovers to try and create a temporary levee until the people have been evacuated. Especially if it starts raining as hard as promised."

"A poor situation as described," Vespasien murmured.

To say the least. Gus was the only thing standing between these people and a flood. Even if the water levels continued to settle, seeping into the buildings and through to the next districts over, it had only so many places to go if the neighbouring districts were themselves flooded.

In the end there was still more than enough water behind this wall to kill and cause untold injury if Gus should set it loose.

"It's going to take longer than six hours," said General Burnstone with an inexorable kind of desperation.

"I know," said Gus.

Just like that. Matter-of-fact. Accepting. And yet, there wasn't even an edge of resignation in Gus's voice. General Burnstone shook her head incredulously and drew in a breath –

Blew it out with a long weary sigh.

"If you're still here when everyone else is gone I'll send a ride to pick you up," she said tiredly, and glanced around. "If I ordered the rest of you to come with me –"

"Not happening," said Tyrian immediately.

"I am no citizen of Prittuni," Yahvanna answered archly.

"I have nowhere I would prefer to be," said Vespasien firmly, and nudged Birdie. "Mistress Birdie, I beg you to take the general on her offer. There is little here you can do that we cannot, and you are unaccustomed to such tribulations."

"And you are?" Birdie demanded, but her tone was thin and small. She bit her lip, glancing around at them. "I know. You've been living in a bog for the last five years."

"Having water constantly up to my ankles feels just like home," said Tyrian sardonically.

"I mean this as kindly as possible," said Yahvanna, "but I think we would all feel much better if we didn't have to watch after you."

It was ungentle, perhaps, to say so – but they had been living in a bog, and Birdie had not. They were fit, and she was not. There was little she could *do* here. They may have to watch Gus in shifts, and nap at intervals; they were accustomed to disturbances, and swift action. She would be more of a burden than an aid.

"And I would not like Schecheya's relationship with Prittuni to sour further if something should occur to you we cannot stop," Vespasien added, far more gently than Yahvanna ever could. "The annex depends on you, Mistress. Master Cheya depends on you. We do not."

"... Alright," Birdie agreed, reluctance warring with relief, and wobbled as she climbed down from her chair. Even so, she raised her narrow chin and set her shoulders. "Don't worry. The annex won't be doing anything stupid if I have anything to say about this."

"I dare say you have a lot to say about it," said General Burnstone with asperity, and looked across them. Her face was tight, her grey eyes unexpectedly piercing even weary. "I'll have someone bring you some provisions. Food and a canvas against the rain, if nothing else. I just have one more question – for Gus, that is."

"Go on, then," said Gus dryly.

"Someone told us exactly where to look for you," said the general flatly. "The only way I can imagine they knew is if you used this – this power of yours after you left the bog. If it's really manipulating magnetic fields, then surely it can be traced by technological means. So, did you?"

... She was right. They'd all been so focussed on other things they'd forgotten to keep asking the vital question of *how*. There was no magical scrying necessary, if whoever was looking knew what skydwellers could do.

"... Yes," said Gus, and now his voice was resigned, and grim. "I used it to find the pocketwatch and fish it out of the water. It wasn't a huge use – and since there was no one around to witness, I didn't think anything of it."

"In a city full of levin a small thing like that would be impossible to find," Tyrian observed, "but out in the middle of a mangrove swamp, if there was a sudden – charge or surge of some kind –"

"Someone's tracking you," Yahvanna said to Gus. "Someone who knows what lodeshaping looks like in *some* fashion or another."

"Someone who knew to expect a man falling out of the sky," said General Burnstone, and swivelled abruptly. "That's it. That's all I had to say. May stars preserve us all."

The last was very nearly muttered as the general strode away, and the quirk of Gus's mouth suggested a fight to contain sudden inappropriate laughter at her choice of words. Birdie looked anxiously toward them one last time, and then followed – more sedately, but at least stable enough on her feet.

"And now we wait," Tyrian murmured.

"Goody," Gus muttered, his voice still quivering. He exhaled as he shifted his weight again in a fashion more like giving his feet a chance to rest than because he was feeling for something under him. "This is my *favourite* part."

Vespasien rose and stretched, a brief moment at his fullest height, and then picked up Birdie's chair to set it firmly behind Gus. Almost at once a wet splotch appeared on the cracked leather.

"If you are able to sit, please sit," said Vespasien, and looked toward the sky as fat droplets struck, slow but heavy with an audible tink against metal, a pat against fabric and skin. "This day promises to be a long one."

Chapter Seventeen

Audiences with authority

Every part of Britt felt so tired it seemed like her joints trembled for naught more than the effort to keep her up. For a mercy, she did not have to, but Britt was conscious that this must be what ageing was like. Except perhaps less acute.

She did not like the feeling of helplessness, and yet: there was nothing for her to do.

General Burnstone's new command post was on the next ring up, safe from the flood and within reach of the outer ring by either lock or by ride. Britt barely saw it, as almost the moment they exited the lock a carriage pulled up before the gate.

"That's for you," General Burnstone told Britt, and handed her a sealed note with her signature over the paper masking where it opened. "Give that to the seneschal when you arrive."

Arrive where, Britt did not have a chance to ask, nor the will to resist as her hand-luggage was taken and she was swept into the carriage – a far nicer carriage than a prison one, and pulled by horse rather than with an engine. Everyone made way for it, nonetheless; and they moved at a hasty clip, very nearly a canter. Not that Britt knew much about horses, but surely it was a mite faster than just a trot.

It had begun to rain just as they commandeered the lock to raise the command post: fat heavy rain, the sort that didn't need to fall thickly in order to fill the air. Britt was slightly damp because of it, and shivering by the time the carriage pulled up, even though it hadn't been all that long. The carriage had to pass through all the rings to get up to – to –

Where was she?

Someone held an umbrella over her head and Britt accepted one of the guard's arms as she came down the steps, if nothing else because her knees were shaky and she didn't fancy *falling* down them.

She almost did anyway, before she looked up before her feet hit ground, and was thusly distracted by her *location*.

Aulerin's Honour was vastly grander than Lammandan's fort, for all that the baroness sometimes lived there. Aulerin had been built long before; it was a tall thing made of stone, like most of the buildings, and currently had water streaming off the slightly outward-leaning wall from the gutters, gurgling into an aqueduct somewhere under the courtyard to join the moat.

"Hurry now, Mistress."

Britt hurried, mainly because she *had* to, because everyone with longer legs certainly were. She didn't get much chance to see the doors, or the main hall, aside from the fact there was a haze of anxiously-chattering people in quite fine clothes. She didn't get much chance to think or do anything before she was swept into a small room so warm she almost cried with relief.

It had been a long – morning. Was it still truly only morning?

It felt like so much had happened, and yet not enough. The scholars and Ryan, and Gus, were still *down there*, and Britt –

Britt firmed up her shaky knees and accepted being escorted graciously to the fire – they must have turned off the levin grids due to the lightning – and having her coat stripped and a blanket put over her shoulders.

A tall man with a bald head and a moustache bowed at her. "I understand you have something for me, Mistress?"

"You're the seneschal?" Britt asked, and forced herself to un-hunch, to sit up straight and lift her chin despite the layer of dampness and the fact that her hair was most certainly limp. Or frizzy. Or perhaps some horrid combination of both. "I was told to give it to the seneschal, by General Burnstone."

"I am he," said the man impassively. His face changed not at all when he accepted the letter, despite the clammy paleness of Britt's hands and the dirt stuck under her nails.

She didn't remember when *that* happened – but she'd been all but thrown to the ground at least once today.

He left immediately, and then Britt was …

Not alone, actually. There were maids. Two, in fact, quiet and soft-footed; they spoke to each other but only quietly, as if Britt herself was – was – either fraught or delicate.

She was *neither*, thank you very much, despite how the tremble in her limbs wanted to tell the tale. She wasn't damp enough to warrant a changing of clothes, but slowly the fire eased away the chill, and one of the maids brought her some scones and tea which primarily served to make Britt realise how hungry she actually was.

Somewhat less, afterward, and yet –

(The scholars, and Ryan, and Gus. Would they have cover? Would a canvas even hold, against rain this heavy, thundering against the stone almost as badly was the floods themselves? How were they going to eat in this? How long could Gus possibly *last*?)

Thought started escaping her, and Britt let it. She was warmer now, and her tired limbs all too willing to sink against the comfort of the armchair. The annex had lovely soft armchairs like these, and yet this one in particular may well have been the most comfortable Britt had ever sat in.

Hurried tapping at the door brought her upright; groggy and warmed by tea and food and flame, but at least not wholly out. If she'd been thinking it would have occurred that she hadn't been sent here just to deliver a message, and the thought *did* occur, chasing itself around her sleepy brain while she pushed herself upright and ground the grit out of her eyes.

Unfortunately she didn't quite hear what was *said*.

"Is aught amiss?" Britt asked, sounding fuzzy to herself, as one of the maids moved the trolley and the other crouched to do – something. Something that entailed the shoes Britt didn't remember taking *off*. "Oh! I can certainly do that myself, thank you –"

But the shoes were already on, and Britt blinked fuzzily as the maids combed her hair, swift but unhurried in that practiced way of hairdressers, and patted down her clothes so that they were at least somewhat better arranged. One of the maids helped Britt to her feet; the other returned from the – bureau, there was a bureau in the corner – and spritzed Britt lightly with perfume, something sharply floral, something that teased the back of Britt's head but didn't yield its owner.

For all that it was only as they escorted her to the door that Britt realised this was not treatment random unkempt guests habitually received unless, presumably, they were about to meet someone *very important*.

The thud against her ribs was somewhat duller than the sharp staccato terror from earlier in the day, but anxiousness did nothing to settle her stomach.

There wasn't time to *ask*, and her tongue had tangled, anyway. One of the maids and the guard outside the door took Britt swiftly past the – goodness, that was a crowd gathering – hubbub in the castle's main hall and through a door into a passage. From there, she had no hope of remembering the directions; but it was not *far*, on the whole, most likely a close waiting room, before she was ushered through another door into a room.

The door looked like every other door they passed. That was probably on purpose, but it still meant that Britt stood blinking fuzzily at the woman in it for some humiliatingly long moments before she remembered herself and sank flushed to the carpet in as deep a curtsey as Britt had ever given.

"My Lady."

The Right Honourable The Baroness was almost as tall as General Burnstone, a fact Britt could tell primarily owing to the extensive experience of being shorter than anyone else even when that person was seated. Britt couldn't actually *see* the seat – Her Ladyship's skirts fanned about them in a way that made her appear to simply be sitting in midair, layers of silk and something gauzy that changed how deep the shade of blue the dress actually was.

Britt got quite a good look at the skirts, and the embroidery on the inner layers, because she didn't dare raise her head until Her Ladyship said: "Rise and sit, Mistress."

She had an unexpectedly low and throaty kind of voice, something Britt never quite imagined from a lady of the baronage. Britt rose but didn't dare lift her face the whole way – just enough to catch another glimpse out of the corner of her eye when she followed the maid to the chair presumably indicated.

Her Ladyship had a delicate face and ivory skin, currently pale and slightly pinched; much younger than General Burnstone. Her brown hair was the thin sort, cut short but exactingly arranged around her coronet in a way that made it, and her face, look fuller than they were. She was thin-lipped, but judging by the crimp in the corners that was compounded by tension.

The chair had cushions on it to raise Britt to the table's height, that was nice, but naturally not so much as to raise her above Her Ladyship. The table itself – Britt's expert eye cast across it – maps, slate, some curling notes in quite-small paper. The map of the city, especially, suggested Her Ladyship was following the crisis *closely*.

And there was the note Britt herself had brought, the general's signature sliced through, sitting oddly close to the teacup on Britt's side of the table.

"That is the message you bore me," said Her Ladyship, her voice as soft as it had been to start with. "Read it, if you will."

It – was an odd request, surely, but Britt could hardly *refuse*. She retrieved the note away from the teacup as one of the maids poured, flattening the paper on the table. It was short and to the point, and made Britt's heart thud.

The man Sch. seeks is a skydweller. I have no doubts as to his provenance. I do not deem him a threat. Msts Birdie knows.

If no commands forthwith I will exercise my discretion and present myself for judgement afterward.

Carefully Britt folded the note along its original lines and wordlessly gave it into the keeping of the maid's hand. Unthinkingly her gaze followed its direction as the maid straightened and moved toward the trolley by the fireplace, casting the note into flames without even a glance sideways.

"Tell me about this man," said Her Ladyship, and Britt swallowed hard, her back prickling.

This was her fault, wasn't it? She *thought* the general had appeared very suddenly behind them – oh, floods, if she'd overheard Britt's careless question –

But *I do not deem him a threat* was – surely – surely that meant something. If General Burnstone herself maintained that Gus was to be defended, rather than turned over for questioning or imprisonment, surely that was better than outright suspicion. And besides, now the game was up –

What use *was* there, in equivocating?

"I hardly know anything myself, Your Ladyship," Britt whispered, and her voice dragged painfully in her throat, her chest taut under her sternum. If this made things worse for Gus, because Britt couldn't keep her damned mouth *shut* – no, she had to hold to the fact that the general seemed positively disposed, despite the magic. "He – he fell into the bog and was found by Ryan and the scholars, and they judged him more in need of aid than to be turned in. As far as I know, all they meant to do was bring him to Lammandan and find him shelter until they figured out what to do."

She hadn't actually *asked*, but – safety and security was always the first step to figuring out future's pattern. Of course they wouldn't want people to look at him and immediately know what he was, but surely that wasn't an unreasonable concealment.

"He looked pathetic," Britt added lamely. "A man who'd ... lost everything." As she had, as many had, in Cantlond. "I couldn't bear to make life worse for him, so when the Ryan and Yoch asked me to hold my tongue until they figured out what to do I – I said nothing. He hadn't, at that point, shown any sign of magic that they spoke about."

Her Ladyship exhaled, and Britt watched her fingers twist together with detached fascination before they flattened on the table.

"We have laws against magicians," said Her Ladyship, "not ... *myths*." Almost to herself, with distant eyes, she murmured: "But how *do* you split one from the other, after all?"

To start with, one was fact and one was fiction – or at least, fiction until it was proven myths could, indeed, exist. Solid. Man-shaped. Flesh and blood and with achingly empty eyes, and despair in his voice and his bearing.

Your people are in danger! Is your hatred of magic so absolute you'd hew to principle at the expense of their lives?

... Right up until he had someone to *save*.

Her Ladyship's blue eyes focussed on Britt. "Ell reported that you do not know about your Master Cheya's orders."

It wasn't exactly a question.

"I don't," Britt said, reigning in the desperation fluttering in her chest. "I'm not even sure he knows Gus is a skydweller himself. I suspect he does, but it is only a suspicion. I think he expected what he was told – a murderer of some description. I only know because ..." Her cheeks flushed dully. "We – we keep the belongings of those in the field. When I went to get Ryan's, I found he and Yoch stealing photographs from the box. They showed me what they were taking and ... and I walked away."

They had not *asked her anything*, that had been a lie; she'd *left*, of her own recognisance, because she could not *did not* believe a man with a stare like his could be anything like the killer they'd been told.

"And then you volunteered to accompany Ell and this man to Aulerin," said Her Ladyship in tones Britt could not in any way divine.

"He looked like a man whose world had fallen apart," Britt whispered, and her fingers clenched on the tabletop, just short of actually catching in the cloth. Her eyes blurred. "I couldn't bear to let him suffer alone. The scholars – may not have been able to help, but I at least could *be there*."

For a moment nobody said anything. Britt took deep breaths, vying for control, swallowing down feeling until it knotted in her throat but stayed.

"You're a very kind soul, aren't you, Mistress?" said Her Ladyship gently. When Britt blinked away the tears and dared to glance up, she found – Her Ladyship not smiling, precisely, save that her mouth was less taut and her face gentler than it had been.

"He reminded me of what I must have been like after Cantlond fell," said Britt unthinkingly, unintentionally honest. "The way he looked after even the barest kindness – what do we truly *have* in this world, Your Ladyship, besides the gentleness we can gift to others? Everything else, *anything else*, might be taken, but never that."

And Britt had grown – not complacent, exactly, but maybe a little stultified, content for now with the worn path of the years before, providing kindness to those put in front of her and no further. Was there aught else she could do? *Should* do? Perhaps the annex could use a better outreach program ...

Or perhaps it needed one in the other direction. If Schecheya understood Prittuni better, what diplomatic incidents could be avoided? Surely the annex was positioned not only to teach those from Prittuni but Schecheya as well. It was a wonder that had never occurred to anyone.

And that was a smile, very nearly a ghost; in the corner of Her Ladyship's mouth, in the changing crease around her eyes, and finally she unfolded her hands to cradle her teacup in her palms.

"Start from the beginning, if you will, Mistress Birdie," said Her Ladyship calmly. "I would know everything you know. If Ell must exercise her discretion in the interim, so be it; her judgement afterwards will be mine to grant."

CHAPTER EIGHTEEN

A DAWNING HORROR

The canvas was delivered to Yahvanna and the others rather too late to spare anyone from being wet, but at least they weren't wet *through*. They all of them had coats suitable for the bog, still, and their underlayers were if a bit damp then at least not liable to chill them to death.

In addition to a small, hastily-erected enclosed latrine, the couriers brought a barrel and a bundle of broken timber and paper. The former looked as though it was debris from a damaged building no longer fit for use in construction; the latter was a stack of low-quality paper which Yahvanna suspected might have been reports and orders superseded and no longer good for anything else. Tyrian spent some minutes cursing at the paper for being a poor means of kindling before he finally got a fire lit and they all huddled around it, squeezing out their clothes such as they could.

The canvas was by rights a pavilion, swiftly erected and sturdy enough against the thud of fat raindrops. Unless a wind started from the wrong direction, they ought to be able to get decently dry. Presuming, of course, the flood did not break loose.

Gus had, in the meantime, sat on the offered chair; slowly and without shifting his attention from the wall, and finally letting his hand drop. He looked almost as bedraggled as Vespasien did, if without the height and the hunch. His hair was long enough to drip down his back and over his shoulders, and he clearly hadn't shaven since he left the bog; all of which lent him an air of misery.

"I hate rain," he said, almost conversationally.

As did, no doubt, his distaste.

"Most people do," said Yahvanna dryly, and tapped on his shoulder. "If I'm able to have your arms, let me have your coat. You'll dry out faster without it."

"Rain's a necessity for crops," said Tyrian with a careful kind of detach, and the barrel clanged as he fed a log into the fire. "How d'you manage up where there is none?"

"We know how condensation works," said Gus, a little snidely, and sat forward in the chair enough to shake loose the coat Yahvanna took from his arms. "And clouds are full of water. It's one of the reasons vessels are authorised to travel so close to the surface of the cloudsea."

"Besides research, I presume." Yahvanna took the coat to the fire to spread it over one of the other chairs Vespasien arranged nearby. There were no seats left for the rest of them, but there was more than enough debris about to suffice, including a large chunk of stone by which the couriers had considerately placed the barrel.

"Besides that, yes."

"What do people research from the ... cloudsea?" Vespasien asked, sitting decorously on the edge of the debris with his eyes unmoving on Gus. Yahvanna wondered if she'd ever looked as hungry, looking at him, as Vespasien did – as he had, when Gus spoke of the stars.

Yahvanna had, waiting for the pavilion, told Vespasien what Gus said on the ride. They had some concept of the words used between them now, or at least a means to easily translate them. For a mercy, Gus's native language appeared to be more descriptive in its proper nouns than many, which made translating them relatively straightforward once Vespasien had the key.

Despite the difference in words and the obvious cadence of Gus's slang, there was a reassuring similarity to the way in which they addressed magnetic fields – or at least magnetic effects, if not the technical terms.

"The changes in its state, mainly," said Gus. "Mine was doing a routine check of the area. We didn't expect anything to change, so we didn't expect the difference in charge."

He went on then, describing the cloudsea in the same fashion in which he'd once vied to describe the stars. And still did; even now, a year on, he struggled to find the words to describe the night sky. They all of them knew that something was being left behind when he did.

The slow careful way he spoke of the colours on the cloudsea surface was the same; only now his wistful enthusiasm overtook his command of the language and there were times he lapsed into his own. On those occasions Vespasien's translations could hardly do justice to whatever depth of feeling and beauty dwelled there.

Listening put an aching yearn in Yahvanna's chest with which she was well familiar: the sort that *wanted*, hungrily and abiding, and may never be sated.

After that the conversation turned, naturally, to the stars and Vespasien's celestial maps. Though he had laboured over a new catalogue, given a first-hand source, he only barely had a grasp of the brightest stars and broadest strokes; and the bulk of that research was currently in storage in Lammandan's fort.

It was a conversation that could, and did, last for some time, leaving Tyrian and Yahvanna with naught to do but to listen and make sure the two of them hydrated and ate.

Their rations were the shelf-stable sort, bread and jerky and dried algae wafers; mostly suitable for putting in Gus's hand without his having to navigate utensils. When Yahvanna handed him the jerky his grimace was belated, cutting off mid-sentence.

It was a reaction he'd always had that slowly faded as he, Yahvanna assumed, became accustomed to their food, but on this instance it prompted her to ask unthinking:

"*Do* you have this sort of meat above the clouds?"

What could they possibly eat up there? It was difficult to imagine any world without large ungulates, and yet equally difficult to imagine fields of grazing cows on floating islands.

"Not like this," said Gus, not precisely glaring at the jerky but fingering it in a manner that suggested he wished he could. "It's mostly – poultry. This comes from those massive beasts that pull the barges, yes?"

"Predominantly, but not only," admitted Yahvanna. "My own people usually keep goats and sheep more often. The meat does come from milk producers, most frequently."

If skydwellers did not have ungulates, did they have *dairy*? If not, then 'goat' and 'sheep' might be wholly useless to him as words. Then again, he hadn't been overly surprised by hard cheese that Yahvanna recalled.

The sound Gus made was mostly of realisation. "We don't eat our milk producers, as a rule," he said simply. "Sometimes if – it might wind up on the royal tables, rarely. But poultry is easier to keep than anything with hooves, and the latter are too valuable to slaughter."

A realm that subsisted mainly on birds – well, it wasn't out of imagination, but it was a bit odd. So many staples, lost to them by dint of having to maintain their nation above the clouds. Oddly enough he hadn't been quite so dubious about fish.

"And your textiles?" Yahvanna asked. "Mostly fibrous, I have to assume, though if you *have* milk producers you may be able to use the hair or the wool. I'm still not quite certain – never mind."

For that was treading a little too closely to talk of when he'd fallen; and if he'd been somewhere dark just prior, then the clothes he'd worn may not be a safe topic. Nevertheless, Yahvanna couldn't help but *wonder*. They'd been light fabrics appropriate for a world which did not see much humidity, and yet at the same time not nearly warm enough for what must surely be cold as a standard.

Not that the fundament was overly warm, given how lacking in sunlight it was; but it was not iced-over, as some scientists insisted it ought to be.

Yahvanna tapped Gus's shoulder. "Eat that. You can resume your lecture afterward, assuming Vespasien's thoughts aren't leaking out of his ears by now."

"I may need some processing time," said Vespasien with the kind of delighted daze of too much information and not enough space, and Tyrian snickered.

Smiling, Yahvanna returned to her seat beside Vespasien for her own meal, such as it was, and though Gus's bearing was reluctant, he did at least eat.

The rest of them found their own conversation, small innocuous things relating to Schecheya and their various studies; subjects of no real import save that they might serve as some small and revealing entertainment to the man holding their lives in his hands.

Every so often Gus asked a question, or inserted a remark; sometimes louder, as the rain grew heavier and then subsided. The smell of water and damp stone and mud became stronger: puddles broke their bounds and water guttered swirling through the pavilion, occasionally hissing as it met the bottom of the barrel.

The sound of the state's guard giving orders seemed to come from further away. The radio the couriers provided had news of the city's state and the evacuation's progression, but intermittently and in general terms, primarily in the way of advising which streets where congested and which were easier to move through.

Conversation withered slowly until Vespasien was the only one who spoke, expounding at length on some divergence of language none of them rest of them truly understood. At first Gus had some input – some questions, some insight given it was an ancient form of his native language on which Vespasien was lecturing – but slowly even his input faded away and only Vespasien's lulling voice remained.

Yahvanna shook her head to shake the drowse away and got up to walk a few paces back and forth, over the rivulets claiming the street and back again. It didn't do *much* to assuage the fuzz, but at least she wasn't just about keeling over where she sat.

Neither was Tyrian, though judging by his closed eyes and sideways list he was likely already asleep, simply – sitting up, with arms crossed.

"Is the rain heavy enough to increase the water-level behind the wall to any detrimental degree?" Yahvanna asked, turning on her pace. Gus's frame had wilted some – not slumped enough to say he was at risk of falling off his chair, but it was abruptly rather alarming the way he'd bowed inward. She hadn't noticed. "Gus?"

Vespasien's voice cut off almost mid-word. As if in response to the lack of it Tyrian's head lifted, his eyes opening clear and without the shroud of grogginess.

Yahvanna's heart beat quick as she cross the streamlets another time, hand outstretched toward Gus. The wall wasn't shifting, not even a groan of metal giving; perhaps it was only that the name was in some fashion unfamiliar to his ears yet –

Gus stirred before she touched him, raising his head with an absent "Mm?"

Yahvanna exhaled consciously. "The rain," she said patiently. "Is it making the wall more difficult to hold?"

He blinked at her slowly, nearly languid thanks to his wide pupils if not for the fact that his face was so pinched; and with a skin-crawling absence of comprehension.

"It's fine," he said distantly, some heartbeats *after* a response would have been most reassuring. "Don't worry about it."

She *would* worry, thank you very much –

Yahvanna bit her tongue. "Very well." It had been *well* over six hours by now, well long enough for boredom and fatigue to set in. How close evening, Yahvanna couldn't tell, given the rain and the thickness of the cloud-cover. For all that, Gus's control over the wall had not slackened, not even a moment, aside from the early mention of his cousin. "You'll let us know if there's aught we can do?"

His mouth quirked, a tucking away in the corner that at one angle looked like sardonic mirth and from another seemed almost a rictus. "Of course."

There was something about his tone. Something – fatalistically patronising. Something that put Yahvanna in mind of a child offering to help a parent with something they could in no way rectify. A response for the sake of being let alone, rather than the genuine expectation of aid.

Yahvanna lingered a moment longer as he closed his eyes and let his head slump. His breathing, at least, was rhythmic – but consciously, in the manner of a man bearing a great burden and withstanding it only by considered attention to himself.

It was possible talking to him now would be more distraction than boon. Reluctantly Yahvanna stepped back and returned to the rock on which they'd made their perch.

"That doesn't seem good," Tyrian said low, more upright than he'd been but still with his arms crossed over his chest.

"The wall isn't screaming yet," Yahvanna pointed out, and tucked herself under Vespasien's upraised arm.

"I doubt we'll get much more than a shriek before we're drowned," said Tyrian, "but I suppose that depends on his control." He shook his head, a slight one that didn't do much more than flick his bangs off his eyes for a moment. "At least it doesn't seem likely he'll fall asleep on us. Not until he's wholly spent, at any rate."

And who knows how long that might take? Far better to ask –

"How far along is the evacuation?"

Their radio was not a powerful one, but the general had wisely loaned them a transmitter so they might contact the command post in the worst event. There would not be much time for them to save themselves – but if Gus's command of the wall failed slowly, there might be enough to bid the remaining citizens to take refuge on their rooftops and wait to be rescued.

Might.

Far more likely a panic would result in a crush of people fit to kill them all, first by jamming the streets and then by the flood. Assuming there were many left, but it was hard to tell. The downpour had long since obscured their vision of the lock in a sheet of grey, and even the sound of people down the street was too muted to hear. Their world had closed to this small damp refuge amidst the rain and the wreckage.

There was naught to *do* but wait.

"General Burnstone said she would send a skyride when the evacuation was done," Vespasien observed. "Might a skyride fly in this weather?"

"... Not well," answered Tyrian grimly, and glanced sidelong, past the two of them and toward Gus, his voice pitched low so as to be concealed by the rain. "Which does beg the question of exactly how the general intends to save our mutual friend from himself."

A question for which they had no answer, not even to offer. *Could* Gus be carried off without breaking his command of the wall? Could he be loaded upon a ride thereby?

A vain point, when a ride could not fly in rain.

It was easing off, at least, and continued to do so by degrees over the next span of time; first light, then heavier again, then once more easing. The drizzle lingered such that it made a view of the lock difficult, and the ominous blackness of the clouds did not assuage overmuch. Yahvanna suspected impending nightfall.

The wall remained sturdy as it had been when its metal finally settled, pressed into a kind of sheet textured by the shape of what the debris had been prior. It did not give; but water oozed between the wall and the buildings where the blocks had sufficiently waterlogged, and sloshed over the top between the eaves. The water level had to be rising in some degree. Enough to leak. Enough to render the street a marsh of pools where stone had been broken.

"The blocks might give out first, at this rate," said Yahvanna grimly, and Tyrian rose sudden and head raised toward the sky.

"Do you hear that?"

There was barely time to listen. For a heartbeat Yahvanna feared he heard the sound of something collapsing. Then skyrides burst from the upper rings, humming with the sound of rain splattering against windshields and their lamps shining blurry but bright, almost blinding with how they refracted in the drizzle.

A dozen of the largest, cargo-runners, descended over the intersection, a few mid-sized more flying further afield. One of the smaller lowered behind them where the command post had been. General Burnstone alighted before it had fully settled, head ducked to exit the open side and water splashing where she landed in a puddle.

Not that there was much of the road that *wasn't* a puddle, at this point – only some deeper than others.

The three of them rose as she approached, hand raised ineffectually against the drizzle. Behind her the ride settled with a quiet thrum in the stone underfoot.

"Good news, I hope," said Tyrian with the jaunty tone ordinarily in evidence when he expected a poor result, in fact.

"This is as light as the rain's going to get," said the general brusquely. "Heading into night, it's only going to get heavier again, and the levees are already at capacity."

"But you have enough rides to complete the evacuation, I perceive," said Vespasien quietly.

"Anyone remaining will be told to get on their roofs," said General Burnstone, her gaze going past their shoulders to rest, presumably, on Gus. "If the stars are in our favour the water won't reach that high – but our chances lower if we let the rain have its way."

For those who could not make the lock or be airlifted out immediately, their rate of survival increased only by the dint of action taken now. Any later and the flood would surely have them, no matter how high on the roofs they hid.

And it meant that for now, they had only to wait until the other rides finished loading.

Yahvanna risked a glance behind her, following the general's gaze. Gus was slumped almost wholesale in his chair, a kind of boneless equilibrium spoken in the rest of his forearms on his thighs, the planting of his feet apart; the slouch of weight so evenly spread that even at rest he wouldn't fall.

"How is he?" asked the general low-voiced.

"He hasn't responded to us recently," said Tyrian grimly as Yahvanna turned, stepping over the rivulets between cracks in the stone.

She didn't try to touch him this time, but crouched before him to see his face. He seemed so very pale, and though his breathing was steady, it was the kind of steady starting to show its labours.

"The general is here," said Yahvanna evenly. "We're evacuating as soon as we're given the clear."

For a long nerve-fraying moment Yahvanna wasn't certain Gus could hear her. Then without opening his eyes or otherwise stirring, in the same kind of too-distant tone as before, he said: "Go on, then."

"Not without you," Yahvanna added firmly, in case this was in any doubt, and because Tyrian had stepped forward with obstinacy radiating from every line of his body.

The smile that touched Gus's mouth was faint, so faint, and yet somehow more genuine than the near-rictus from before.

"I'm not done yet," he said, sounding somewhat less distant and calm in a fashion that made Yahvanna's back prickle rather than assuaging her fears. "Just mark me a safe place to which to escape, will you? Somewhere visible."

"I dare say we can manage that."

Yahvanna pushed up on her knees to straighten, glancing at the rest of them past Gus's shoulder.

"The ride can hold above the street and set its lights to max," said General Burnstone. "But I don't see how that's going to help when he can't damned reach it."

"He can fly," said Yahvanna matter-of-factly, "of a sort. Levitate at the very least, I dare say. That chair is made of metal."

And he'd told them float was easier with something under him.

Tyrian made a comprehending noise. "He did say the worst that would happen if the ride fell out of the sky is he'd have to slow our descent. No reason why he couldn't go up as well as down, if he had something to stand on."

General Burnstone's eyes creased, her face becoming substantially more fixed than haggard.

"Assuming he has enough time to do it in," she said, "but fine, since none of the rest of us know what he's *Surge-sodden* capable –" She cut herself off so hard her teeth clicked, and pressed her fingers to her brow. "Fine. Pack up and get ready. We'll leave once I have word everyone else is clear."

"Only at the last, hm?" Tyrian's mouth quirked. "I could almost like you, General."

The look General Burnstone shot him was mingled amusement and chagrin and irritation, but Tyrian didn't stick around to wait for a riposte. The three of them scattered to pick up their personal belongings and stow them in the ride, while the pair of the general's aides dismantled the pavilion and whatever else could be rescued. All the gear was secured in the ride's hold, the soldiers silhouettes of movement within.

Yahvanna shook rain off her coat, but it trickled down through her collar regardless, chilly down her back. In the distance, rides which had vanished behind buildings lifted off again, one by one becoming a swarm battered by the once-again thickening rain.

The ride's copilot leaned from her half-open door, one hand motioning and the other on her headset. "All clear," she called. "The lock's raised and set for flooding. We're ready, General."

"Everyone in."

General Burnstone jerked her head to the open well of the ride behind her and offered her hand to Yahvanna, callused and solid and with fingernails suggestive of a woman with an unexpected taste for manicures despite the filth currently on them. In one strong lift the pelt of rain on Yahvanna ceased, replaced by the hollow vibration of the ride's hold and the memory of how *solid* Gus had been even mid-lift, as though he wore weighted boots.

Yahvanna's things were already secured. She made way for Tyrian and Vespasien but stayed by the entrance, her heart pounding as she glanced out toward Gus's figure, oddly small on the width of the street.

Either they'd all make it out alive or they were about to witness a man sacrifice himself for people he knew not at all, and who knew him even less.

Vespasien made space by the door, his hands well secured by the net in the ceiling and one of the general's aides keeping him steady; but the rest of them gripped handholds and stayed where they were. The ride's hum intensified, gravity briefly pressing them into the floor as it lifted. Only then, finally, did Gus stir from his slump in the chair.

He pushed himself to his feet, hands on his thighs, as though the weight of him was too much to bear; looked up at the wall. Yahvanna wished she could see his face, but the angle was wrong even if they were near enough for her to parse his expression.

For some moments all he did was stand there. The ride reached altitude and stopped, its side open to the sky, the splatter of fat raindrops growing thicker until the headlights cast a corona against the sheeting rain. Yahvanna's heart fluttered, vying toward panic, and she could not help but recall how Gus stood before the waterfalls in the bog, so close to the edge as if teetering on the brink of a fall from which there could be no return.

"Come on," Tyrian breathed. "Don't do anything stupid."

With an ear-ringing twang something inside the wall of debris shifted, and something else crunched. The entire edifice loosened with a spurt of gushing water; a long groan of surprised relent from metal which had spent hours being pressed into one tangled piece.

Gus swivelled on his heel, not urgent enough to be a whirl, his face lifting blankly toward them. Yahvanna's heart thudded.

There was naught of comprehension *there* –

Debris screeched. Plumes of water jetted into the street. One moment Gus stood before the wall; the next the levee burst and Gus –

Appeared before them with a rattle and a thud on the ride's threshold. He tilted dangerously on the edge, his feet in the ride but weight leaned over the street. Tyrian lunged and yanked him into the ride so forcefully they both went over. The floor shuddered with their fall.

Beneath them water rampaged down the street in a long shuddering roar, scraping plaster from walls and glass from windows and tiles from eaves. Yahvanna thought she caught a glimpse of the chair eddying helplessly in the froth before it vanished from sight.

Someone thumped on the wall between them and the pilots. The ride's hum briefly intensified as it lifted away, and then dulled as the general pulled the door shut against the wind. The howl of air and rain both ceased, leaving Yahvanna's ears throbbing.

Yahvanna's limbs were weak as she crouched, her heart pounding so hard she felt sick to her stomach. Tyrian pushed upright primarily by virtue of Vespasien's body and arms behind him, while Tyrian himself cradled Gus. Gus was so very pale, and damp through; but he *breathed*, at least.

"I don't know what I expected," said Tyrian, sounding rattled. "But that wasn't it."

He'd just about – *teleported* – from one place to another. Surely that had no bearing whatsoever on *magnetic fields*, and yet there was no other description.

Unthinkingly Yahvanna took Gus's limp hand, put her own on his forehead. She had always read an individual body like its own system of water, governed by its natural tendencies; and in this instance Gus's was a desert wrought by exhaustion, if one mercifully short of collapsing wholesale. There was some will in him yet, and yet –

Yahvanna frowned. Something about the leys of his body seemed ... wrong. As if ... as if there was something filtering into him from some source she could not divine.

He opened his eyes, his gaze half-focused, dazed and baffled in one; and made more so for the fact his pupils were so very large. "Who *are* you?"

The general turned sharply from speaking softly to one of her aides, and the blood drained from Tyrian's face. Yahvanna's back bloomed with cold chill.

"Yoch," she said as calmly as she could muster. "We met a year ago."

"Did we?" The bafflement was coloured by tired bemusement. There was no recognition at the name, no comprehension –

As there had been none before. The prickle intensified.

"Yes," said Yahvanna, and then half-desperately – not knowing quite what to say, but surely if he could only be induced to remember what had only lately passed, the *effort* he had bestowed – "You've just saved thousands of lives."

"Have I?" The smile that touched his mouth was the same as before, faint and indulgent and wry all at once. "Well done, me. I wonder if I can keep that up?" He closed his eyes, resting his head against Tyrian's shoulder; exhaled so long that Yahvanna's heartrate spiked in the too-long gap between that and when he inhaled once more. "I'm so tired."

It was almost too faint to be heard, too much a statement of fact to be a confession. The voice of a man whose burden was not yet *done*, for all the rest of them couldn't see it, and this was the barest release he had – to state it so baldly unadorned, weary beyond weary.

"Then go to sleep," said Yahvanna for lack of anything else to say. There was nothing in his body's cycle that would threaten his life were he to rest. Whatever this – unidentified strength – seemed to be subsiding.

She wasn't even sure if he *heard* her, such was the weight he put on Tyrian, bonelessly heavy in a way he hadn't been even in his chair.

But he breathed. Still, he breathed, nerve-frayingly long and nearly unheard in the rattled silence.

"Most likely to be panic attacks, you said," said Tyrian over his shoulder.

"The likelihood of one cause does not rule out the possibility of another," said Vespasien, sounding strained, though whether that or Tyrian's weight on him in turn – it was hard to tell. "I stand by my assertion. Such behaviour as Gus has exhibited is most likely to be caused by anxiety."

"Until now," said Yahvanna, and gently set Gus's hand on his lap. She bit her tongue on attempting to describe what she'd felt in him; the last thing they needed was for her to identify herself also as a magician to over-stressed Prittune.

"Professor Alvin would be able to diagnose him more specifically," Vespasien said.

"And where's your professor?" asked General Burnstone flatly. "Schecheya, I assume?"

Vespasian exhaled slowly. "Yes."

A long, long way away. Even if the baroness was willing to ask for Professor Al's professional opinion, the request would take time to get there and return. And that was presuming no one interfered, or found out about Gus in the meantime.

The intercom between the hold and the cockpit crackled. "Approaching the Honour, General."

Yahvanna's gut coiled, but it was tired, the cold sour of too much adrenaline. General Burnstone pressed her hand to her face and mouthed soundlessly into her palm: "*Fuck.*"

But when she raised her head, as tired as she looked, her gaze was steady on Yahvanna. "There's a lot of people in the Honour's courtyard," she said brusquely. "People rescued and being counted, and so forth. And it's still raining. If you don't stick close after we disembark it'll be easy to lose you in the crowd." Her eyes bored into Yahvanna as greyly inexorable as the firmament. "Do you understand?"

"I understand," said Yahvanna quietly, holding her gaze. "Tyrian can carry him."

"As we began, then," said Tyrian in tones of fatalistic resignation, and shifted with a grimace, shifting Gus's weight in his arms. "Help me get him situated."

Between them they got Gus onto Tyrian's shoulder. The general nodded, once and short, and thumped the wall with her fist. "Take us down."

Chapter Nineteen

Many hands and heavy work

It seemed as though the nobles of the court never ceased talking. At each other, at Her Ladyship; at no one at all, in some cases, only as *loudly* as possible as if in the hope someone might engage.

Britt had been given a chair with Her Ladyship's ladies-in-waiting, in a corner of the throne-room not so close as to be considered having undue influence but near enough that if Her Ladyship needed something, they were there. Never had Britt felt quite so much like a beast in the water, wallowing just short of drowning, and certainly not where she ought to have been. All of these ladies wore finely spun and tailored woollen dresses, while Britt was grubby and worn. Even her coat – among the finest things she owned – was not on the same level. Not least owing to how sorely taxed it had been today.

And the ladies all smelled wonderfully of some perfume or another. The spritzing Britt received from the maids seemed long ago.

She was tired, and wished she could curl up in that comfortable chair by the fire and go to sleep; but even if she was given leave, her nerves had overtaken exhaustion. The audience with Her Ladyship had been thorough, and ended with the delivery of reports and the necessity of Her Ladyship to return to the hall. Though for all Britt could see, she mostly said nothing and waited patiently for her court to stop *talking* before she said anything herself.

For a mercy the ladies-in-waiting did not oblige Britt to say anything or engage much. Whether that was presumption that Britt didn't have the knowledge to contribute or a matter of courtesy to her fatigue, Britt wasn't sure, and altogether too weary in body and spirit to care.

They spoke primarily to each other, quiet murmurs Britt didn't wholly realise related to events at hand until the first courier came to them to deliver a report. Every so often one of them rose to go to Her Ladyship and report to her in equally quiet tones, while the rest wrote – perhaps edicts; perhaps simply letters. Britt could not initially be sure as to the topics, but when she realised it, she rose to wordlessly fill the inkpots and tidy the desks despite that there were maids standing by.

She simply needed something to do.

It wasn't everyone decrying the state of their future. The guard had the actual suppliants in some kind of order, most of whom had some wealth to them if their clothes were any guess; but others were there on behalf of still others. One of them was a black-skinned woman in a white suit who represented the trustee of a farmstead west of the city.

The farm and its greenhouses were obliterated in the flood. The woman was trying to determine how many of its residents survived, including the owners. And she wasn't the only one already vying to find something to grip, for all that solid news was still like so much water as the flood itself.

With the flood now claiming significant parts of the plains, there was no way to know as yet who on the outskirts had lived and who had died. Two of Her Ladyship's other officers had already departed to oversee surveillance and recovery, along with a string of brave volunteers from a variety of houses but most notably the Yew and Pigeon.

The sight of their livery and coat-of-arms called to Britt's mind the tarnished pocketwatch dangling from General Burnstone's hand what seemed like an eternity ago, and the man who had bothered to recover it, and her heart ached.

No, most of the fearmongering came from those who had the right to be present and seemingly nothing better to do but overlook proceedings in the vain search for gossip.

The most recent update related to the extent of the evacuation and the stability of the waters. The levees in most places were holding. The city's east had not evacuated at all; to the north and south, only the westernmost districts.

It was the city's west that was most sorely tested, especially its westernmost lock. Britt did not need to listen to the updates there for her heart to ache, but did anyway – at least as far as hearing that there *were* updates that did not include the sudden and catastrophic failure of the levee there. She stopped listening after that.

No one seemed to know how the levee was being held, at least not that Britt overheard. There was some gossiping about the engineers cutting it close – but that was all she heard on the subject. Maybe, just maybe, despite the witnesses – maybe Gus's identity was safe after all.

Currently there was chatter, but not so loud as to overtake the sound of rain against stone and tile, the incessant thundering wash of water dripping down the windows. It had eased some, earlier, light enough not to hear it; but now it was back, and if nothing else subdued the voices of those inclined to grumble.

Britt was seated quietly beside the ladies with the quickest hands, ready to seal the letters and deliver them to the tray where they would be sorted by – someone else – for delivery – elsewhere. This was not fine paper, not at all; fine paper was, after all, expensive. Wherever these notes were going were confirmation of verbal orders, a paper trail to ensure anything left undone was rediscovered, and meant to be discarded to flame afterward.

The *fine* paper was being used by the ladies on the other side of the circle, their letters carefully written and exactingly worded, for the loved ones of those already known to be lost.

It was a dull kind of waiting, half-drowsy, leaning on the habitual to surmount the exhaustion. Broken, sharp as cracking glass, as the doors scraped open and someone cried with startled surprise: "General Burnstone!"

At once there was a hubbub, a pushing-forward followed by a pulling back as the guard forced curious onlookers to give way to the throne. Britt's heart thudded, clearing some of the groggy malaise, and for a mercy there was a line of sight between the ladies-in-waiting and the floor or else she wouldn't have seen anything.

General Burnstone looked exhausted, her windswept hair barely constrained by its braid and her face haggard; but her pace was brisk and steady. And leaving a trail of water one of the footmen hastily polished up in her wake.

Britt couldn't tell whether aught had happened or not, her face was so flatly granite.

"Report," said Her Ladyship, clear and calm and cutting into remaining whispers, as the general stopped before the throne and saluted.

"The western outer ring is evacuated," said the general, and a dozen sighs cascaded around the room, including

Britt's own. "Once the rain has stopped someone will need to fly over to see if there's anyone in need of rescuing from the rooftops – but the west-cardinal lock is cleared."

"And the levee?" asked Her Ladyship.

"Broken shortly after the evacuation," said General Burnstone flatly, ignoring the increased whispers. "It was my judgement that the continued rainfall would cause it to break sooner rather than later, so in the interval of light rain I had as many skyrides as could fly ferry the remaining evacuees at the lock. General Greatoak supported this order by placing his rides at my disposal."

She brandished a folded, dampened note received by one of the ladies-in-waiting, who slit it open to read.

"The western outer ring is flooded, then," said Her Ladyship steadily.

"Almost the whole quarter, My Ladyship," said General Burnstone, "but fewer lives lost than could have been hoped-for, frankly. The levee held just enough."

"Come now, general!" cried one of the grizzled courtiers across the way, one of those with rights to stand near the throne and wearing the bright blue belonging to the Reed and Swan. General Burnstone's jaw visibly clenched. "We all know you had a magician on hand, a man entrusted into your custody! Why, dozens of people saw you and your guard at the ward in the outer ring, and further dozens saw him stopper the flood!"

All the breath went out of Britt and she sank into her chair, forcing herself to inhale. Slowly. Her ears rang, but it could have been shock or the agreeing murmur of anxious courtiers.

"Surely he's in custody still, is he not?" asked a lady just down from the Reed and Swan's patriarch, clad in subtle shimmering greens whose house Britt could not immediately identify from the distance and with her head swimming.

"He's gone," said General Burnstone flatly without so much as turning her head toward them, and Britt's heart clawed into her throat with dread while the rising babble clashed. The general's voice rose. "Upon the ride's landing he vanished in the crowd of evacuees. We might catch him if we closed the gates, Your Ladyship, but that seems a poor use of strength with a portion of the city flooded and the rest overburdened."

– Wait. *Gone*, not dead. Did that mean –

If no commands forthwith I will exercise my discretion and present myself for judgement afterward.

Britt's heart did not cease its yammer, but at least it eased enough not to be trying to *choke* her with it. Gone, not dead. Gone meant *safe*, at least for now.

But what of the scholars –

"You let him *go*?!" exclaimed the patriarch of the Reed and Swan, and even from the wrong angle, the sharp turn of General Burnstone's glare was evident.

"I put the wellbeing of my people *first*," she retorted. "What would you have had me do, wade into the fearful crowd with sword and gun drawn to seek out a fugitive who isn't even of the state? I judged my efforts better placed elsewhere. If my judgement was erroneous, let Her Ladyship condemn me."

"I will never condemn earnest efforts to preserve the safety of my people," said Her Ladyship, and the patriarch of the Reed and Swan huffed, folding his arms across his chest but making no reply. Her Ladyship held out her hand, and it took too long for Britt to realise it was in her direction. "Mistress Birdie."

Well, now Britt's heart yammered for other reasons. Tongue tying in her mouth, she slipped off her chair and moved toward the throne, curtseying low. For a mercy she didn't *have* to speak, because she *couldn't*. All these eyes on her back …

How grubby a thing she must appear to these nobility.

"You're to remain here as my guest until the route is assessed as safe," said Her Ladyship, "at which time I will send you to Lammandan with a letter on the subject to Master Cheya of the Schecheyan Annex." A low, not-quite-belligerent grumble echoed around the room. "As it was Schecheya's request that this man be taken into custody on behalf of an unknown state, and this man's escape in the middle of an unforeseeable crisis equally unforeseeable, I do not see that Prittuni is culpable for the loss of their fugitive, nor that this business remains within Prittuni's purview. Only a fool would remain within the state when his face is known, and I will not compromise my people's welfare in the wake of such a crisis for Schecheyan designs."

"But a magician, Your Ladyship!" exclaimed the patriarch of the Reed and Swan.

"Have you a place to put him, even if we should capture him?" asked Her Ladyship quietly. "Your estate, perhaps?" The patriarch's mouth snapped so cleanly shut that the click was audible from across the room. Her Ladyship's low voice continued, as relentlessly inexorable as her silence had been calm. "The ward in the outer ring was last prison suitable for containing a magician, and it is now flooded. It seems to me a confrontation is more likely to place Prittune lives in danger, where if we simply let him be he would soon be shot of our borders. If Schecheya desires his capture so greatly, let them risk theirs rather than ours."

Her gaze swept the room slowly, awaiting denunciation or denial, but no one spoke. General Burnstone stood upright and unbending, a savage twist to the side of her mouth in Britt's view – one that seemed very nearly satisfied.

Her Ladyship's eyes came to rest on Britt, her voice gentling. "If you wish to write a short letter to send prior to my own, I will see that it is delivered to the annex as expediently as possible."

"Thank you, Your Ladyship. I do." Britt curtseyed again, ignoring the burning white in the corners of her vision, straightening while refusing to let it cause her to buckle despite the weakness of relief.

Condemnation, perhaps, in Her Ladyship's tone; but most people feared magicians, after all, in some ways more than they had when magicians were more common. The unknown always was the more terrifying.

Regardless of tone Her Ladyship had, tacitly, allowed General Burnstone's judgement to stand – her *discretion* to stand. And General Burnstone had chosen to *allow* Gus to escape; of this Britt had no doubt. Where Gus was, no doubt the other three would be: but so long as no one *realised* Gus had compatriots, there would be naught to report to Schecheya in the way of condemnation, either.

They would be fine. They would be *fine*.

Though perhaps Britt would dare to ask for clarity on the scholars' and Ryan's status, once it was safe to do so.

"Escort Mistress Birdie to a guest room and see that she has all she needs," said Her Ladyship to the lady-in-waiting who delivered her the general's note, and then looked toward General Burnstone direct. "General Burnstone, you are relieved from duty. Pray go and rest; others will oversee the city and further evacuations. Your next task will be to investigate the breaking of the dams and the cause of the floods."

General Burnstone saluted. "As you wish, My Lady."

She turned smartly on her heel, still as upright and dignified as could be despite the fatigue obviously in her frame. For a moment her gaze met Britt's, piercingly unblinking; and although there was no wink, no indication of subterfuge or that they might share a secret –

Nevertheless, Britt felt seen, those frayed nerves of hers soothed enough that exhaustion weighed as heavy as a thick blanket. Wordlessly, relievedly, she followed the beckon of the lady-in-waiting, her knees rather shaky.

There was *so much* work to be done, but for Britt at least, it would only begin tomorrow.

Chapter Twenty

Grounding

Erasmus swayed with a gentle rattle, a soothing kind of rock which deepened the warmth currently shrouding him. He didn't *want* to wake; he was too warm, too comfortable, and had the awful inkling that waking up meant having to deal with something unpleasant.

Unfortunately *knowing that* didn't stop his sleepy mind from paying idle attention to the sounds around him, in the kind of clinical way seeking to catalogue while forgetting that the act of doing so brought wakefulness closer.

The rattle wasn't just under Erasmus's back. There was a more distant echo, a tap of footsteps so numerous that at first Erasmus only heard it as white noise. Every so often, a groan of timber; sometimes accompanied by a curse in a language Erasmus felt he ought to recognise but heard as nothing but soup.

There were people somewhere close by, surrounding him like a vast crowd whose dimensions he could only read by the ferrum in the tack. He could be floating, but on his back instead of upright, the way he'd been shown ...

And with that realisation came the one that there were people closer-by yet, breathing somewhere in his *very* near vicinity. Alarm jolted under Erasmus's ribs, a punch that made his exhale waver. The inhale took effort to keep steady.

"Are you awake?" Yoch asked, quiet somewhere off to the side.

Alarm unravelled into the weight of resignation, the duality of relief and dread both. Erasmus wasn't in immediate danger, or among those from whom he needed to hide; he wasn't *home*, this wasn't a nightmare from which he could escape just by waking.

... Why did he feel like he was waiting for dead air to come to him?

Erasmus raised his hand and misjudged the distance, smacking himself in the face while trying to rub the grit out of his eyes. "What ...?"

His voice ground out of him tiredly confused.

... The city. The *flood*. The levee.

Alarm punched him in the ribs again, harder than before, and Erasmus jolted half-upright before his head spun. A hand on his shoulder stopped him from getting any further than his elbows.

"Peace," said Passion gently. "We are safe, for now. We have exited the city from the southern gates along with many others seeking berth elsewhere."

The area around them was dim and enclosed, and the only light from the end, partially blocked by Ryan's silhouette; and they were definitely moving. A wagon, probably, judging by the large huffing and snuffling and the movement past Ryan that reminded Erasmus of the barge oxen.

And also the smell. There was something sharply earthy about the smell of the barge oxen that Erasmus had never experienced before, and didn't particularly want to keep experiencing now. At least it was just – passing; here and there only. Mostly he smelled people, warm and weary and familiar, lacking the acrid scent of waterlogged metal prevalent in the bog. Something still smelled damp, but it was more distant even than the oxen.

"What happened?" Erasmus asked blearily, lowering himself again to the – bed? No, more like a swaddling of blankets and things. The act of trying to push himself upright told him he might be rested but not hale; his limbs felt wrung and if not shaky then lacking strength.

He'd pushed himself. He'd pushed himself *hard*. Sad to say, this wasn't even the first time, because he know how it felt.

"How much do you remember?" asked Yoch, and Erasmus squinted in the dim light until he found her silhouette seated on a long low crate to his side. She was harder to see than Passion, whose complexion was nearly the brightest thing visible. There weren't any lamps lit.

"The levee," Erasmus said. "We're alive, so – I assume I didn't drop the lode, but I don't remember the end."

It hadn't been so bad, at first, but it never was. They'd distracted him with conversation so he didn't notice the slow seeping weariness, the strength eking out of him. But sooner or later there was always a point – like there had been when he held the skimmer in float – where the weight was too much and it was all he could *do* to breathe, and hold.

He didn't remember anything after that. Just the slow segue from weight to weariness to the abject, grimly desperate clinging to consciousness and lode. It'd taken longer this time, that was all.

"You held the lode long enough," said Yoch, very nearly gently, and Erasmus's breath came out of him unexpectedly rattling. "When the rain eased the general sent a fleet of skyrides to pick up the remaining evacuees, and came for us herself. You let the levee go once we were all boarded."

"*I* managed to hold an anchored lode while moving and exhausted?" Erasmus's laugh was more like a huff, thin and scattered and amusedly disbelieving. "Wish I remembered doing *that*."

Lodes could be made in motion, but that wasn't the kind of lode it had been. It was too rooted in the earth, the deep unyielding stone. A lode that was meant to stay *stayed*. A lode made in motion was ephemeral and made to collapse to yield to another. Only the most accomplished of lodeshapers could move around an anchored lode while holding it, and although Erasmus knew the theory, it wasn't something he'd really done before. Remembering the experience would be nice.

Truthfully he hadn't really thought ahead far enough to consider how he planned to escape. He'd gone in to anchor, and anchor he had. And himself thereby.

The telling silence, caught only by an aborted breath, made dread crawl up his skin.

Ryan turned his head, not quite swivelling to join the conversation proper, and said low: "I hope *we're* not planning on concealing things, at this point."

"No," said Yoch, her silhouette's head angled toward Ryan. "But I'd like *you* to find the words at swift notice." She glanced downward, and something icy gripped Erasmus's gut. "Mistress Birdie told us that you feared possession. That you believed you might be."

Very suddenly Erasmus's mouth seemed dryer than it ever had been. He tried to wet his lips – realised how *thirsty* he was – and then Passion's arm slid under his shoulders to lift him up enough to drink. Passion didn't release his hold on the cup, and it was probably just as well; Erasmus's hands were entirely too shaky for it.

When Passion lowered him it was to a mound of – something – behind his back. Bags, maybe. They were soft enough for now but he felt the edges of other things inside them.

Focusing on that was better than actually looking at either of them in the face. The fact he could barely see wasn't *much* of an excuse for the fact his gaze skirted around them.

There was no point in hiding it. He hadn't been able to even in Aulerin.

"I thought it went away in the bog," Erasmus whispered, and pressed his knuckles to his sternum as if that would at *all* assuage the tautness under it. "... I *hoped* it went away in the bog. But then I ..."

His tongue tied, his breath coming short while he struggled for words.

"When did it start again?" Yosh asked.

"I fell in the sea," Erasmus said, hardly able to raise his voice any higher than before. "And it was – big. Booming. Everything ... distant. Unmoored. Sometimes it was like I could almost hear voices, but – they were too far to know what they were saying. It felt just like ... when I escaped the prison ..."

The escape he barely remembered, and only snatches, wild and hazy; like a dream. He didn't remember landing, just – before. Before and the crushing weight, the panic binding his chest, the certainty that he couldn't bear to be imprisoned any longer and had to *go*.

(The wild exhilaration of being unfettered, unchained, knowing that the prison couldn't *hold*; the unexpected hysteria of freedom from any chains or trappings, even those he loved, tipping on the edge of a fall that might *end him*.)

They weren't saying anything.

"I don't remember landing," Erasmus said, very small.

Tell me your name *and we can* end this.

Just like he didn't remember the end of Christopher's interrogation.

Just like he didn't remember –

His chest squeezed. "D- did I –?"

"You didn't harm anyone," said Yoch. "You didn't even try. You just stopped responding after a time, and when you did – it seemed as though you were only half there. I thought at first it was simply that you were overtaxed."

"When General Burnstone came to our assistance, we loaded the skyride," said Passion in his deep, most measured tones. Mostly he used them when he was lecturing, Erasmus thought, but right now they were – *dis*passionate. Soothing. "The skyride held above the street beyond the reach of the flood. You released the lode and – and – might lodeshapers be able to teleport?"

"What?" Erasmus's voice was teary and incredulous. "I did what? That's not – we don't. Is that how I –?"

He didn't remember *falling*.

"I could accept stress making him unresponsive," Ryan said, still low. "I could even accept the burden of that stress making him forget where he was and who was around him." Erasmus's heart vaulted into his throat and clutched it. "But magic that even a magician knows nothing about doesn't bode well for who was using it."

"I forgot what?" Erasmus asked, very small.

"You asked who I was," said Yoch. "What I took to be unresponsiveness proved to be a lack of knowledge. You didn't remember me at all. And the others, presumably, but it was me to whom you were speaking." She hesitated a brief moment, with an in-drawn breath and then another. "You said you were tired."

Did he?

Something hysterical, either laughter or tears, bubbled up until Erasmus trembled trying to keep it in, his breath catching and catching again.

Tell me your name *and we can* end this.

Had it really been him who said that?!

Erasmus caught his breath and drew it in deep and shuddering. A few more and he managed to swallow down whatever yawing panic tried to claw its way out. And they waited; oh, they waited for him to breathe, until the air settled, as if there was any way for this to stay steady and *civilised*.

"The murder of which you're accused," said Yoch softly. "It was your cousin, yes?"

"... Yes." What was the point of denial? They were smart enough to know. "But I – I don't remember." Erasmus's voice caught in his throat, came out cracked. "I went to see him – and then I was sitting next to ... next to ... his body ... and I d- don't remember anything in-between."

And now they knew he was either damned or killer, that truly he had *nothing* to hope for and no life to which to return that would not be forever shadowed.

Action fleeting, the brief driving intent of purpose even to save lives was not enough to adequately stand between where he was and where he'd *been*.

Every fraying edge unravelled. The sob came bucking, and Erasmus curled in – as best as he could, with them on either side of him and no real recourse to *privacy*. Unexpectedly Passion's hand smoothed over his head and landed on his back, pulling Erasmus more properly into his lap.

"Peace now," said Passion gently overhead. "This too shall pass."

How, Erasmus had no breath to ask. If anything the gentleness made the dam break faster, so there really wasn't anything Erasmus could do but *ride it out*. The last time anyone had held him like this had been Alexander after his mother died, and that comparison too was a lancing stab that only served to excise tears afresh, his chest an aching knot of guilt and grief and confusion.

For a long time no one said anything. Passion hummed something not wholly tuneless, his hand passing over Erasmus's hair again and again until Erasmus's tears were spent and he lay in a dazed kind of half-doze, barely aware of what was happening. Or at least, barely wishing to.

"The Professors Al would know better how to proceed," Yoch said, steadily matter-of-fact as though Erasmus's revelations weren't all that bad, really. "But Schecheya is very far."

"Indeed," Passion agreed, "but I believe it to be the best course. Professor Alvin has made a study of possession and will have insight I do not."

For the briefest moments Erasmus considered *trying* to say something, but –

What did he have to lose, to give it all over to them? He had already, in the bog. Even if it was for nothing more than an academic interest in where he'd come from and what new knowledge he represented, it wasn't as though he had any idea what to do with himself otherwise. Maybe it would be – fine – to live out a life as a subject of curiosity for those who dared.

He didn't know what help this professor might have. Even if possession could somehow be cured, no one at home would believe he had been. The price was too high if they were wrong.

"We'd have to cross the mountains," said Ryan. "And Gus will have to avoid using any magic outside of any town with a levin grid. They were able to track him from the mangroves, remember."

Passion's fingers carded through Gus's hair. "Did you hear that, Gus?"

Wordlessly, his damp face still buried in Passion's robes, Erasmus nodded.

"Then we must decide what to do about the pass," said Yoch. "There'll be a hard border, and we have insufficient papers. Leaving aside how difficult it might be to get there – some of the roads might have been flooded."

"If we want to avoid it, we'll have to decide soon," Ryan warned. "The road diverges ahead. *Closely* ahead, in fact."

Almost on the heels of his words came a bellowing from some distant beast, as if one of the barge oxen was vexed. There came a rustling of cloth somewhere over Erasmus's shoulder, and Yoch's voice came a little further – but low, as if she was looking out while trying to contain the conversation to just them.

"Best to move to the edge while you can, then," she told Ryan. "Keep south. Our best course is to find help crossing the mountains elsewhere."

There came a dull sound, like leather against leather, and Ryan clicking his tongue. Erasmus flinched against the pillow of Passion's lap. The steady rhythm of hooves against stone shifted, and the mass of the wagon around them tilted ever so faintly as it turned.

"There aren't many who know these mountains," said Ryan conversationally.

"And I know where they are," said Yoch, her tone warmly confident. "I'm taking you all home."

About the author

Pur Durance is the co-author of Broadsides, an urban fantasy series written with Makari Clove. She looks forward to adding Helix fantasy novels to her repertoire. Aurichalcum Publishing is her self-publishing vehicle (vroom vroom).

ALSO BY

Makari Clove & Pur Durance

Voice & Vein

(https://books2read.com/u/mgEN90)

***

Sunlight & Bone

(https://books2read.com/u/mgEN7v)

***

Blood & Nerve

(https://books2read.com/u/4EKELO)

***

Breath & Name

(https://books2read.com/u/bpaN8X)

www.ingramcontent.com/pod-product-compliance
Lightning Source LLC
Chambersburg PA
CBHW020227260626
47156CB00002B/570